WHO KNEW PHILANTHROPY COULD BE SO DEADLY?

Katie Nelson, a program officer at Atlanta's largest charitable foundation, has the job everyone wants, giving away other people's money. But when her latest grant recommendation literally goes up in flames, killing a nameless Latina woman, everyone becomes a suspect. Was it a hate crime, an inside job or something more insidious? She enlists the help of foundation trustee Jim Hunter, but as they begin to unravel the mystery, they discover a burgeoning romance growing between them that complicates their investigation. As Katie unearths more evidence, Jim becomes less cooperative and more distant. When Katie accidentally discovers that Jim is not who he claims to be, she has to choose between trusting him or giving up on their relationship. As she struggles to find the culprit and trust her heart, headstrong Katie unwittingly places herself in mortal danger. Who's looking out for her and who's trying to do her in?

"Elizabeth Russell has crafted a compelling and most intriguing narrative sure to make the reader smile with satisfaction and delight."—*Mark Constantine, author of Wit and Wisdom: Unleashing the Philanthropic Imagination*

"Exquisite! There is an honesty and humanness about these characters which is enormously refreshing."—*Janine Lee, President, Southeastern Council of Foundations.*

"Foundations need not be mysterious, but this novel about grantmaking by someone who knows foundations well clearly belongs on the mystery-lover's bookshelf."—*Dorothy Ridings, Former President, Council on Foundations.*

OTHER PEOPLE'S MONEY

Elizabeth Russell

Moonshine Cove Publishing, LLC
Abbeville, South Carolina U.S.A.

FIRST MOONSHINE COVE EDITION NOVEMBER 2014

This book is a work of fiction. Names, characters, places and incidents are products of the author's imagination or are used fictitiously. Any resemblance to actual events, locales or persons, living or dead, is entirely coincidental.

ISBN: 978-1-937327-54-5
Library of Congress Control Number: 2014952424

Book design by Moonshine Cove; cover illustration and design by Claire Newbury, used with permission.

Acknowledgments

Although this story is a work of fiction, it would not have been possible without the hundreds of very real people who work ceaselessly for the greater good in charitable foundations and nonprofits across the country. Thank you for the work you do and for sharing your stories, hopes, fears and frustrations with me. Particular thanks to Jera Stribling, who told me my first great foundation story, and to Brenda Rambeau, who made me realize that these were stories worth telling.

A big thanks also goes to other experts in their respective fields: Buddy Thompson, Asheville Arson; Amanda Sullivan and the staff of the Old Edwards Inn; Tim Saviello, John Marshall Law School; Dawn Dowdle, who isn't my agent, but was a big help anyway; Mark Bloom, editor and coach extraordinaire; Mary VanClay, who actually makes proof-reading a fun process; Laura Lowe, for taming the online lions; and Claire Newbury for years of awesome design and friendship.

To all of you early readers and advisers, a hearty thank you for patiently wading through multiple drafts: Anne Battle Shultz, Ginny Thomas, Katharine Pearson Criss, Janet Rechtman, Doug Aiken, Luci Hansson Zahray, Linnea Linton, Gerry Cooke and Mark Constantine.

And of course, huge hugs to Debby Maugans, who made me believe, and overwhelming love and gratitude to Mom, Mitch, Anne Elise, and Owen, who gave me the time and support to make it happen.

Dedication

For Pop

Also by Elizabeth Russell

Donor Intent - Forthcoming

For Mona,
Happy Reading!

OTHER PEOPLE'S MONEY

CHAPTER 1

The light drizzle didn't matter; the fire would still catch easily enough. Even in the hands of someone who'd never done this before, someone who didn't really understand the nature of fire, nothing would remain but smoke and ashes in half an hour. It wasn't much of a structure anyway—just a wooden frame inside a shell of ancient brick and crumbling mortar. It didn't even have a sprinkler system. I'd checked.

The man paused before leaving his car. Maybe he had a sudden attack of nerves. But no, he was just struggling with a black ski mask. He pulled it over his head and emerged without a sound. He wore only black, but I'd know him anywhere. His loafers whispered across the pavement as he made his way around to the back of the old building.

The rest of the block consisted of abandoned warehouses, decaying factories and vacant lots strewn with trash; there wasn't another soul in sight. Only the homeless and the junkies hung out in this part of town, and they were all sleeping it off or out committing crimes. No one saw him but me, and that's the way I wanted it. Not that I gave a rat's ass what happened to this guy. The building was all I cared about. It took some doing to get to this point, some intricate negotiations. There were a million reasons that this building had to go. I just happened to know the best one, and in a few minutes, the plan would ignite, if you'll pardon the pun.

He stood at the back wall by an old, single-pane window. Whoever renovated this piece of crap did it on the cheap. Or maybe they were going for "rustic." Whatever. It would burn all the faster because of it.

He glanced around, nervous as a middle school shoplifter, but I knew he'd never spot me. One quick overhand hurl and the first bomb crashed through the window, followed swiftly by a second. The sound of breaking glass gave way to a muffled bang and then a whoosh as fire raced along the floor and worked its way up the walls. If the strikes were as true as they sounded, nothing would survive.

The explosion itself disappointed me, but a louder bang would've attracted unwanted attention. The fire spread, visible now through the windows, mesmerizing to watch. The man stood there, frozen. The awe of fire can do that to you. But he needed to get a move on, get out of there before the cops came. I threw a rock—not a big one—at his back to shake him out of his trance. He glanced around, but I ducked away, out of sight. Maybe he'd think it was a projectile from one of those little explosions that kept coming from inside. Pop! Pop! Pop!

He looked uneasy, though, as he scurried back to the car. He started the engine and silently drove away, slicing through the early morning darkness until even the trace of taillights disappeared.

I wanted him gone so I could watch in peace as the whole thing unfolded. I like the progression of destruction as a fire chews every bit of fuel it can reach, eating its way to its own death. First the ceiling, then the walls and then...well...then she screamed.

I was the only one who heard her, the only one who pictured her trapped inside, the only one who heard her life end as the heat and smoke stripped the air from her lungs. I was the only one who wondered if, mercifully, she suffocated before the flames found her flesh.

When the fire began to slow, I heard the sirens as the first fire engines approached. I knew before the firemen did what they'd find. A charred body of some nameless immigrant. Some clues about how that fire had started, but not enough to trace. He might get away with it after all, that lucky, stupid bastard.

I could just picture him. By now he'd have a glass of wine in hand, toasting his night's work. In his mind, the task was all done, the hard part over.

But I knew better. It takes time to learn that setting a fire might end one thing, but it always starts something else, sets something else in motion. The minute he lit the first fuse, he unleashed something he couldn't control. He didn't know that, but I did.

That's why I was there–to make sure that whatever this fire set in motion moved in the right direction. I didn't start this, but I was pretty sure I would have to finish it.

CHAPTER 2

"What the hell am I doing here?" Katie Nelson pressed her trembling palms against her 14th story office windows, almost willing the thick glass to dissolve so she could fly away. Outside, rain streamed down onto Midtown Atlanta. She blinked back the hot tears that wanted to fall as well.

Her face still burned with the sting of what had just happened in the foundation boardroom. Guy Porter, a foundation trustee, hadn't slapped her physically, but his verbal assault hurt every bit as much. She reached up with her left hand to grab a wavy strand of her long brown hair, pulling it over the front of her shoulder and threading it over and over, over and over, through her fingertips, pausing only to wipe a threatening tear with the back of her hand.

"Katie, it happens to everyone. Eventually." Chris Montez, her only fellow program officer on the Hartwell Foundation staff, offered an explanation.

She knew he meant to help, but it just made her tears more difficult to contain. She swallowed hard and with her back still turned away from him, spoke to his reflection in the floor-to-ceiling window. "Really, Chris? Can you honestly tell me that you've been skewered by Porter like that?"

Chris glanced at the floor for a moment before meeting Katie's reflected gaze. "The board has turned down my grant recommendations plenty of times…" he started, then stopped as Katie cocked at eyebrow at him. "But no, not like that."

Of course not like that. For almost a year now, the board had trusted her judgment as a program officer for the city's largest charitable foundation. Katie rotated her fingers faster, twisting the strand of hair to a point just shy of knotting. The board never shot down Chris's proposals unless funds just weren't available. They practically ate out of his hand, approving his solid, safe…and boring proposals with hardly any discussion. Like Chris, some of Katie's grant recommendations didn't end up getting approved because of limited funds. Unlike Chris, Katie intentionally pushed the envelope sometimes, hoping to open the board's minds and their hearts to new ideas. She considered it her mission, the value she brought to her work. After all, she'd been in the trenches, hadn't she? She knew what it was like to beg for funding to provide services to those who needed them so desperately. It was a lot harder than writing a damn check.

"Look," he said, "you tackled a difficult issue. Not everyone feels the same way you do about immigration and illegals. You have to admit, even if you don't agree with it, even if he didn't express it well, Porter has a right to his opinion."

Katie's mouth tightened at the irony in his words. Chris, the one Latino on the foundation staff, was trying to defend the board's biggest bigot on his anti-immigration stance. She spun to face him, the words exploding out of her mouth before she could even think. "Really, Chris? Do you think he has a right to scream at me like that? Does he have a right to tell everyone I should be fired?"

"That's not *exactly* what he said. But even if he did, it's not what he meant. At least not about you."

"Why the hell did I leave the food bank? It didn't pay worth a damn, but at least people didn't attack me when I was doing my job!"

She glared at her colleague, then looked away as the harshness of her words echoed between them. Unlike Porter, Katie rarely cursed, and she knew that while he could get away with being a brash, knife-tongued bully, the rest of the board and staff frowned upon such outbursts. A fresh wave of shame poured over her. The swell of water building behind her eyes threatened to burst, and she'd rather die than cry in front of a coworker. Especially here, in the esteemed offices of the Hartwell Foundation, where calm always prevailed. *Unless you're Guy Porter*, she thought, clamping her teeth down on her bottom lip. *Then you can rant and rave all you want.*

"Hey, you know we don't all think like that. Just chill for a bit and then let me know if you want to talk." Chris shot her a sympathetic look, then disappeared down the hall.

Katie crossed her office to shut the door as the tears began, silently thanking Chris for knowing when to leave her alone. It was embarrassing, really. She could watch the saddest movie ever made and not shed a tear. She hadn't even cried when her beloved grandmother passed away last year. But when she got angry? Frustrated? The waterworks began. Ridiculous.

The tears came now. Her head whirred as she replayed Porter's harsh attack in front of the entire board of trustees, all because of her request for grant funds to the Viva Latina Health Clinic. Okay, so maybe sometimes she'd pushed a little too far with this proposal, but *no* trustee had ever attacked her so viciously, or personally. In a matter of minutes, he'd ripped her professional reputation to shreds, pummeling her like a school yard bully while the rest of the room looked on in silence, cowed by the raw juxtaposition of unbridled aggression and naked helplessness.

"This is the most irresponsible recommendation I've ever seen!" he shouted across the polished oak table at his fellow trustees. His gaze snapped to Katie, shooting daggers across the room to where she sat next to Chris along a side wall. "If this is the kind of suggestion we're going to get from our program staff, why the hell do we pay their salaries?" His piercing look left no doubt whom he meant by "program staff."

"This clinic will attract nothing but illegals, and I don't see how we can justify that when we already can't do enough to help care for our own citizens. We've already funded programs for immigrants at the charity hospital. Why the hell do we have to keep supporting people who keep breaking the law?"

As a well-known corporate attorney, Porter never hesitated to say whatever he wanted. But Katie had never seen him attack anyone else on the Foundation's staff so vehemently. None of the other six trustees volunteered an opinion one way or the other. Maybe they too didn't see the value in her work.

Worst of all, the outburst caught Katie completely off guard, giving her no time to prepare a defense or even guard her own countenance. She kept her eyes on Porter's hands as he talked, trying in vain to stop the wave of heat surging up to her face. If she tried to meet his gaze, the knot in her stomach would have risen to join the one in her throat and she might have lost her composure, so she simply sat there, expressionless and paralyzed, watching Porter's hands jab back and forth like a boxer's as his barrage of words surged over her.

"The sheer *idiocy* of this proposal puts me in shock, in *shock*! And I thought I was a pretty tough guy to rattle." Porter stood up as he levied these words at Katie, his large frame demanding her acknowledgment. "If you're not going to give your work any more thought than *this*…"—he waved the proposal in the air with one hand and smacked it hard with the other—"…then I think you'd better go back to the soup line!"

If anyone in the room had doubts left about whom Porter was attacking, then his final outburst left no doubt.

In the end, the trustees denied the recommendation without further discussion.

Now, alone in her office, Katie glared out the window as a new wave of indignation replaced her tears. No one had defended her in the meeting. Not Chris, not any of the other trustees. Why would they? As a close cadre of white men, long past their sixtieth birthdays and steeped in tradition, they set the tone for all things Hartwell.

But damn it, the proposal was solid! *All* of her work was solid! Katie always dotted every "i" and crossed each "t" with care. It took her months to examine every piece of each proposal she brought forward to the board. Viva Latina was no different. Every penny of the proposed grant would go toward saving lives and curing the sick. Wasn't that the purpose of the Hartwell Foundation? Wasn't that her job?

Maybe Porter is right. Maybe I should be somewhere else. She closed her eyes as she pressed her forehead against the cool glass, forcing herself to take deep breaths that fogged the thick pane.

Did I miss something? Anything? She cast about for an answer as she rolled first the backs of her hands, then her wrists against the cooling window. Viva Latina provided a much-needed service to an underserved population. The organization had a strong, committed leader and an impressive track record. It had decent finances, but was hard-pressed to continue, much less grow, without an influx of cash. The foundation most definitely would have seen a positive social return on its charitable investment. Other than Porter being a complete jackass, she hadn't missed a thing. She had vetted that proposal well, maybe even better than usual.

Thinking about the Viva Latina proposal, she felt a fist tighten in her stomach. More than one casualty had emerged from that board meeting.

How am I going to break the news to Jorge? she wondered.

CHAPTER 3

"Knock, knock." A voice and simultaneous knock on the door of her office made Katie jump.

Rubbing the spot where her forehead had pressed against the glass, she turned to see Jim Hunter, the foundation's newest and by far youngest trustee. At thirty-one, he was just two years older than she. With the exception of Chris's modest reassurance, no one else on the staff had said a word to her since the meeting. It was just as well; she preferred to lick her wounds in private.

She cocked her head at the intruder. What was he doing here? They'd met and spoken before, of course, but only in the formal confines of board meetings, where staff sat at silent attention unless called upon.

"I hope you weren't thinkin' of jumping," he said with a small smile. He leaned one shoulder against her door-frame, his feet crossed, tie loosened and hands resting in his trouser pockets. "We'd hate to lose you."

Not like you'd really care, Katie thought, struggling to suppress a scowl.

His smile disappeared when he saw her reaction. "Sorry. You okay? That was some venom Porter hurled at you today."

"I'm fine," she said through clenched teeth. "It's not the first time one of my recommendations was denied. I'm sure it won't be the last either, since Porter made it pretty clear he doesn't trust my abilities."

Jim shook his head at the suggestion. "Listen, Porter doesn't speak for all of us, you know."

"No, but apparently the rest of you don't care to speak for yourselves."

Jim's mouth flattened into a thin line, and she took a quick breath. *Oh great, now I've offended two board members in one day. Way to go, Kate.*

"I'm sorry." A flush crept into her face. "That wasn't fair. I'm just…I really believed in that proposal, and I worked hard to make sure it was airtight before I brought it in there." If the board decided to fire her, at least she'd go down defending her work. She crossed her arms in front of her and leaned back against the glass. The cool pane calmed her anger. She let out a breath and realized how tight her shoulders felt.

His face relaxed, and a boyish grin that she had seen before settled into place. With his relaxed stance and slightly tousled hair, he looked as if he had just stepped out of a prep school catalog. "I would hope, Miz Nelson," he said with a mock-formal Southern drawl, "that you'd do your best to make sure that *every* proposal you bring before the board is 'airtight,' as you call it."

Katie suppressed an eye roll and her knotted stomach unwound a tiny bit. "Of course. It's my duty as the humble servant of the late Mr. Hartwell's wishes." She could play the mock-formal game, too, although she hoped she didn't push it too far. The late Mr. Hartwell was also Jim's grandfather, and Katie had no idea how deep the family bond might lie.

Jim seemed unfazed by her comment and appeared to be enjoying their little game, his eyes sparkling along with that dazzling grin.

"In that case, Miz Nelson, I would invite you to join me for a quick libation. You've had an exceedingly difficult time of it, and I happen to know of an establishment that will have the appropriate distilled beverage to restore your spirits. My treat, of course."

She took a small step toward her desk and clutched the back of her chair. Did a board member just ask her out? What did foundation protocol dictate for *this* situation? Since all the other board members rivaled or exceeded her parents in age, she'd never even considered the possibility.

"Aw, come on," he said, dropping the fake formality. "It's the least I can do to make up for the board's bad behavior. And it would make *me* feel better."

"All right," she said, letting go of the chair and standing up straight. "I can come for a little bit." She hesitated as a new thought occurred to her. Maybe he was just being nice in preparation for letting her go. It would make sense, taking her away from the office to avoid a potential scene.

"I can't stay long, though. I have to get home and feed my cat." If he was about to fire her, he would have to make it quick.

"No worries," he replied, gesturing with his hand for her to precede him down the hall to the elevator. She grabbed her coat and purse, flipping off the light switch as she passed Jim in the doorway. In that brief moment of closeness, an odd bolt of electricity surged up her spine, as if the poles of the earth had just been knocked askew.

CHAPTER 4

Out on the busy sidewalk, the noise of rush-hour traffic and nearby construction equipment prevented much conver-sation, so Katie shot silent sidelong glances at Jim as they walked. He had sandy brown hair and blue eyes, stood almost a head taller than her five-foot-five and had a lean, athletic figure under his suit and coat. The grin wasn't the only thing boyish about him; he ambled along with a laid-back air and seemed to take in the streetscape with interest. He appeared to make eye contact with every person who crossed their path, waving at several, all of whom waved or at least smiled back.

Katie felt the back of her neck prickle with the heat of uncertainty. For a trip to the chopping block, it felt awfully friendly. *Maybe it was just one of those Southern things. Lord knows they raise their men to appear charming and confident, even if they're clueless. Not really a skill cultivated in the New England of her childhood.*

She compared her own reflection to his as they passed several glass-fronted buildings. Her dark brown hair had an unruly wave in it, and her hazel eyes and dark brows contrasted her fair skin. Although younger than Jim, a passerby might likely think her the elder of the two. Unfair but typical, as Katie's mother often told her that her serious countenance always made her look older.

Jim was somewhat of an oddity when compared to the rest of the board. In addition to his young age, his politics and connections appeared to diverge from those of the other trustees. He seemed more forward-thinking, progressive even. And of course, the whole family scandal that surrounded him made for interesting conversation.

From what Katie had heard, when Joseph Hartwell created the foundation, he had stipulated that in addition to some of his closest friends and cronies, every male member of the next two succeeding Hartwell generations could serve on the board if they so desired, beginning on their thirtieth birthdays. But developments that Joseph didn't count on upended his carefully laid plan. His only son died tragically in an auto accident and his daughter Camille rebelled against him, traveling around the country in the 1970s, following the stoner rock band the Grateful Dead with various boyfriends, eventually becoming pregnant.

Joseph refused to communicate with his daughter after she left his home and therefore never learned about his illegitimate grandson until Camille visited his bedside just before his death. Joseph had threatened to change the foundation's charter before he died, but didn't. Whether because of physical weakness or a new sense of forgiveness, no one could say. Either way, since the charter placed no restrictions on legitimacy and since Jim was a bona fide third-generation Hartwell male, he became eligible for service at age thirty. And because board members enjoyed a lifetime appointment, Jim could become a fixture on the Hartwell Foundation's board for decades.

This story circulated with many others through the social fabric of the Atlanta foundation staff via quiet conversations. Although the foundation was cloaked in a cape of propriety to the outside world, insiders often deemed the stories behind foundation doors too good *not* to share. The foundation's announcement of Jim's ascension to the board simply stated that his mother was Camille Hartwell Hunter, who lived with her husband Bailey Hunter in Landrum, South Carolina.

"In here," said Jim, opening the squeaky door of the Rose and Crown, an English-style pub on a Midtown side street a few blocks from their office building.

Katie entered and waited for her eyes to adjust to the dim light. After the din of street noise, the pub's quiet emptiness belied its proximity to Midtown's many law, accounting and consulting firms. Then again, on most chilly, drizzly Tuesday late afternoons, the professional crowd probably had more pressing engagements. Even Katie normally would work late or scurry home to change into her sweats and curl up with her cat Babka and *Sex and the City* re-runs.

"So, what'll you have?" Jim asked, waving a friendly hand at the bartender. With a light touch on Katie's elbow, he steered her to a booth along the pub's back wall.

She ordered a red wine while he opted for draft beer, an English brew, not the usual American light beer she and her girlfriend Rita sometimes ordered on their rare nights out.

"You've got sophisticated tastes for a South Carolina man," she said, trying to keep the conversation light.

"Weeell, you can take the boy out of the castle, but you can't take the castle out of the boy. Or something like that," he said, smiling. "And hell, I'm heir to the Hartwell fortune, right?"

"What?" Startled, she swallowed hard while trying desperately to look casual, as if his declaration of impending wealth held no more consequence than his mentioning what he'd had for lunch.

He laughed. "Just kidding! The entire Hartwell estate went into the foundation. My mama never saw a penny. I won't either and that's just fine with me. I think I've had it pretty darn good without the old man's involvement. Used to want it, but then I learned better. So many people seem to think I'm sittin' on money, though, and I can't help playing with 'em. You should've seen your face. I thought you were gonna hit me for a minute. Just one of the reasons I think you're good for the foundation."

Katie released a breath she hadn't realized she'd been holding. So he wasn't going to fire her and he apparently valued her work. Better yet, he wasn't some mega-rich spoiled heir with a warped sense of entitlement. Maybe she could learn something else about his past, something that could fuel or suppress that family gossip. She looked up at him and asked, "Since you brought it up, do you ever resent not getting to know your grandfather? Is that why you joined the foundation board? To feel closer to him?"

"No, no. Didn't even know about the foundation until one of the partners at the firm told me I should pursue my seat. Actually, it was Porter who told me about it. He thought it'd be good for the firm and good for my resume."

"I knew you two worked at the same firm, but your addresses are in different places. Is Kinsey & McMillan really that big?"

"Yep. Really is. Porter's on the real estate side. I'm in litigation. He's in the Buckhead office. I'm in Midtown."

Oh, Lord, not another litigator! What am I even doing here listening to another attorney? Katie held all attorneys in disdain. There was one in particular, Michael, a promising young partner in another local firm. Michael had considered attorney-client privilege a suitable excuse for not sharing that he slept with one of his former clients for three months while he and Katie were engaged. She had returned his ring with enough force to cut a two-inch gash in his cheek, and the resulting scar had turned him from cute and clean-cut to ruggedly handsome, damn it.

"What, you got somethin' against Midtown?" Jim eyed her with a puzzled look.

When she realized her face had shifted into a scowl, she smiled. "No, not at all." She took a deep breath and stretched her shoulders. Old ghosts were hard to shake off sometimes. *Okay, so he's another attorney, but he's also a board member of the foundation. Technically, that makes him my boss. Be nice, Kate.*

"I've gotta admit," Jim said, "I didn't wanna pursue it at first, because of the family history, but Porter insisted. Once he got my supervising partner on board, I couldn't say no. Now that I've sat through a couple of grant cycles, I find that it's really fascinating and a lot more difficult than I imagined. I mean, you'd think it wouldn't be hard to give away $150 million a year, right? But then you see how much need there is, and how committed all these people are to their causes, and you realize that $150 million is a drop in the bucket. So you've gotta figure out how you're gonna make the greatest impact for the most folks. It's a real challenge, and I take it more and more seriously every day."

"I know what you mean," Katie said, shifting in her seat, "but can I ask you something, just person to person, not staff member to trustee?"

"Of course. My friends and I have a saying—what happens in the Rose and Crown *stays* in the Rose and Crown."

She gave a small chuckle as she chose her words. It was a delicate question, one she'd longed to discuss with a trustee for a while, and Jim seemed like a good bet now that it was clear he wasn't going to fire her. "Well, it's just that...don't you ever get frustrated with the charter of the foundation, the way it still controls everything we do? I mean, I'm sure it made perfect sense in 1954 when your grandfather wrote it, but now there are so many great things out there we can't fund because they don't fall into his description for using the money."

"Like your Latina health clinic?"

"Yes, exactly. Immigration wasn't a problem back then. But there're other things, too. Environmental issues didn't exist. No one could have imagined AIDS. There was no such thing as foster care. Women's issues were totally different. Atlanta has changed since the fifties, and it's crazy that the foundation can't change as well."

"The other board members would tell you that no matter how a city changes, it still needs good schools and churches and hospitals."

She squirmed in the booth, crossing her legs. "Yes, but you know what I mean. Isn't there a way to serve some of those newer, more pressing needs? Would your grandfather really have opposed offering health care to immigrants?"

He shrugged. "Who knows? Never met the man. A lot of how that charter is interpreted depends on the board, and practically everyone there has some sort of personal tie to my grandfather that I don't have. They're all incredibly loyal to their memory of him. It's kinda touching, really. You'd think that as his actual descendant, I might have some sway in our deliberations, but that's not the way it works...But yes, in answer to your question, I'd love to see us branch out a little more. We just have to work the system to make that happen. It takes a while."

"I know," she sighed. *Why did everyone want to change so slowly? What was wrong with speeding things up a bit?* "I try to stay focused on all the good the foundation *does* do. When I started, everyone told me, 'We have the best job in the world. We get to give away money to help make the world a better place.' But I get so frustrated. It's like I'm always on the outside and can't ever really tackle a problem. At least when I worked at the food bank, I actually helped people on the front lines. Here, I'm not physically contributing anything to the actual people who need it, and I certainly don't make any decisions about where the money goes."

"You worked at the food bank?"

"Yes, I was the development director before I came to the foundation. Long hours, really bad pay. This is a better job, hands-down, but sometimes it's just not quite as fulfilling as I thought going into it."

"Especially after today, huh?"

Katie blanched. In talking about the foundation's work with Jim, she had momentarily forgotten about her personal work there and how viciously Guy Porter had attacked it—and her—only hours before. It all came pouring back down in a chilling deluge. In some ways, it was worse than the rejection from Michael. She took her job very seriously, and Porter had tossed it on the carpet and stomped it flat. The feeling started in the pit of her stomach and radiated outward. She took a long sip of wine to stifle a growing tirade of rage.

"Definitely," she said at last, setting her glass down with a rattle.

"I didn't see that coming at all, but sometimes Porter's a loose cannon." Jim seemed eager to console her. "After you staff folks left the room but before we voted on what to fund, we talked about it some more. He still insisted we couldn't fund it, but enough of us decided we might entertain another request next quarter. He didn't like the idea, but he was outvoted."

"Really?" Katie's face flushed with the possibility. "But what would keep Porter from shouting it down again—and me with it?"

"Who knows? Who knows why he did it today? Personally, I thought it had great merit and you definitely researched it well. So next go-round, if you want, I'd be happy to work on the recommendation with you."

"By next go-round, do you mean the next grant cycle? June?"

"Sure. I think it's a safe bet Porter will have something else to rant about by then. Tell you what, I'll even present the recommendation myself so he can't just yell at you." His wide grin sent a ray of hope through her.

"You will? That'd be awesome! As long as Porter doesn't fire me for conspiring with a board member." She smiled, sitting up a little straighter on the booth's cushy seat. Finally, she might have an ally! "There aren't any rules against that, are there?" she added with a smirk.

"No, not at all," Jim replied, looking straight into her eyes. Her heart skipped a beat as he added, "Believe me. I checked."

CHAPTER 5

The next morning, Katie called Dr. Jorge Ramirez to share the bad news about the board's decision not to fund the clinic, but also the good news that a possibility for funding remained in the next round of grants. Her brain buzzed with the potential that still existed for the clinic, and on a whim, she asked Jorge if he could to meet her for coffee.

At the appointed time, she arrived first. The coffeehouse, one of several local joints holding its own despite the ubiquitous presence of Starbucks, bustled with an interesting mix of slackers and businesspeople. She ordered a latte and perched at a table near the door to watch for Jorge. A warm spring wind had carved its way through the brisk air, blown away the rain, and paved the way for bright sunshine that fought through intermittent clouds.

The weather reminded Katie of a day long ago, in the summer of her tenth year. Her family had taken a vacation to Maine, and on an unseasonably cool day, her father had led her and her sister on a hike along the rocky cliffs above the ocean. The wind blew strong then, too, and the sun burned just as bright as it fought to catch hold of the sky.

Katie had skipped along ahead, the sunlight dazzling her eyes and the wind lifting her spirit skyward. As her father and sister stopped to inspect a flower back down the trail, she stood there, mesmerized on the cliff's edge. She felt that if she held out her arms at that moment, she surely could have soared into the sky, completely carefree and unfettered. She could do and become whatever she wanted. She felt no fear, only freedom and possibility. Ever since, she'd craved that feeling, but never got as close to it as she had that long-ago day. Lately it seemed so out of reach.

She watched Jorge enter the coffeehouse, blushing slightly as her gaze lingered on his face while he searched for her.

When they'd talked about the clinic before, his deep brown eyes had burned with an intensity and passion for his work that hovered on the border of sexual. An immigrant himself from Cuba, he had worked his way through medical school at Stanford and delved into the work of helping others.

Katie found his passion contagious. Foundation protocol forbade relationships between staff and grantees, and Katie blushed more deeply now, remembering how she'd wrapped that rule around her like a safety net as Jorge told her about his plans with the fire of enthusiasm that enveloped them both. Together, they'd talked for nearly three hours about all of the center's potential uses. In addition to health care, they discussed adult literacy training, student tutoring or mentoring and possibly even working a daycare center into the plan down the road.

She couldn't help but study him now from a distance. His skin, smooth and olive-toned, displayed only the tiniest hints of wrinkles from frequent smiles and a brow often furrowed in concentration. His fine, dark hair showed just a trace of gray, the kind that made men look distinguished and women just old. She had no idea of his age, probably mid-to-late forties.

Then, he caught her staring and she quickly waved to him, face reddening all the more. As he placed his order at the counter, she chided herself. *How unprofessional. Get a grip. He's strictly off limits.* For a brief moment, Jim's face flashed through her mind as Jorge approached and sat across from her.

"Hello, Katie. What a wonderful idea to meet for coffee," he said, smiling, his melodious Cuban accent melting her toes.

"Thanks. I…I'm glad you could make it on short notice." She squirmed a little in her seat, then took a long, steadying sip of her latte. "I wanted to tell you in person how sorry I am that our…um, I mean your…"—she blushed—"proposal didn't make it this round. If it were up to me…well, you know I'm a fan. But I have hope that it may get funded yet."

"Ah yes." He still smiled, but a faraway look drifted into his eyes and then flickered away. "There is always hope. There is always more than one way to accomplish a goal. Sometimes it just requires a different approach."

"Well, actually, I don't know that the approach needs to be all that different. We, well, *technically*, I mean *you*, just need to supply some more ammunition for your case."

"What sort of ammunition?"

"Information that goes beyond the clinical outcomes. Data or projections about how your services might provide an economic benefit for the whole community, clear the path to citizenship for those it serves, that kind of thing."

"The clinical outcomes are not enough? Saving lives and providing human beings with access to health care is not valuable in its own right?" He didn't sound or look offended. Rather it was as if he weighed the pros and cons of the argument in his own mind as he spoke.

She bit her bottom lip. On one hand, she agreed wholeheartedly that the clinical merits of Viva Latina should stand on their own. On the other hand, her role as a program officer obligated her to respect the views of the foundation board whether she agreed with them or not, and present them in the best light to the rest of the world.

"It's not really a question of one versus the other," she said, frowning down at her cup. "The clinical merits are definitely impressive, but the board looks at how every grantee functions within the greater community and the local economy. If you're working in a silo or a vacuum, sometimes that makes it harder to fit with the foundation's mission."

"I understand," he said, looking directly at her. "It is not my money to give away or my place to criticize. It is just that, like every other nonprofit leader in this city, I want everyone to see why my work is so, *so* important, and I get frustrated when they do not. But we each see the world in our own way."

He paused a moment, looking down at his hands, then brought his eyes up to meet hers with a smile and said in a brighter tone, "So, what do I need to provide you with?"

"Well, actually, I'm still working on that." She raised her cup for a quick sip before sharing the good news. "I recently found one board member in particular who has taken an interest in your organization, and he wants to work with us to pull the information together. I've given him all the background from your last proposal, and he promised to get back to me with ideas in the next few days."

"That *does* sound promising. This board member, what is his interest in Latina health? Is there a particular area of our work that appeals to him?"

"I…" Katie hesitated, her coffee cup hovering halfway to her lips. She realized she had absolutely no idea why Jim cared about the clinic's work. "You know, I don't really know the answer to your question," she said, placing the cup back in its saucer. "I think it must be a sense of social justice that makes him want to get involved."

Jorge looked confused. "A board member wants economic data from my clinic to satisfy a desire for social justice?"

She couldn't help but laugh. "I said that *might* be his motivation, but he's only one of several board members. I think it's in your best interest to cover all the bases. We really do try to look at *all* angles of a proposal."

"Ah, good point. Very well. I look forward to working with you and this board member…" He raised an eyebrow at her.

"Jim Hunter," she said, trying her best not to blush yet again.

He looked at her with a knowing smile. She could practically feel his eyes piercing her thoughts. "Jim Hunter. I see. I look forward to working with both of you."

I see? What exactly does he see? Katie cursed her uncontrollable blushing. It always happened at the most inopportune times! What could he possibly see? Other than drinks and conversation last night, she had barely even spoken to Jim Hunter before. They had two glasses each, and then he walked her to her car. Not even a handshake passed between them. It was strictly professional.

"He's a smart guy. You'll like him," she said, glancing at him with a weak smile.

He looked amused. "Of course I will, Katie. I am happy that you have someone on your side, on *my* side, in all of this. I look forward to meeting him."

No, no, no! It's not like that! She yelped to herself. Nothing in his words implied anything other than professional assumptions. But what she saw in his eyes, that wasn't something she could counter with mere words. She held her embarrassed smile as he bid her goodbye.

Once he'd left, Katie dropped her forehead into her open palm. Now Jorge thought she had a thing for Jim Hunter.

It was ridiculous. She closed her eyes for a moment.

Ridiculous…and very possibly true.

CHAPTER 6

Over the next week, as spring began to unlock Atlanta's wealth of dogwood and azalea buds, Katie committed almost all her extra time to strengthening the Viva Latina proposal. Jim, true to his word, asked for her notes and reviewed all the information with methodical relentlessness. He even agreed to visit the clinic site to meet Jorge in person and see the operation first-hand.

Jim asked questions she would never have thought of, such as his request for the estimated value of the clinic's property, which it owned outright. "Why does that help?" she'd asked him, and he explained that since Porter's work focused primarily on real estate, showing the property value would help to show a stronger financial position for the organization.

He grew more intriguing. She wondered about his family history. Had his mother found it difficult to walk away from a fortune like that? Or was it easier than she could imagine? The rift between Camille Hartwell and her father must have run incredibly deep. Did a single incident ruin an otherwise happy childhood? Or had Camille been miserable throughout her youth?

Katie knew that people treated you differently when you had money. She did it herself. Because she spent a good portion of her professional time around the city's wealthiest families, she had to learn to mask her reactions to wealth and the wealthy—which usually included either a desire to drop her jaw in amazement or else attack their motives and principles—with a studied layer of indifference. The very wealthy were, to her and to so many others, unreachable beyond their walls of cash.

Maybe Camille hadn't wanted that role. Although Katie colored when she remembered her reaction to Jim's joke about inheriting the Hartwell fortune, she also had to admit that it would have changed her opinion of him. She would have treated him differently, wouldn't have felt as comfortable with him as quickly.

Another mystery surrounded Jim as well. Did his interest extend beyond the desire to fund the clinic? Twice he "just happened" to stop by her office to discuss something that he could easily have taken care of with a phone call or an email. Once more, they'd gone for drinks after work, under the guise of discussing the proposal. Two rounds of drinks had turned into dinner, and then a long, lingering glance when he walked her back to her car. The electricity had surged, no doubt, and at times she could absolutely swear he felt the same—but then he would once again become all business.

At first, she chastised herself for spending time turning the possibility of a romance with Jim around in her mind. She needed to focus on getting that clinic funded and moving the foundation out of the Dark Ages. Romance could wait. Michael had shown her that.

Their breakup had rocked her world. While it all happened just over a year ago, those wounds still ached. Michael's betrayal went deeper than a mere love lost; he had derailed her entire life plan. She had intended to follow in her older sister's footsteps and live up to family expectations. Until Michael, all had been on track. She'd graduated cum laude from a high-ranking university and begun a respectable career. A stable and loving husband was next on the agenda, but Michael had pulled the rug right out from under her. Whip-smart but manipulative, he'd turned every argument they'd had in his favor. Exactly what made for a good litigator.

She had buried herself in her work after that, building a thick wall of practicality around the weakness that allowed "the Michael situation" to arise in the first place. Michael always made her feel a little off-balance, out of control of her emotions. It was a tough lesson, she'd told herself, but it wouldn't happen again.

Since breaking her engagement, Katie had only gone out on two first-and-last dates—and then only when Rita threatened her with a listing in the online personal ads. She just wasn't ready.

Dating your boss certainly wasn't a good idea, she knew. Yet despite all of her internal protests, a new desire was awakening with the spring season. Jim was smart. He was funny. He shared her interest in broadening the foundation's horizons. Could he have an interest in broadening their personal horizons as well?

Jim added to the confusion when he called to schedule dinner with her on Saturday night. That was definitely a date night, but when he called, he also suggested that they talk about the clinic site visit scheduled for the following Monday. "Sorry I can't get together before Saturday and I hate to ask you to give up your weekend time for work stuff, but one of the partners is wrapping up a trial on Friday and I'm part of the team."

A weak date invitation or a business meeting? Katie had no clue.

***

Late Friday afternoon, Chris popped his head into Katie's office. "Got a minute?"

"For you? Of course."

Although barely thirty-five, as the senior member of the foundation's two program officers, Chris had achieved rock-star status in the city's nonprofit community. He represented the key to grant fortunes, and charity staff and board members spoke his name with reverence. While this may have gone to another man's head, Chris' humility and selfless approach to service earned the respect and admiration of his peers at other foundations. Understated and soft-spoken, he was viewed as wise and thoughtful. He rewarded their respect with extreme diligence, even if the proposals he brought to the board didn't necessarily excel in creative solutions to social problems.

He'd taken a rough-around-the-edges Katie under his wing without ruffling a feather, explaining foundation processes and answering her many questions in detail—but rarely uttering a single word about his life outside the foundation walls. Chris was an intensely private person, despite his modicum of celebrity. Katie was happy to respect his wishes. And if he needed something, she'd help without hesitation.

"You appear to have bounced back from the board meeting," Chris had given her space, but she knew her recent smiles and humming in the hallway as she passed his office door had likely not gone unnoticed. Although quiet about himself, Chris was a keen observer of others.

Katie blushed. "Yes, but I don't think I ever properly apologized for snapping at you."

He tossed a hand loosely. "Don't mention it, please. It was nothing."

He paused as he slid into one of the two carved wooden armchairs in front of her desk. "I wanted to ask you something." He crossed his legs, placed his elbow on his knee and rested his chin in his hand as he studied the mess of papers between them.

Whereas Katie often started ranting without thinking, she knew Chris liked to choose his words carefully before he spoke. She waited until he lifted his eyes.

"It's more of a favor really. I know that you've been working with Jim Hunter on that Latina clinic proposal."

"Yes?" Crikey! Did *he* suspect she might have a thing for Jim? Or vice versa?

"I know that's a very important project for you, and I admire the way you've stuck to it even after the board shut you down like they did. I believe your chances for funding are decent in the next cycle." He took a deep breath, searching her eyes for a reaction. "But I wonder if I could ask you to back off, just for this round."

What? Katie sat back in her chair as if pushed there, her hand moving instinctively toward a strand of hair to twirl.

"I…I don't know. We've done a lot of work, and Jorge—I mean Dr. Ramirez—is ready to reapply for funds. Why do you want me to wait?"

"I know my request is odd, but I have a proposal I've been working on for almost two years that is finally ready to bring forward. It's for the Rainbow Theatre, you know, the gay youth theater group. The board has never funded anything like it, but I think the time is right to try. And that's thanks to you, by the way, for opening that door just a nudge."

Katie understood this grant's importance to him. He was gay, she knew, but kept that aspect of his life quiet at the foundation. An unstated "don't ask, don't tell" policy permeated the office. While the foundation tried to make a conscious effort to hire a diverse staff, the conservative roots of most board members meant that they didn't necessarily want to know the details or the true meaning of that diversity. Good for Chris for deciding to push the envelope! But that still didn't fully explain his request.

"What does that have to do with Viva Latina?"

"I just don't want us to give the board more than they can handle at once. I know you're passionate about Viva Latina, but I've got *two years* invested in this, Katie. This theater group needs the money to buy a building for a permanent home. Viva Latina already has a building and more potential funders from other places. Couldn't they wait just a little longer for expansion?"

"And you think the health of all those women should wait?" Her fingers were flying through the lock of hair now. Arguing with Chris was uncharted territory.

"I'm saying that compared to tackling an immigration-related issue, funding an under-the-radar gay theater should be a piece of cake for this board. And Rainbow could pave the way for Viva Latina. Once they see they've stretched a bit and the sky hasn't fallen, maybe they'll do more." He raised his chin off his hand and gave her an imploring look.

She couldn't have felt more surprised if he'd stripped naked in her office. To see him step from behind his wall of reserve and criticize the board, however discreetly, made her jaw drop. And what he was asking practically sent it through the floor.

"But Chris, I don't get it." Her voice rose an octave. "I thought you'd would want to support the clinic, too."

He straightened up, gripping the arms of his chair as a deep flush crept into his face. "Why? Because my name is Montez? Katie, I'm a third-generation U.S. citizen. Just because I have a Latino last name doesn't mean I identify with illegal immigrants. Frankly, I think your Dr. Ramirez has done just as much to aggravate the problem as to solve it. You've seen the protests; you know how his work divides people. My family has lived here legally for decades, and you know what? It kinda ticks me off when people assume that I automatically support illegals, but they never even stop to consider that I might be more interested in helping gay people. Because *that's* my community."

He looked extremely uncomfortable, and she realized that this was probably the first time he'd ever spoken about being gay inside the foundation office, or displayed this much emotion within these walls. Her heart went out to him, but she simply could not, *would not*, back away from Viva Latina at this point.

"I'm sorry, Chris. I really am. I didn't mean to assume anything, and I totally get why you want the theater funding to go through." She took a deep breath. "But I can't back off Viva Latina right now. Jim is committed, I'm committed and it would make the foundation look terrible to Jor…to Dr. Ramirez."

Chris shook his head at her, scowling. "You still don't get how all this works, do you?" He pointed at the calendar on her wall. "*Two years* of playing by the rules. But hey, since you have it all figured out, maybe I'll just do it your way this time. We'll just present both proposals and keep our fingers very tightly crossed."

He banged the chair against the floor as he stood, cutting off any chance of a response. "Oh, and one more thing. I'd think twice about how closely you choose to work with our board members. Especially Mr. Hunter. That might not turn out so well."

Before she could ask what he meant, he disappeared down the hall.

CHAPTER 7

That might not turn out so well. Of all Chris's comments during his shocking loss of decorum, *that* was the one that Katie heard over and over as she sat at her desk, fingers on both hands now worrying her wayward strand of hair. She was annoyed with him for asking her to delay the clinic proposal, but his comment about Jim overshadowed those thoughts. Chris wasn't the type to hold a grudge or to nurse petty jealousies about a coworker's success, but his last barb had certainly sounded that way. Totally inappropriate. And so unlike the Chris she thought she knew.

But what if something *did* happen between Jim and her? What if it ended badly? It would be awkward, to say the least. It might mean she'd need to find a new job, too. On one hand, that wasn't a risk worth taking. But on the other hand, working closely with Jim looked like the best way to get Viva Latina funded. And she hadn't made any sort of romantic move—she would leave that up to him.

She needed an expert's perspective. It was time to call Rita.

She stilled her fingers, released the now-frazzled lock and picked up the phone. As usual, she dialed with mild trepidation. Rita had an unsettling ability to read her like a dime-store novel; Katie wouldn't be able to keep Jim a secret once Rita saw her face. But that was okay. Rita also excelled at "claiming her power" as she called it, recognizing when a woman should seize an opportunity and when to call bullshit.

"Where the hell have you been?" asked Rita as soon as she said hello. "I thought perhaps you'd forgotten you had friends."

Katie cycled through every poor excuse for not returning calls and sending only cursory emails over the last two weeks before she got to the point. "Look, I know it's short notice, but do you want to get together this evening?"

"Well, it just so happens that I just dumped another loser man, so my schedule is completely open. I'm planning a little girls' night out tomorrow with some of the women from my office and you could jump on that if you want, or we could do something tonight. Endless possibilities, girl!"

Katie shuddered at the idea of hitting the bar scene with the man-hunters from Rita's office. They were loud, brash, fearless and overtly horny. On the one occasion Katie had joined them before, she had been way out of her league and shrank to complete invisibility. Not that Rita didn't also take on the hunt when just the two of them went out, but she had a certain air of sophistication and control that made Katie feel more like an honored guest than the weakling who gets trampled by the rest of the herd.

"Let's just get a drink tonight." They agreed to meet at the Dark Horse Tavern.

***

The Dark Horse wasn't exactly the quietest spot to meet and talk, but it usually provided Rita with fertile hunting grounds. As Katie walked through the door, she spotted her friend on a stool at the bar, surrounded by three young men in shirts and ties. All three appeared enthralled. And why not? Her curly red hair and large green eyes were designed to stun her prey. And the emerald green silk blouse with the plunging neckline didn't hurt either.

When Rita saw Katie approaching, she interrupted her admirers, hopped off the barstool and with a loud "Heyyy!" came over and gave her a hug before leading her to a small table in the corner. A waitress appeared the second they took a seat, and Rita quickly sent her off with an order for two glasses of pinot noir.

"Aren't you going to introduce me to your friends?" Katie asked in mock seriousness.

"Those babies? No way." Rita rolled her eyes. "They're seniors from Emory trying to pose as lawyers from Charlotte. I had fun pretending to buy their story, though. Kind of get their hopes up, among other things." Rita's sparkly laugh echoed through the bar, causing more than a few heads to turn.

Rita always held forth as a master of flirtation and a quick and brutally honest judge of the men she attracted. Katie served as a one-woman audience, but that was all right—kind of fun, in fact. Watching Rita work a room was both awe-inspiring and entertaining. She was the ideal person to spend a girls' night out with because she would never abandon her friends. She had one standing rule, never go home with men you meet in bars no matter how strong the chemistry or how promising the conversation. "If he's really interested, he'll call me for a proper date," Rita once declared. "I have no interest in that morning-after moment when one of you realizes that you just made a big mistake."

"Too bad. One of them was kind of cute."

"Oh, don't get me wrong. If you had stood me up, I might have done a little cradle robbing. But that's a sad commentary on my current state of affairs—or lack thereof. Let's talk about you instead. What's up? What's *hapnin'*?"

"Well…" Katie began, but Rita cut her off.

"Oh my God, you're getting laid! Who is he? Spill it, sister!"

"It's not what you think. At least not yet. But there *is* someone…"

"Yeeeesss?"

"I haven't known him that long. Well, I've known him for a while but we only just started hanging out a couple of weeks ago. It's Jim Hunter. You know, that younger trustee from the foundation board? The lawyer?"

"Oh, score!" Rita's feet did a little tap dance under the table. "That's awesome!"

"Yes, but it's complicated." Katie filled Rita in on the events of the past two weeks, including his asking her out on a questionable "date" and ending with the afternoon's conversation with Chris.

"So let me get this straight," Rita said, sliding her finger around the lip of her wineglass. "You may or may not have a date with a coworker—okay, technically a boss—who may or may not be interested. You are obviously interested…"

Katie started to protest, but Rita held up a hand.

"Or we wouldn't be having this conversation. Hanging out with Jim could make your job more rewarding, but will piss off Chris and probably turn awkward if things go south. That about it?"

"Um…yeah. That about sums it up."

"So really, it's simple. You have the choice between being happier at your job with a potential boyfriend or leaving things just as they are at this moment to keep some queen from having a hissy fit."

"I wouldn't call Chris a queen, and he's not the hissy-fit type, at least not usually. I respect him."

"And he'll get over it. *You* need to think about *you*, and from where I'm sitting, girl, that's a no-brainer."

"I guess it wouldn't hurt to see what happens tomorrow night. At least I'll go into things with my eyes open."

"Amen to that," said Rita, toasting Katie with her pinot. "Here's to a good decision. Just don't be afraid to own it, sister. I'm glad that at least one of us will be getting lucky soon."

"Oh come on, you're the queen when it comes to attracting men. Don't tell me you don't have a date somewhere in your back pocket."

"Nope, I made a rookie mistake and put all my money on one horse, so to speak, and I just got thrown off with no one there to catch me."

"I'm sorry to hear that. But I thought you said you did the breaking up?"

"It's easier to think that way. Actually, it was for the best. He works for one of the firm's big developer clients. They moved him to Jacksonville, and he said he wasn't interested in a long-distance relationship. By the way, that's really code for 'I'm not that interested in *you*,' in case you ever find yourself in that situation."

Rita paused as her eyebrows arched. For a moment, she almost looked forlorn, but she rebounded, a smirk creeping into the corners of her mouth. Katie marveled at her resilience.

"But let's not let him ruin our Friday night. I see two very acceptable men at the bar who do *not* look like college students. Be my wing-woman, and I promise you won't have to pay for any drinks tonight."

"Uh, hello? Did you miss the part of our conversation where we talked about Jim?"

"Nope. I heard every word. You've hung out, you like him, but your possible 'date' isn't until tomorrow night. In my book, that means there's no obligation on your part—at least not yet. And you know my rule about meeting men in bars, so you're perfectly safe."

And with that, Rita caught the eye of the taller of her two intended targets and began to make the evening hers.

CHAPTER 8

Katie spent Saturday morning looking through her closet to find something that said "respectable, smart and possibly interested if you are."

After lunch, she did her regular workout at the neighborhood YMCA, but added a few extra rounds of crunches. She told herself that she did it so she could have dessert at dinner and not because she had a reason to make her stomach look flatter. That evening, she showered and put on the outfit she had chosen, a plain black skirt that skimmed the top of her knee and a sheer shirt over a decorative, decently fashionable camisole. She slipped on tall black boots to ward off the evening chill.

They had agreed to meet at Nolo, a trendy urban spot in the heart of Buckhead, Atlanta's lively entertainment district north of Midtown. Buckhead was the city's mothership of capitalistic excess, where two high-end malls and swank fine dining destinations integrated seamlessly with tourist-grabbing restaurants like the Cheesecake Factory and even cheesier souvenir shops.

Katie didn't often venture into Buckhead, preferring the smaller neighborhood bars and restaurants that peppered the Druid Hills neighborhood where she lived, to the east of Midtown, near the Emory University campus. She recognized her luck in finding a converted carriage house apartment behind one of the neighborhood's historic homes. A friend of a friend of her parents knew the owners, who wanted a single, quiet tenant. She rarely saw her landlords, a childless, retired couple who traveled a great deal.

Getting to Buckhead always involved an ordeal of snarled traffic and a maze of twists and turns, no matter which route she took. She left a little early to give herself time to make the trek, find a parking place and still arrive on time at 7:30, looking relaxed and unfazed. It was a good plan, but by the time she made it across town, she was already 15 minutes late. That meant she'd have to either add another 15 minutes to find a parking place on the street or use the restaurant's ridiculously expensive valet.

She wasn't above keeping Jim-the-potential-date waiting a little longer, but she didn't want to annoy Jim-the-pseudo-boss. Cursing under her breath, she pulled up to the valet. "I've got to remember to go to the cash machine before I get my car back," she mumbled, thinking of the lone dollar crumpled in her wallet.

Jim stood waiting by the valet stand when she pulled up. "Beginning to think you stood me up," he joked as she gave the classic Atlanta excuse, "I'm sorry. The traffic was crazy."

The restaurant bustled, but its padded booths and curtains kept the noise at bay and allowed the conversation to flow—along with a very tasty wine that Jim ordered. Katie forced herself to sit still and keep her hands away from her hair as they talked about "safe" topics first, the threat of rain that lingered in the air, the fact that both of them liked to run for exercise, the restaurants they frequented, activities with their friends and how they typically spent their time away from work. He told a story about attempting to keep up in Atlanta's citywide tennis league, but being unceremoniously dumped from his team. She shared a story about training for the city's annual 10K, the Peachtree Road Race, and then injuring herself at the starting line.

The warmth of the wine soothed her. It became easier to sit still. Jim was so easy to talk to and she wanted to learn more. "Tell me about your family. What's your mom like?" she asked.

"She's more down to earth than you'd think, after being such a Deadhead in the seventies. She did all the usual mom stuff with me—you know, like little league, library trips—we spent a lot of time outside. She keeps a big garden."

"Any brothers or sisters?"

"Nope. Just the three of us. Every now and then I wished I'd had some brothers, but there were lots of kids in the neighborhood."

"You didn't want any sisters?"

"Hey," Jim laughed. "Didn't really like girls until it was too late for sisters, if you know what I mean. What about you? Sisters? Brothers? Typical American childhood?"

"I have one sister. She lives in Boston with her husband and my niece. My parents live in Connecticut."

"That where you grew up?"

"Actually, I was born in Boston, then we moved to Connecticut when I was in high school. My dad was a professor. He's retired now from U-Conn."

"That where you went to college?"

"No, I went to Emory, and then just stayed here. What about you?"

"I got lost in the sea of thousands at Clemson, then went to Georgia State for law school."

"What made you decide to be a lawyer?"

"Watching my dad all those years. He'd always work so hard for his clients, and you could always tell he was practicing law for all the right reasons. He never did it for the money. We weren't wealthy like the other lawyer families we knew. My dad took a lot of pro-bono cases and really helped some folks change their lives. I wanna do that, too."

"At Kinsey & McMillan?" Katie asked, raising an eyebrow.

"Oh, good God no, but I wanted to get some trial experience, and it's a good place for that."

"I guess the foundation is one way to balance that out, huh?"

"Sure. Even though we have to stick to my grandfather's restrictions and we only have enough money to fund a fraction of the proposals we get, I still think we're helping. Don't you?"

"Yes, most of the time, but then I get frustrated. Maybe it's because I learn so much about these organizations, but I never get to make any decisions about who gets funded. I know it's not my role, but I feel like I know a lot more than most of the trustees do about what's really needed."

"I can buy that, but you know that we take your recommendations very seriously, don't you?" Jim's eyes found hers. "Especially me. I think the work you do is brilliant, and I love the heart you put into it. You're intelligent, you're passionate about helping people and you do great work."

He hesitated for a moment, glanced away, and then looked back directly at her again. "I also happen to think you're incredibly attractive."

Bam! There it was. Katie's heart flipped over in her chest. With one sentence, Jim had cleared away any question about the purpose of this Saturday night dinner.

She took a deep breath. "This dinner really isn't about business, is it?"

"Well, I did want to talk a little bit more about our strategy for Monday, but I also admit I was hoping that there might be something more to it." Jim's amiable grin took on a sheepish quality, which made it even more captivating.

"I think there might be." She smiled.

"Good." He sat back and let out a long breath. For a moment, neither of them said anything.

"I suppose we should at least talk about the best questions to ask Jorge on Monday," she said, not knowing what else to say.

"Right, right, of course," he said, shifting and settling into his seat.

They spent the rest of dinner talking about the visit to the clinic, the kinds of information they'd need to strengthen the existing proposal even further and the best way to deal with Porter's very adamant stance against serving illegals.

"Has Porter said anything to you at work about this?" Katie asked. She needed to clear up this last little sticking point so she could give in to the warmth of the wine and the different kind of heat that she felt radiating across the table between them. It seemed to grow stronger every minute.

"Nah. We hardly ever see each other at the office. Different divisions, different buildings. I haven't said anything about working with you on this. He'd be quite pissed if he found out, though; he'd say I was trying to stab him in the back. Fancies himself as my mentor. Likes to give me advice whether I want it or not."

Katie rolled her eyes in sympathy.

"It's not all bad. I do get some perks now and then. But he also likes to remind me constantly that I owe him. He'd see this clinic thing as a definite breach of loyalty."

"What if he finds out that you've come by my office? Other staff have seen you there, and I've told them that you've had an interest in this proposal. Not that they'd blab to Porter, but he could find out."

He flashed a big grin. "If he asks, I'll just say that I was just pretending to be interested in this proposal to get you into bed. That line of reasoning is right up his alley."

"God, he's disgusting!" Katie groaned.

"What? You don't like the idea?"

"Not if you're talking about Porter."

"Actually, I was talking about myself in that respect. Still opposed?"

"I'm not sure." She looked down at her hands as a flush began to creep up her neck. "It's only our first date, and I don't know what I might be getting into. It's too early to make that kind of call." The hot flush rose into her face the moment those words left her lips. *Might as well own it.*

"Au contraire, Miz Nelson," he replied, adopting his mock drawl. "I believe this makes the fourth time I've had the pleasure of your company for drinks or dinner. So, according to the unwritten rules of dating, we're past that magic 'third date' and some physical contact is now allowed—which, I might add, I will wait for you to initiate, whenever you are so inclined."

"Keep talking like that, and I may be inclined to punch you." She giggled.

Just then, the waiter arrived to offer the evening's dessert selections.

"We could try something here," he said in a velvety voice, "or you could try some homemade chocolate pecan cake that my mom brought from South Carolina earlier this week."

"Your mom brings you cake? Really?"

"Oh yes! It's in my apartment, right next to my etchings…"

She laughed and turned to the waiter. "I think we'll just take the check."

As they exited the restaurant, he placed his hand on the small of her back. Katie felt the heat radiating through her core.

CHAPTER 9

Jim lived within walking distance, but they decided to take her car the few blocks to avoid the light rain that had begun to fall. Without a word, he stepped up to pay for the valet before she had a chance to confess her lack of cash.

Katie's head buzzed during the short drive. *Is this more because of the wine or because I might actually do something I haven't done in too long?*

He'd left the next move up to her. An unfamiliar mix of power and apprehension swirled in her chest, and she tapped her fingers on the steering wheel. If she moved too fast and got burned, she would have no one to blame but herself. But if she didn't…well, she didn't believe she had the strength or the inclination to end the evening without at least a kiss. More than one if Jim was good at it.

They parked in the lot below his high-rise and rode the elevator to the 10th floor. Jim unlocked the condo door and stood to one side, gesturing Katie over the threshold.

"Welcome to Chez Hunter. It's a perfect example of modern thirty-something bachelorhood, complete with the crowning jewel, Mom's chocolate pecan cake. You'll find it in the fridge in the kitchen to your left. If you don't mind getting it out, I'll be right with you."

She stepped to the kitchen, casting a glance around. The small dining area doubled as the entry. She saw the living room at the back of the apartment beyond the kitchen counter, which acted as a dividing wall. Jim had disappeared down a hallway that hooked to the right after the entry.

The apartment seemed surprisingly nondescript and sparsely furnished for a rising young attorney. He appeared to have no interest in collecting status symbol décor, like antique armoires. He didn't even have a flat-screen TV. Instead, a simple sofa sagged next to a coffee table littered with magazines, newspapers and an iPad. An ample CD collection stood in neat rows in the entertainment center, along with a modest television. An ancient-looking recliner sat in one corner next to a weathered iron side table holding a couple of sad-looking plants. No pictures hung on the walls or adorned the entertainment center shelves. Only one photo—of a pleasant-looking blonde woman who appeared to be in her fifties—clung to the door of the freezer with a magnet advertising the number for the local pizza delivery joint. Katie took a moment to study it. The woman's brown eyes radiated a warmth that her smile echoed. This must be Jim's mother, Katie realized, Camile Hartwell Hunter.

All in all, the apartment was clean, spartan and somewhat depressing. Katie took the cake out of the fridge and set it in its Tupperware container on the counter. She opened the upper cabinets to hunt for plates and practically gasped at the flour, oils, vinegars, cans and boxes of staple goods that filled the shelves. Spices stood in orderly rows, some run-of-the-mill varieties and some with exotic names she had never seen before. Intrigued, she peeked in to the lower cabinets and found rows and rows of pots, pans, baking sheets, a pasta press, an industrial-looking mixer and food processors.

"Ah-ha!" Katie jumped, almost hitting her head on the lower lip of the counter. "You've discovered my deep dark secret," said Jim, holding both hands up, as if he were under arrest. "I confess that I love to cook. Does that make me less of a man?"

She stood up and shot a questioning glance at the chocolate cake on the counter.

"Yeah, that's mine. Figured if you didn't like it I could blame my mom. Been working on that recipe for a while. I think it's finally ready for company."

"Well," she said, her surprise melting into deeper warmth for this man. *A heart placed well outside the rat race* and *a potentially phenomenal cook?* "I suppose there's only one way to find out."

He took two plates from a cabinet on the far side of the kitchen and set them on the counter. "You may do the honors."

Katie cut two slices while he fetched forks. Then he led her to the living room couch. Among the magazines and junk mail on the coffee table were copies of *Epicurean* and *Bon Appétit.*

"Well?" he asked as she took a bite.

The chocolate emerged subtly at first, but then grew in intensity. It warmed with the heat of her mouth, mixing with the salty pecan as she rolled it around on her tongue, its flavor growing richer with every millisecond until it exploded with an unexpected burst of deeply seeded orange essence.

"Oh my God! This is phenomenal! What's making that orange flavor?"

"Grand Marnier infusion. Took me weeks to get right. I'm glad you like it."

"Like it? Are you kidding? You're in the wrong line of work, mister. You should definitely make *these* for a living."

"Oh, no, that's a hell of a life. I only like to cook for people I care about." He looked right at her.

She blushed as she took another bite. "Where did you learn how to *do* this?"

He shrugged. "My mom's a good cook. And I had a girlfriend in law school who taught me some things. It's a good way to unwind, make some space between work and the real world."

Old girlfriend? No surprise there. He was a desirable catch for a number of women. Yet now he was genuinely interested in her. *Own it.*

"So, if I decided to kiss you right now, and exercise my option, so to speak, would that be this good, too? Or should I stick to the cake?"

"I suppose there's only one way to find out."

"Well, then," she said, setting her plate on the coffee table and leaning toward him. "You may do the honors."

CHAPTER 10

At 2:00 a.m., Katie woke with a start and looked around the darkened room as she tried to get her bearings. Then she realized she was still in Jim's apartment, wrapped in his arms on the couch, in fact. The memory of the evening came to her. Although she had wanted him, she'd managed to maintain her vow not to move too fast. She craved speed at work, where change couldn't come fast enough, but relationships were different territory and required more caution. Michael had seen to that.

She'd put on the brakes, and they had both fallen asleep. Now, as the thought of Michael flitted through her mind, she decided it best, and potentially less awkward, to slip out and go home.

She looked out of the living room window and saw that the rain had stopped. She tried to slip out of his grasp and retrieve her shoes—and her sheer shirt, which had apparently managed to work its way off her body during their session of brain-searing kisses.

As she tried to make a silent exit, Jim stirred. "Hey, what's up?"

"I've got to go. I need to…I need to…"

"You need to stay here and sleep more. I make a great breakfast," he said with drowsy lidded eyes and tousled hair.

Katie wanted to stay more than she'd ever wanted anything. But she needed to go home and clear her head—after replaying every moment of the evening, every shred of conversation, every bite of that fabulous cake and every magnificent kiss, of course.

"I'd love to stay, but…" No words seemed adequate.

"It's okay—this time. One day, you'll realize that it's okay for us to hang out together. There really *is* no rule against trustees dating staff. I think of you as a lot more than that anyway."

"I know. I just need some time to think."

"Look, there's absolutely no reason we can't spend time together, as long as it doesn't affect our work. Don't know about you, but that's a risk I'm willing to take. I'm also willing to take the fall if this doesn't work." His voice softened, beckoning her back to the couch. "So far we've been really good together, Katie. And just a little while ago, we were great, and I think you know we can be even better."

His words sank in, and her feet stuck to the floor, not knowing whether to walk toward him or toward the door.

"But look, I really don't wanna rush you," he said, shifting to a brisker tone, as he got up off the couch and fetched her coat. "So I'll walk you to your car if you promise to lock your doors, drive home very carefully and take my call when it comes in the morning."

"Yes to all of the above." She paused for one last kiss in the doorway of his apartment, which turned into another rather long one in the elevator, another leaning against her car and a last one on her forehead just before she started the ignition and backed away.

Driving south on the nearly deserted Peachtree Street at 2:30 a.m., thoughts of Jim and dozens of questions swam in her mind. She allowed them to float there without probing for answers. She couldn't make any real sense of it all here in the wee hours of the morning. Good thing there wasn't much traffic.

She stopped at a light, her eyes wandering as her brain floated back to Jim's apartment. For now, she just wanted to dwell on the evening.

Suddenly, she sat bolt upright in the driver's seat, eyes wide open. There, across the intersection in a black Mercedes, waiting to head past her in the opposite lane, sat Guy Porter.

Katie froze. What if he saw her? What if he figured out the direction she was coming from? Did he know where Jim lived? She looked down at her console for sunglasses, a hat, anything to hide behind, but she found nothing there. Her heart pounded.

She glanced at Porter again and realized that he hadn't yet seen her. He stared straight ahead, his hands drumming on the wheel as he gazed ahead, stone-faced.

When the light changed, he drove right by her without so much as a sidelong glance.

She breathed a huge sigh of relief and continued through the intersection. Now nightmares of Porter supplanted her reverie of Jim. What if he'd seen her? What if he found out and got angry like Jim said he would? What if he demanded her resignation, or worse, termination? Jim said he would take the fall, but he couldn't be fired as a trustee. Could he keep her from being fired? She didn't think so, and she really couldn't blame him if he didn't.

When she reached her carriage house, she ran up the steps and bolted her door. With the click of the lock, waves of fatigue began to lap around the edges of her mind. She threw on her oldest, most comfortable and reassuring pair of pajamas and climbed under the covers to hide in sleep. She would deal with whatever she had to in the morning.

***

The piercing ring of the phone startled Katie awake. What time was it? A pale light, barely enough to distinguish itself, peered around the edges of the window shade. Her alarm clock said 7:30. The phone rang again.

"Hello?" She struggled to make her voice sound clearer than her head. It all came to her at once: the dinner with Jim, the cake, the kisses, a cozy slumber and then Porter. Oh God, was this Porter calling now?

"Hi, Katie, it's me." Her chest unclenched a little at the sound of Jim's voice, but he sounded odd, strained.

"Hi. It's a little early, isn't it? Did you miss me already?" Her weak attempt at a joke failed miserably.

"Yes, I did…I do, but that's not why I'm calling."

Her pulse quickened. Had Porter called him?

“Turn on your TV, Katie. Channel 2. The clinic—it’s gone. It burned to the ground.”

CHAPTER 11

Katie drove on autopilot towards the site of the fire. Stark gray morning light did little to lift the fog in her mind. She drove for blocks before she noticed the tears on her face. *All that work, for nothing.*

As she neared the street, she detected an acrid tinge hanging in the air. A wave of nausea swirled up from the pit of her stomach. She found a parking spot near the police barricade that cordoned off the block where the clinic once stood. She hugged her sweater around her as she walked toward the site. The Sunday morning streets of this part of downtown Atlanta were practically deserted—not surprising given the wasteland of abandoned warehouses and vacant lots. She walked past crumbling masonry and cracked windowpanes encased in layers of dust and grime. If she hadn't known the clinic had been on this street, she would never have missed it. Just one less teetering roofline to block the weak morning sky. Only a lone fire truck remained at the steaming ruins of the building, keeping watch for any last sparks.

As she approached, she noticed with horror that the front and side walls of the clinic had partially collapsed, scorched by the flames that had engulfed the interior. Through the gaping holes of the now-shattered windows, she saw that the back of the building and the roof were completely gone. Smoky black chunks of charred wood and twisted metal poked up at odd angles past the crumbled walls. Ash and puddles of water from the fire hose leaked from the guts of the building, a slow hemorrhage of devastation. Yellow caution tape circled the perimeter of the site, rippling halfheartedly in the chilly breeze.

Next to one of the fire trucks was a large pickup truck with the Atlanta Fire Department seal on its door. Firemen walked through some of the rubble, searching for remaining hot spots or clues to the blaze's origin. Jorge stood, stock-still and staring, from the sidewalk in front of what once was the clinic entrance.

She stepped to him and rested her fingers on his arm. "Jorge," she said, "I'm so sorry."

He turned to face her, his eyes sad and weighed down by dark circles. "Me too, Katie. I knew that many people were not happy about the work we did here, but I had no idea they would be so, well, inhuman about it."

"So definitely arson? Not an accident?"

He shrugged a shoulder toward the firemen walking through the rubble. "That's what they say. That's what it looks like. The investigator wants me to answer questions about people and groups that might have had something against us. How am I supposed to answer that?" His voice rose and he raised his hand to his eyes for a moment, exhaling loudly. "We get regular phone calls and hate mail from all kinds of wackos. There are protests here every other week. They either hate us because we serve 'illegals,' or they hate us and call us 'spics,' or they hate us because we're 'baby killers,' even though most of our clients are Catholic. Maybe they hate that, too. There are more threats than I can count, and any evidence we would have had was in there," he said, nodding his head to the building's remains.

She followed his gaze and for the first time realized that one of the men walking the rubble was dressed not in firefighting gear, but in coveralls and boots. He had a shovel and was picking through the rubble at the back of the building. Occasionally, he would pick something up in gloved hands or take a picture of the rubble with a smartphone.

"Is that the arson investigator?"

Jorge nodded.

Just then, a hand touched Katie's shoulder and there was Jim, who followed up on his initial touch by wrapping his arm around her with a soft, "Hey, there. You okay?"

"Actually, you should ask Jorge," she said. Realizing that the two men had never met face to face, she introduced them.

"Jorge, this is Jim Hunter. He was coming with me tomorrow for our site visit. Jim, this is Dr. Ramirez."

Jim extended a warm hand to Jorge while keeping an arm around Katie. Jorge looked at Jim with a blank expression.

I bet to Jorge we look like a couple, Katie thought and took a half step away from Jim as she explained, "The firefighters tell Jorge they suspect arson. They want him to answer questions about all the hate mail and phone calls the clinic received. It's such a waste…"

She trailed off as two women walked up on the other side of Jorge and began a conversation with him in rapid Spanish. She thought she recognized them as workers in the clinic, and Jorge introduced them as his medical director and lead patient case manager.

"If you'll excuse me," Jorge said, "they have just reminded me that although we do not have a building, we still have patients who will want to know how and where to get help tomorrow morning, and we need to start making plans for dealing with them." A small smile played around his lips, and the old spark reappeared in his eye. "It just goes to show you that even if I wanted to give up right now, they would not let me. We are a blessed enterprise."

"Of course," said Katie, and Jorge returned to his conversation with his coworkers while she and Jim moved a few paces down the sidewalk.

"So, are you okay?" asked Jim again, giving her a questioning look.

"Yes, I'm fine. I'm not the one whose life's work just went up in smoke." She looked again at the rubble and wiped her eyes with the sleeve of her sweater before turning back to him. "I'm sorry. You didn't deserve that. I'm just tired, and with this and with you and…and everything, there's a lot going on right now. I think I need to go home."

"I could come with you."

"No thanks. That's sweet, but I'd like to be alone for a while."

"I understand. But I'll come over and make dinner for you tonight. Won't take no for an answer."

"Okay." She mustered a smile. "You're the boss."

"Please tell me you don't really think like that."

She shook her head no and turned toward her car. It was nice that he didn't like to be reminded of the authority he held.

"Hey, wait. One other question," said Jim. "Did Jorge say what it was that made the investigators suspect arson, what they found?"

"No, he just said that it looked like arson. Why?"

"Blame it on the litigator in me. If there's enough evidence, there'll be a criminal investigation, which could turn into a civil suit, and there's also making sure the insurance company pays the claim. Maybe I can do something. Help Jorge get some of his losses back. Anyway, I'm gonna hang out for a while and see what I can learn from those guys." He hooked a thumb over his shoulder at the men sifting through the building rubble.

That surge of warmth from the night before returned for a moment, even as Katie fought off a growing weight in her muscles and a desire to just collapse in a heap on the sidewalk. "That would be awesome. Let me know what you find out."

"I will. I'll come over around five to start cooking. We'll see what the evening news says about all this. Call you later for directions."

Katie waved and walked to her car. On the way home, as the rest of the world was waking up for a full day, her lids grew heavy, matched by her mood. Everything was working against her desire to help Viva Latina—foundation policies, the older foundation board members…and now this fire.

Her lips pressed into a hard, thin line, and her fingers on her right hand teased at a stray curl as she drove with her left. Ironic, she mused, that Porter's attack on her had been wasted. Now the whole project was literally up in smoke.

She pulled into her driveway and stumbled up the stairs to her apartment. Babka the cat, who resembled a kitty-sized version of Jabba the Hutt, meowed loudly to protest his empty bowl. Katie absentmindedly fed him, then collapsed into bed, pulling the covers over her head and letting the sound of the wind carry her off as it knocked tight spring dogwood buds against her window.

CHAPTER 12

Just like the arson investigators and the cops, I watched who showed up after the fire. There were the usual suspects, like the spic doctor who runs the place and some of his staff.

I'd expected them. It's the people you don't expect that you have to watch out for. Like the girl. She focused on the doctor and didn't stay very long, but I could tell she was upset. She cared about this fire. She'll also be upset about the body once they find it. Could be that it would just make her sad, but it also could spell trouble.

I'll have to ask the boss who the girl is. Find out if she could be a problem. Figure out what to do about her if she is.

Like any violent crime, arson and murder can bring out a different side of people. It can make them feel afraid for a long time afterward. Because even if you know the reason someone torched a building or even if the murder was an accident, they can still feel like completely random crimes. If one nut job could burn down your office or your house or your church and kill someone in the process, who's to say it wouldn't happen again? Chances of that are pretty damn slim. Real arsonists don't commit random acts. They don't "accidentally" kill people. They aren't kids playing with matches. So once they've lit a fire, they're usually inclined to move on.

But a crime like that can also make people angry. It can make them feel like they were treated unjustly and make them want to right what they think is a wrong. That's the way the girl looked when she left—angry.

I wasn't worried about the arson investigators or the cops so much. They would find some clues, no doubt. But they had protocols to follow and rules of law that would only let them proceed in sanctioned ways during their investigation. Their work could only take them so far. And a hate crime with a nameless body wasn't going to be a priority.

But the girl, she didn't have to answer to anybody. Depending on who she was, she could ask questions and point fingers if she wanted to. And she very likely could become a problem. Her I'd have to watch. I'd have to learn her story, how she fit into all this.

CHAPTER 13

Katie awoke around noon and took a shower, but still couldn't shake the gloom that had slogged home from the fire scene with her. She kept thinking of Jorge and his staff and all of the women and families who looked to them for help. What kind of person could do something like this? What kind of hatred or deep-seated anger would it take to drive someone to strike the match or lighter or whatever had been used to start the blaze? Did that person feel vindicated now? Powerful? Patriotic? Was it even possible to catch them?

Maybe she could take her mind off things. A bad TV comedy was simply too trite. A walk around the neighborhood in the chilly afternoon only painted the world a dull gray. It was no use. At 4:00 p.m., she lay on the couch, hiding behind closed eyes and a drooping pillow, more miserable than ever. It just wasn't fair. *I hope they catch you soon, you bastard, whoever you are.*

The phone rang, jolting her eyes open. She swung her feet off the couch and shrugged herself upright.

"I've got homemade minestrone on the menu for tonight." Jim's voice was warm and reassuring. "Need anything from the store?"

She declined and went to put on some fresh clothes before he arrived. She chose a pair of black fleece warm-up pants and a well-loved cotton fisherman's sweater. Comfort was more important than sex appeal now. "We'll see how Mr. Hunter reacts to the real me," she said to Babka as she shuffled back into her living room.

The carriage house apartment wasn't large, perched above the main house's two-car garage and storage area below. It contained just four rooms: living room, kitchen, bathroom and bedroom, but it had never felt small. Instead, it was cozy and comforting—her personal, private sanctuary. In it, she had placed a mix of yard-sale furniture and family hand-me-downs. "Heirloom" was too strong a word for the wooden double bed with turned posts that took up most of the bedroom or the glass-fronted secretary in the living room with scratches from her grandmother's long-ago cats.

The prints on the walls hung in inexpensive frames. Most were generic, plucked from the bargain bins at Crate and Barrel or Pottery Barn, but a handful were purchased as souvenirs from art exhibits at Atlanta's High Museum.

In addition to the secretary, the living room held an old sofa with a plain canvas slipcover with a set of faded floral pillows, perfect for napping, and a low coffee table that Katie had reclaimed from a yard sale and painted white. She hoped it was more "shabby chic" than "shabby cheap." Two slipper chairs—her only new furniture purchases—divided time as dining chairs for her small table and extra seating should she ever have visitors, which was unlikely, since the carriage house was her refuge from the world.

Now, with Jim coming over, she began to pace, repeatedly twisting her hair into a bun and then letting it drop again. When she heard his footsteps on the stairs, she unbolted the door and opened it.

"I guess since you showed me yours…" she began, but then deflated. Joking took too much effort.

"Nice place," he said, leaning down between two armfuls of grocery bags to give her a peck on the forehead. He squeezed past her and made his way to the kitchen, which was easy enough to find.

Katie gave him the quick but complete tour, pointing out her meager selection of cooking implements. She felt thankful that she at least owned a decent soup pot, a cutting board and a passably sharp knife. She didn't require many kitchen tools for frozen Lean Cuisine, canned soups, salads or pints of Ben & Jerry's. She did, however, have take-out menus from every nearby restaurant stuffed into a drawer, which definitely was *not* part of the kitchen tour.

As the gray daylight began to fade, Jim chopped and sautéed onions, garlic, carrots and a little celery, filling the apartment with a delicious odor. Katie opened a bottle of wine he'd brought and poured two glasses.

"Where did you get wine on a Sunday?" she asked. Georgia's arcane "blue laws" forbade the sale of alcohol on the Lord's Day.

"I keep a small cellar. You never know when you're gonna need a glass of Zinfandel to round out a weekend. I like to be prepared."

He was trying to cheer her up, she knew, but she stood against the fridge, her wineglass clutched close to her chest in both hands. She wanted answers, and she hoped Jim would provide them.

"Did you find out anything else from the firemen this morning?"

"Talked Jorge into letting me serve as his attorney, but we didn't get much information from the investigator on the site. They seem pretty durn sure it was arson. Said it looked like two separate 'incendiary devices'"—here he made air quotes with his fingers—"likely thrown through a window. They've got all Jorge's contact info for follow-up questions. Don't seem to suspect him, though."

"Suspect *Jorge*? Why on earth would they do that? That clinic is his passion!"

"Crimes happen for reasons of passion all the time, Katie. But I agree with you. Doesn't seem like something Jorge would do. On the other hand, his building was insured, so he had somethin' to gain."

Her brow furrowed as she gave him a deep frown.

He stopped chopping and took a deep breath. "Katie," he said, "there's one other thing you should know."

"What?" She swallowed hard. This couldn't be good news.

"In the rubble at the front of the building," he said, staring down at the vegetables. "They found a body. After you left, they found it."

Her stomach lurched. "Who…?"

He shook his head. "No one knows yet. Dr. Ramirez insisted that no one should have been there. His nurses had already accounted for all the staff. The coroner will have to make an I.D. because of the condition of…"

He stopped short, but her mind filled in the rest. *The condition of the body*. Probably burned beyond recognition.

"Oh, poor Jorge! He'll feel responsible."

"I think he's okay. We talked for a long time. But you should probably call him tomorrow just to check in."

"Do you think it was intentional?"

"Hard to say. From what I could pick up, it sounds like a hate crime against the clinic is the most likely reason for the arson. Coulda been racists or pro-lifers or both. Once they found the body, though, the medical examiner and the Hat Squad showed up. They…."

"Hat Squad?"

"Yeah, that's what everyone calls the Atlanta homicide detectives. They decided a few years ago that they weren't getting enough respect or recognition, so they decided that they'd wear suits and fedoras, like they used to in the forties and fifties. Not sure what it did for the quality of their work, but it does give them a pretty cool film noir vibe.

"Anyway, they asked Jorge some questions, but like I said, it didn't sound like they suspected anything other than hate. I'll see what else I can find out. I'm not a criminal attorney and I'm not well versed in the procedure, but I'll do what I can to make sure Jorge has what he needs to at least get his claim filed. I can make sure he has good representation for questioning, too."

"But he won't really need that, right?"

"Nah, I doubt it. The Hat Squad says hate crime, at least for now. And hell, there was a protest there just yesterday. All kinds of wackos come out for those things."

It was true. Like Jorge had pointed out this morning, the clinic had received plenty of anonymous threats. If dozens or even hundreds of people had hated the clinic, how would they ever find a single arsonist? *No, not just an arsonist: a murderer.*

The thought of someone burning to death in Jorge's building squelched Katie's appetite, but with a little coaxing, she agreed to at least try some of Jim's soup.

They took their bowls and a loaf of crusty bread to the living room couch and flipped through the local news channels. The fire and the discovery of the body headlined the top stories of every local station. The reporters confirmed the suspicion of arson, but offered no speculation as to who the victim or suspects might be. Despite her horror and sadness, Katie's stomach began to grumble. She took a few tentative mouthfuls, soaking up the warmth and comfort the soup provided.

After the news, they channel-surfed until tendrils of sleepiness wafted into her brain. She leaned against Jim, who put his arm around her. They sat in silence, watching the screen, and then he began kissing her temple. His lips were soft and searching as they worked their way along her cheek, her jaw line and her neck, finally finding her lips. She kissed him back, but neither her mind nor her body wanted to give into this tonight.

"Dinner was wonderful," she said, pulling back and looking into his eyes. "And *you* are wonderful. But tonight's just not a good night for this…for me."

"Are you sure? 'Cause it feels like a good night to me." He smiled at her. But he looked tired too.

Part of her longed to ask him to stay, just to sleep curled up with her all night, but she needed more time to herself to process everything that had happened during this eventful weekend. "I'm sure. For tonight. I need to get my head together for the week, and I'm pretty sure work tomorrow is going to suck."

"No doubt. But I betcha at least one or two other folks there will feel like you do. It's a big shock, but ya'll can support one another." He gave her shoulders a comforting squeeze. "And hey, if you're still worried about people finding out about us, then don't be. We can just do our thing and to hell with 'em."

"No, no. It's not that at all. It's really all *this...*" She gestured toward the television set. "But you're right. I still don't want to advertise about us seeing..." She stopped suddenly and sat up straight. "Oh! That reminds me. Last night, on the way back from your house, I saw Porter at a traffic light. It scared me to death for a minute, but he didn't see me."

"So what if he had? You have just as much right to be out driving at—what, 2:30? 3:00?—as he does."

"I know, but it still gave me the creeps. What do you think he was doing in the middle of the night? He was coming north from downtown, but his office is up by you in Buckhead."

Jim grinned at her. "Same thing you were doing. He either had a late night with the cronies at the City Club or else an early night with his mistress at her condo downtown. Who knows? Who cares?"

"Mistress? Really?"

"Oh, yeah. He's very open about it. Doesn't give a damn who knows. Brags about what a looker she is. I've never seen her, though."

"What does his wife say about that?"

"He doesn't care. Porter and his wife hate each other. He stays married to her for her money and social standing. She's old Atlanta. She stays married to him because he shows up at events when he's told to and otherwise leaves her alone to do whatever and buy whatever she wants. She spends a ton of time vacationing up in North Carolina, in Highlands. It's a match made in heaven."

Katie shuddered. *What a pig. Why did I ever care what he thought about me?*

"I wonder if he's ever made soup for her?" she asked, tracing her spoon through what was left in her bowl.

"Doubt it, and I bet he's never done this either." He leaned over and gave Katie a long, deep, slow kiss that made her rethink her desire to spend the evening alone. Would it be so bad to have some company?

"Wow, you're making it very difficult for me to ask you to leave."

"Then don't," he said, raising an eyebrow.

"Jim, I really like you, but I…I…"

"I know, I know." He stood up and stretched his arms out, leaving an empty hollow on the couch. "I don't want to screw this up either." He smoothed the front of his shirt and extended a hand to her. "So, until next time, Miz Nelson, I will bid you goodnight."

"Thank you. For everything." She took his hand and stood, placing a lingering palm on his chest.

"I'll be in touch soon," he said, giving her one last peck on the forehead. He stepped to the door, opened it and then turned back to her. "If you don't want to eat all the leftover soup over the next few days, it will freeze well," he added and left, closing the door behind him with a click.

Katie giggled. *It will freeze well?* How could a man sound so passionate one minute and so borderline gay the next?

CHAPTER 14

Monday morning, as she drove to the Foundation offices, Katie called Jorge to extend her sympathies about the death in the clinic. He sounded tired and distracted, which was to be expected, and politely declined another impulsive invitation for coffee.

"I understand," she said, wishing she could look him in the eye and know that he was all right. "I just wanted you to know that this isn't your fault. I worry that you'll think it is."

"Ah, no. It is no one's fault is it? She was an illegal, homeless, a cousin of someone who works for the cleaning service. She had only been in the country a couple of months. She wanted to see a doctor and didn't have a place to sleep. Her cousin let her into the building and locked the door after she was inside. She could not get to a door or window. The coroner says she died of smoke inhalation."

Katie gulped and pulled her car to the side of the road. She squeezed her eyes shut, pressing her thumb and forefinger against them. "Oh Jorge, that poor woman! How horrible! And the cousin…how stupid to leave someone in a building like that. Why couldn't he have taken her to his house?"

"I cannot blame him. He thought the clinic was a safe place. And he has lost a member of his family. He is tormented enough."

Katie heard a muffled sound through the phone. A sob? "But it's not your fault either, Jorge! You didn't even know she was there!"

Only silence came through the line for a moment before Jorge choked on whispered words, "She should not have been there. It was not right. That was not the way we…"

"But you didn't *know*! You would never have allowed it."

"Right. I would have stopped it. It should never have happened." Jorge almost sounded as if he were responding on autopilot. He paused again, and then spoke so softly Katie could barely hear him. "Her name was Angel. Now she is one."

Katie didn't know how to respond. He sounded so defeated, so morose.

But then he continued, once again regrouping to face the adversity. "But we go on. We will go on for her. We will grow bigger and better, Katie. And to do that, I must get back to work."

"Of course," said Katie, marveling at his fortitude. "I…just take care of yourself, please."

Katie moved through Monday and Tuesday as if in a daze. At the office, the other staff commented on the fire and the death. "What a tragedy." Everyone knew this project held a special place in her portfolio, and many of her coworkers treated her with kid gloves. While she gratefully took advantage of the leeway the other staff gave her, she knew they couldn't appreciate how fully, how deeply this tragedy had shaken her. Viva Latina had become a symbol of change for her. If the board had funded it on the second attempt, it would have meant a professional step forward for her and a personal victory over Porter. Now, just like the ashes that had swirled around the burning clinic, she was floating in limbo.

Chris, who she hoped would offer some words of wisdom, barely met her gaze as they passed in the hallway, and he closed the door to his office the second he stepped inside. She didn't know whether to be angry with him or sympathetic. Her other coworkers tried to engage her in chitchat, but she didn't really hear their condolences. Because of the fire, because of the death of some unknown woman, everything had changed. The clinic proposal was dead now, too.

And the image of a woman burning simply would not leave the back of her mind.

She tried to focus on her work—after all, the next really great funding idea could turn up just around the corner—but an unshakeable cloud loomed over her. The weather didn't help. The brief sunny spell had dissolved again into gloomy rain and chill. In the evenings, she warmed up the leftover soup and curled up on the couch with a glass of red wine, watching British sitcoms. Jim called her twice each day, but didn't push to see her, and for that she was grateful, although she missed the feeling of having him next to her. They agreed to meet on Wednesday for dinner.

Katie clung to that prospect like a lifeline. Jim understood her, knew how deeply Porter's words had cut and understood how fighting for the clinic had become more than just a grant. Surely he would have some news, some great idea, for setting her world back on its axis and making sense of everything. Maybe together they could help Jorge submit a different proposal, one to help the clinic rebuild or relocate. Or if nothing else, surely Jim would provide a distraction from the gloom.

***

The March board meeting, the one in which Porter had attacked her, was the first of four quarterly meetings. The next was scheduled for June, and to prepare for it, Katie had to review the proposals that kept trickling in. Late Wednesday afternoon, she took a pile of new proposals—accumulated over several days—out of her cluttered office and into the spacious and austere foundation boardroom. Aside from the quarterly board meeting and occasional staff gatherings, the room was rarely used, but its large table gave Katie room to spread out and concentrate on each new proposal without any distractions.

Katie took this stage of the proposal process very seriously because during this initial review, she would decline the majority of submissions. For the sake of fairness, she had to give each one as much attention as she could. She was a gatekeeper, sifting through dozens and dozens of documents to find the gems that both adhered to the foundation's grant guidelines and offered promising ideas that could successfully address a community need. Those she would explore more fully and, if everything added up, forward to the board with a funding recommendation. Those that were approved stayed in

Katie's portfolio, where she monitored the grantees' progress and ensured that each grant agreement was honored.

She always read through each proposal twice, giving her full attention, as if it were the only one she had to consider. She made a conscious effort not to compare the merits of each against the others—at least not yet, anyway. That would come later and would be the board's role.

After the first read-through she would put each proposal into one of three piles: "no way," "ho-hum" and "very interesting." Those that made the "very interesting" pile she'd have to discuss with Chris later, assuming he would talk to her at all.

When the now-defunct clinic proposal had first come in, she remembered with a sad smile, she had placed it into the "very interesting" pile right away and had followed up with a request for more details. Since that proposal had literally gone up in smoke, she wondered if there would be anything as inspiring to take its place. She also hoped this new pile would offer some sort of a sign for her personal future—if even one proposal sparked the same level of interest, then that would mean she should stay at the foundation and continue her work. If not, then she should quit being so idealistic about other people's money and get real about what she could do by herself, which in reality meant going back to the nonprofit front lines.

Usually, she dove into the review process, tempering the inevitable tingle of power with a healthy dose of humility. Each proposal represented months or years of blood, sweat and tears on the part of the nonprofits submitting them, and even the ones destined for the recycling bin deserved her respect. But today, just thinking about the review process that lay before her and the proposals that would pour into the foundation offices over the next few weeks made her head ache.

She pulled the first proposal from the stack. Another request from St. Mary's Day School, most likely destined for ho-hum-dom. But she owed it a fair read. She leaned over it, her dark hair falling on either side of her face, and began.

With the door closed, the boardroom's three walls of silent bookshelves muffled any noise from the rest of the office. The one long wall of gauzy shaded windows let in waning light from the southwest. It cast a sober, studious air, and she became engrossed in her work as the hours tiptoed by. Whenever she read like this, her hands moved constantly of their own accord. If she wasn't torturing a stray curl, she flipped a paper clip over and over around her thumb or played an imaginary piano on her knee or, as she did now, twirled the thin silver bracelet she had been wearing around and around, slowly, then quickly, slowly, then quickly. The unconscious rhythm sharpened her concentration and kept her mind from wandering elsewhere.

As she concentrated on a new proposal, the silver bracelet twirled too fast and flew from her finger, clattering across the length of the oak board table and landing with a metallic clink somewhere across the room. Katie almost jumped out of her skin. "What the…?" She glanced up where the sound had come from, trying to place it, bringing her mind back to her surroundings. Then she looked at her wrist, at the spot where her bracelet should have been. "Oh. Ooops."

She rose from her chair, rubbing the slight stiffness in her neck and stretching out the cramped muscles in her back, and strode around the table to the narrow corner where the bracelet had disappeared. A quick glance at the carpet and on the chairs where she thought the bracelet ought to have landed revealed nothing.

"Damn, now where did you go?" The bracelet wasn't particularly valuable, but it had belonged to her grandmother and was therefore special. When Katie was only six or seven, Gran had shown her a jewelry box full of beads and pins and other treasures and told her she could pick out whatever she wanted to keep for herself. She chose the silver bracelet, although now she couldn't remember why. Her mother had admonished her to keep it safe and not to wear it to school, and Katie had followed her instructions. In fact, she had packed it away so well that she had only rediscovered it when moving into her carriage house apartment. Now she wore it whenever the mood struck her.

She searched the floor again, this time on hands and knees on the lush woolen Oriental rug that covered almost the entire floor. She crawled under the table and felt around in the dark with her hands, even though the bracelet should be easy to see. Nothing. She then systematically checked the creases in the leather upholstery of the chairs, squeezing her hands in between the backs, seats and sides. Again, no luck.

She remembered the sound of a bracelet hitting something more concrete than a chair. Could it have landed on one of the lower bookshelves? She checked them all, running her hands along the tops of the volumes. Was there was space behind the books where the bracelet could have fallen? No, not there, either.

Next, she turned to the trash can. It wasn't far from the edge of the table, innocently sitting in the corner. Definitely worth a shot. She peered into it. "Ugh. Don't they ever empty this thing?"

The trash can wasn't large, but was deep enough to appear empty to a cleaning person scanning the room from the other side of the table; however, it was by no means empty. In addition to strewn pieces of paper—some flat, some ripped, some wadded—there was a Styrofoam cup of rancid coffee, old enough to have grown an impressive array of mold that no one would want to touch. There was also, of all things, what appeared to be a navy blue sock with a considerable hole in the toe. Katie chuckled to herself as she pictured one of the straight-laced board members quietly removing his shoe and the offending sock under the table during a board meeting and surreptitiously tossing it into the trash can as the meeting broke up.

With a grimace, she knelt by the trash can and forced herself to extract the Styrofoam coffee cup, placing it an arm's length away on the carpet. The sock received the same treatment. Katie still couldn't see to the bottom, where her bracelet could have easily slipped, so she removed a sheaf of flat papers that listed to one side of the can. As she picked them up, her bracelet clattered in the bottom of the can, and she dropped the papers to her side and lifted the loop of cherished silver out of a pool of undetermined stickiness. It would need a rinse and a rubdown with the antibacterial gel she kept in her desk, but otherwise it appeared not much worse for the experience. She put the bracelet on top of the stack of papers in order to avoid making a sticky mess on the carpet and then deposited the sock and coffee cup back into the can. As she reached for the stack of papers, words on the top page caught her eye, and she flipped through the stack.

These were copies of proposals from the last board meeting, apparently dropped into the trash by a trustee after the meeting. But what piqued Katie's interest were the notes scrawled in the margins. Although she often heard board members discussing proposals, she could never know their personal opinions, and so she couldn't resist looking to see what one trustee had written. Any clue as to how a trustee thought could be helpful.

The first few pages were copies of the approved proposals, mostly with notes about financial questions and long-term support. Nothing really unusual and nothing to give Katie an idea as to who this trustee might be. Whoever it was apparently went along with the general consensus of the board.

As she neared the bottom of the pile, her thoughts about this trustee being a complacent follower flew out the window as his identity became crystal clear. Scrawled across the top of her proposal for the Viva Latina health clinic were the words "Fuck No!!!" Only Porter would be comfortable enough with that term to commit it to paper, not to mention being so violently opposed to the proposal itself and so overwhelmingly unfair to her in the process. She could hear his voice just as clearly as if he'd been yelling directly at her—just like he'd done only a few weeks ago. She clenched her jaw and continued scanning the page.

The rest of the proposal was devoid of any comment, which she suspected meant Porter had formed his initial reaction quickly and had felt no further need to read the details. A wave of resentment nearly choked her. With all the hard work and research she had put into the proposal, the least that arrogant bastard could have done was read the damn thing. He must have reacted purely from racial prejudice. What else could it have been? And how could the other trustees put up with that?

Maybe this was a sign to leave for sure. On the last page of the proposal was one other quick note: "Call Sutter." Great. Now he was using her work as a memo pad for his daily tasks. Thanks a lot, Porter.

She paused and looked at the note again. *Sutter.* She had seen that name before. But when? Where? She sat wracking her brain for a moment, trying to remember if Sutter was the name of someone in another grantee organization, someone at another foundation or someone completely unrelated...

"Katie?" Louise Jackson's voice startled her so that she dropped the papers, scattering them onto the carpet around her. Louise was the foundation's executive director and a stickler for protocol. "Katie, what are you doing down there?"

This must look odd to her boss, finding an employee huddled on the floor amid the debris from the trash. "I...I lost my bracelet in the trash can. I was twirling it, and it just flew off...but I found it, see?" Katie held up the bracelet sheepishly. "They really don't empty these cans often enough, do they?"

Louise gave her an odd look. "I didn't realize anyone else was still here. It's after six. Why don't you walk out with me?"

Katie had no idea so much time had passed. Babka would be hungry. "Okay, just let me clean off this bracelet and get those proposals back to my office. I'll be right with you," she replied, nodding at her piles on the table. She scooped the papers off the floor and placed them back in the trash, Porter's "Fuck No!!!" note now glaring from the top of the stack. She longed to show it to Louise and discuss her frustration at what appeared to be blatant racism. But as much as Louise might share her sentiments about Porter, Katie knew she had overstepped her bounds by looking at his notes. Louise would most certainly disapprove.

"Okay," Louise replied, "I'll meet you by the elevators." After censorious glance at Katie's messy piles of paper, she headed back toward her office.

Katie gathered up her proposals from the table and dumped them in her office. Then she hurried down the hall to the bathroom to rinse her bracelet off. She stared at her reflection for a moment in the mirror. *I don't belong here anymore.*

On her way to the reception area, she passed the conference room and couldn't help herself. She peered up and down the hallway to check for Louise. Then she ducked into the conference room and went straight to the trash can, where she extracted the offensive page, folded it into sloppy quarters and slipped it into her purse. She thought about showing it to Jim, although she wasn't sure if she should. Either way, she wasn't ready to let this go. Not yet. For whatever reason—and she'd figure that out later— she wanted to keep this memento of her anger at the way Porter had treated her.

CHAPTER 15

Sutter. The name kept popping up as she drove home. She fed Babka, then rushed out again to meet Jim. How could she ask about Sutter without saying where she had seen the name written? As much as she disliked Porter, his notes on grant proposals were his confidential business.

She met Jim at a small Italian place in Virginia Highland, one neighborhood over from hers and not too far from Jim's Midtown office. "Va-High" sported less of the elitist "see-and-be-seen" attitude that flourished amidst Buckhead's trendy clubs and restaurants. It was quieter and more pedestrian-friendly. While Va-High's narrow streets of cute bungalows drew mostly recent college grads and young families, it also offered a number of cozy restaurants, bars and small shops that attracted its share of tourists.

"So you heard they identified the victim?" Jim asked as soon as they had taken a seat.

"Yes, I talked to Jorge on Monday. He sounded terrible. Have you seen him? Is he okay?"

"He feels responsible, but the police still don't consider him as a suspect. I'm no criminal lawyer, but I've got a friend who is on standby just in case Jorge needs him. Step One is finding out who started the fire, but there doesn't seem to be much headway yet. They're still sayin' it was a random hate crime, and I tend to agree. I wouldn't get your hopes up that this will ever be solved, Katie."

"Oh." There was nothing else to say. A woman named Angel with no face or voice disappeared into smoke as silently as she arrived in this country. Katie sensed that there would be little else said about it here, but somewhere south of the border, someone would probably miss her for a long, long time.

"What if they *do* find the person?" she asked. "Would they be accused of murder even if they didn't know she was in the building?"

"First, they'd have to determine that the person who died did indeed die as a result of the arson."

"Jorge told me it was smoke inhalation."

"Right, so that means whoever set the fire was responsible for the death of the woman inside. Arson is a felony. In Georgia, a death that's the direct result of a felony is automatically a felony murder. So the person who started the fire, if they catch him—or her—would be tried for felony arson and felony murder. If they're convicted, that gets them mandatory life in prison with a possibility of parole."

"But the likelihood of that happening…? Catching the person?"

"Next to nil." Jim dropped his head to stare into his drink, a bourbon and water.

"But we can still help him, right? He could still apply for funding to rebuild or relocate, can't he? We'd still be supporting the same kind of work…"

Jim shook his head. "Not this time. I know Jorge is overwhelmed, and I've got a lot on my plate. You may just need to let this one go, darlin'." He looked tired.

A new trial was keeping him busy, and Katie knew he was debating whether to return to work after dinner or take a much-needed evening off. She was preoccupied by competing thoughts herself, as her mind wandered back and forth between the dead woman and the puzzle of her trash can find. The conversation lagged, filled with intermittent silences. She wondered if these were the kinds of silences that heralded a deepening, more comfortable relationship or one already heading toward the rocks. If it faded now, she could still work with Jim and remain friendly, but it would be a shame to be this close to something deeper and have it slip away.

Her question about Sutter could be a test. If Jim were looking for a way to distance himself, this could present him that opportunity. He could use his role as a foundation trustee to admonish her and reinforce the formal relationship between them, or he could choose to overlook this minor indiscretion and help her to solve the mystery.

She swirled the wine in her glass and began to speak before she even looked up. "I want to ask you something."

"Something kind of funny happened today," he said at the same time.

"What?"

"No, ladies first. What's on your mind?"

"Mine can wait," she replied, happy to delay her "test" now that Jim was apparently interested in a different line of conversation. "Tell me what was funny. I could use a laugh."

"Well, I had lunch with some of the guys from my department at the City Club, and Porter and some of his colleagues were at the table next to us. When they got up to leave, he stopped by our table to say hello. Sam, one of the senior partners, asked Porter what he did last weekend."

"I don't know if I want to know the answer to that."

"Didn't you say you saw Porter in the wee hours of the morning after you left my place?"

"Yep. Scared the hell out of me."

"And you're absolutely positive it was Porter?"

"No question. He's pretty unmistakable. Why?"

"Well, Porter told us all that he'd been in the mountains all weekend with his wife. Some historical society benefit up there or something. Complained about all the little two-lane roads and the local yokels. Said there was no satellite reception so he couldn't watch the game and no bar open after 11:00 p.m. so he couldn't escape the wife."

"But you told me that Porter had a mistress downtown. Maybe he was covering for that."

"That's the funny part—he never covers for that. Unless..."

Katie tilted her head, waiting, as a slow grin spread across Jim's face. "Unless he has someone new that he's trying to keep a secret!"

"Ha. Ha. Very funny," she scowled. "I fail to see the humor in that pig having yet another mistress."

"Aw, c'mon. It's funny because you saw him. He's busted!" Jim practically crowed.

"And what, I'm going to tell on him?" She rolled her eyes. "I don't have a death wish. Besides, the way you describe him he wouldn't care anyway. I'd just like to forget I ever saw him. I certainly don't want to sit here speculating about what he was doing downtown in the middle of the night that he wouldn't want people to…oh, my God! The fire!"

She looked at Jim, wide-eyed. The hair on the back of her neck stood at attention and her heart threatened to jump out of her chest. *Could it be?*

Jim stared at her, speechless for a moment, then held up his hands. "Whoa, whoa! That's a big leap there, Katie! I was just wondering if there's a new, secret woman somewhere, and you're turning him into an arsonist and a murderer. I know you hate him, but let's hold off on making him a criminal, okay? Remember, in this country, we rely on a system of evidence."

"And out comes the trial attorney." She took a sip of wine to slow her thumping heart. "I'm sorry, but doesn't it make you even the tiniest bit suspicious?"

"No." He shook his head. "Porter's too smart to commit a crime like that. He may be a racist and quite possibly a first-rate asshole, but that doesn't make him a criminal mastermind. Besides, he's the type who would pay someone *else* to do the dirty work. He wouldn't do something like that just because he hated the clinic. Hell, he hates a lot of things, but he always expresses his anger verbally, not physically."

Katie placed her wineglass on the table with a shaky hand. Her eyes went cold as she squinted at him.

Jim watched her a moment, then added, "Sorry, I didn't mean he hates you. I meant that he's all talk and very little action, especially if it doesn't affect his personal bottom line." He kicked back the last of his bourbon. "Maybe he decided he couldn't stand being in Highlands overnight and snuck down to Atlanta for a little late night nookie. It's only a two-hour drive from there to here, so he could have conceivably made it down and back in the course of a night."

"Wouldn't he have just picked up some girl in a bar or something?"

Jim grinned. "They close at 11:00, remember?"

"That's true, I guess, but it seems like a long way to drive for sex."

"You forget we're talking about Porter."

Katie returned his grin. "I didn't forget; I was trying not to remember. There's a difference. Why would he bother covering that up, anyway? Didn't you say he always bragged about his, ah, conquests? He could let his wife think he was going to visit his regular mistress, couldn't he?"

"Could be. Or maybe there's something more to it. Maybe this new woman demands more discretion. I can see Porter getting a thrill from hunting 'bigger game,' as he'd put it."

"Ugh. You're making me ill just thinking about him—which leads me to the question I had for you." This was as good a time as any to bring up what she'd found in the trash. After all, they were talking about Porter's trashy behavior already. "Have you ever heard the name Sutter?"

"Like Malcolm Sutter, the developer? Sure. He's one of our firm's largest clients. In fact, he might be the single most important client Porter has. Keeps kind of a low profile, but he's got his fingers in a lot of projects all over the city. Why?"

She shared the story of the flying bracelet and the subsequent find in the boardroom trash can. "I can't believe that he didn't even bother to cross out his comment about my proposal before tossing it into the trash. And why would he write Sutter's name on it? Was he just using my hard work as a frickin' notepad?"

She scanned his face for interest in her theory or sympathy for her outrage. Instead, his incredulous look and slow, disapproving nod sent a knife straight into her heart. "Katie, you know those were confidential documents. Why did you go through them? You had no right."

"What?" No words came for a moment, but then the blood rushed to her face as a flash of anger spurred her on. "Are you actually standing up for that jackass?"

He smacked his glass down on the table. "No, but I'm thinking about the rules at the foundation, and you overstepped your bounds. Yes, Porter's an ass, but he's technically your boss, and you've gotta respect that. Just 'cause he doesn't agree with you doesn't mean you can go through his personal notes. Just give it a rest already!"

"Well." She breathed hard, battling the hot tears building behind her eyes. "I see how it is. You're my boss, too, aren't you? That trumps everything else. I get it now!" She jumped up and fled to the ladies' room. She would *not* let him see her cry.

The restroom was mercifully empty. She grabbed a paper towel, soaked it with cold water and began dabbing at the red splotches growing ever brighter under her eyes as the tears trickled down. How could he side with Porter on this? Yes, of course she had gone a *little* over the line, but it wasn't like she had rifled through Porter's briefcase or broken into his office. The notes couldn't have been *that* personal, or else why would he have just tossed them in the trash? And what if he *did* have something to do with the arson—and that poor woman's death?

But it was more than that, she realized. As long as she worked at the foundation and Jim was a trustee, he would always be her boss. That would always take precedence over any personal relationship.

"This is never going to work," she said to her reflection as she dried her tears. She took a deep breath to steady her frayed nerves. Time for one of them to begin the big break-up speech. Maybe she could leave now, using this little fight as a cover before he had a chance to start the conversation. She could go home and plan what *she* wanted to say to break up with *him*. She began to put the words together in her head: "Look, I really care for you and respect you, but this just isn't going to work out as long as we have this work relationship, and it would be crazy for either one of us to leave our jobs…"

Thank God I didn't sleep with him yet.

A knock on the door startled her. "Katie?" Jim's voice echoed on the other side of the door. When she opened it, he was standing there with her coat and her purse.

"Let's go for a walk." He looked grave, and she couldn't think of a way to say no, so she simply took her coat and purse and followed him out of the restaurant.

Pedestrians clogged the narrow sidewalk out front, making it difficult for her to walk next to him at first. She followed a pace behind him down the block, fuming. When the hungry diners and bar-hoppers thinned, he waited for her at a side street crossing. They walked for several blocks in silence, side by side but not touching. She paid no attention to their route, concentrating instead on keeping her tears in check. Why couldn't she just stop right here, scream her anger at him and walk away? Instead, she bit her lip, hard, and kept her eyes on her feet.

He guided her farther away from the restaurants and deeper into the neighborhood. The pedestrian traffic disappeared, and they came upon a small park. At any other time, it would have been romantic with its wrought iron and wood benches and gas lamplights. Tonight, it felt ominous. Dark shadows stretched from the park's trees, and she realized how very alone they were. She hesitated as Jim led her into the gloom.

He cocked his head as he looked at her. "It's okay. Let's sit down," he said. Taking the lead, he sank onto the end of a dark bench just out of reach of the streetlights. She sat at other end, on the very edge. She studied his face, tears forgotten. He looked different now. Serious. Preoccupied. He stared at the ground a few feet in front of them and wrung his hands.

For a moment, she almost felt sorry for him. Then the memory of his tone in the restaurant came flooding back, along with a fresh surge of anger. "Look, Jim," she began. If they were going to break up, they would do it on her terms.

But he held up his hand and turned toward her, eyes steady. "No, please. Listen to what I have to say." He clenched his jaw once, twice, and then the words began to trip and tumble from his lips.

"I know this is hard for you. It's awkward 'cause technically I'm your boss. Plus Porter treated you like shit, and he's kinda *my* boss. Can't you see that puts a lot of stress on me, too, being caught between the two of you? Plus, I didn't think it would, but it turns out being a trustee is a pretty big deal to me. Even though I didn't really know my grandfather, I feel like I kinda owe it to him to be good at this. I'm supposed to look out for things.

"That *really* puts me in a tricky place when it comes to Porter. Helping you with the clinic, which," he added with an affirming nod, "I think was the right thing, didn't win me any points with him. And he can make my life pretty difficult if he wants to.

"But on the other hand..." He let out a deep breath and leaned back against the bench, bringing his hand to his eyes. "On the other hand, I wanna to support you and *not* be the boss. You've got good ideas. You're passionate. And that makes it all so damn complicated because I'm falling in love with you, and it really gets hard for me to know what I'm supposed to do. I just wish you'd cut me a little slack and forget about Porter so we can just get on with what really matters and..."

"I'm sorry," Katie interrupted with wide eyes, frozen in place, her hands absolutely still in her lap. "What did you just say?"

"I said that I wish you would forget about Porter and..."

"No, no. Just before that. What did you say?"

Jim paused and blushed and looked away for an excruciating moment. Then he turned back to Katie and looked into her eyes. "I said that I'm in love with you. Honestly, you can't really be surprised by that?"

"I...no, I guess I'm not. I just didn't realize...I..."

"Look, it's fast, I know, but it's just how I feel. You don't have to say anything right now. Just want you to know where I stand. I love you, Katie Nelson, but this whole thing with Porter is screwing everything up. You know what I think of you professionally and what I think of Porter personally. But

Katie, he's just one little part of a bigger picture. I'm just asking you to realize that when you get all bent out of shape about him and the clinic, it makes things a lot harder."

She started to protest, but he reached a finger out to silence her. "It's done. Let's move on. Yes, I'm sorry it burned down and that woman lost her life, but we'll probably never know why. We'll get it funded again. Hell, it was fully insured, so maybe it'll even come out ahead. Can't we just drop it? Can't we just concentrate on what's ahead?" He gave her a small, pleading smile. "For us? Don't you want to see where this goes?"

Katie's heart rose in her chest. She suddenly felt that she might float right off the park bench. Instead of a break-up, here was Jim, wonderful Jim, considerate Jim, conscientious Jim, *her* Jim, saying that he loved her and asking her to love him back. Porter and the clinic and the horror and the death…everything fell away. Katie wanted nothing else but to slide down that bench to be closer to him.

So she slid.

"I'm sorry. I had no clue that I was making it so hard for you. I've really been wrapped up in my own head." She swallowed and pressed her forehead into his cheek as he twined his fingers in hers. "I really would like for this to work, too." She paused, then lifted her head to look into his eyes. "But honestly, I can't promise I won't keep driving you crazy. And we both know this boss-employee thing won't go away…"

"If we can just let the stuff with Porter drop, the rest will work itself out, I know it."

"Consider it dropped." She moved closer until her whole side pressed into his.

"Look at that, you're doing it already." His voice dropped to a hoarse whisper as his lips caressed her ear.

"What?"

"Driving me crazy."

His kiss burned its way to the bottoms of her toes. In the flickering heat, her mind's eye saw their future in a whir of activity—nights of lovemaking, lazy Sundays over paper and coffee, a house in this very neighborhood, babies—yes more than one—Jim coaching Little League, vacations at the beach and much later, quiet hours spent together in front porch rockers. Her sudden hunger for him overwhelmed her, and she would have gladly consummated their relationship right there and then on the shadowy park bench.

She heard herself whisper, "Jim, I think I might love you too," and she knew it was true.

His lips were hungry on hers as he threaded his fingers through the hair at the nape of her neck. She held his face with her hands for a moment before sliding them down to his chest and slipping them under his coat. He pressed her body against his, then held her that way for several long exquisite moments before he slowly pulled away and wrapped his arm around her shoulders with a long exhale. "Can't believe I'm sayin' this, but I've really got to finish up with this trial. In fact, I was supposed to be back at the office an hour ago, since everybody's burnin' the midnight oil."

She leaned into him and snuggled her head on his shoulder. "That's so not fair."

"Tell me about it, but I didn't exactly plan this…not tonight."

"Mmmm. Well, even if you didn't, I'm glad it happened." She snuggled deeper.

"Tell you what. Let's do something special next weekend. I'm thinking that we can get away, out of town, and really spend some quality time together. Maybe up in the mountains?"

"That sounds perfect. And I think we probably agree on what 'quality time' means." She winked into his beautiful blue eyes.

"Oh reeeeally?" He smiled. "That's still completely up to you. No pressure; I'm just offering a getaway."

"Oh really?" She mimicked his tone. But she knew she'd never been more sure of anything in her life.

He held her for several minutes, caressing her hair, then kissed her again. "I'd better get you to your car before I change my mind about work."

Together, they strolled back toward the restaurant, this time with Jim's arm snugly around her shoulders.

***

Later, alone in her bed, Katie could still feel the warmth of Jim's arms around her. For the first time in weeks, she felt calm, floating in a bubble of contentment. *I love you.* Her fingers spread over the sheets and then relaxed. Jim was right. Porter was a pompous, bigoted windbag prone to outbursts—but not so out of control as to commit a hate crime against a homeless woman he'd never met.

With sleep fast approaching, Katie's mind drifted back to the woman in the fire. Had *she* been in love? Was that why she came here?

In her dream, she walked along the edge of the seaside cliff she'd visited as a child so long ago. A brilliant sun lit up the sky, reflected in the faces of the bright daisies and black-eyed Susans that grew along the path. The ocean breeze wafted across her face and arms, delivering a refreshing coolness and causing tickling goose bumps that made her giggle. She walked along, practically skipping with delight at the beauty of it all, when she came upon a beautiful woman with dark hair gazing over the edge. As Katie approached, the woman, startled, turned to her, losing her footing on the rocks. She screamed as she fell. Katie screamed too, as she ran to try to catch her, but was too late. She peered over the ledge, and the sea below had turned into a seething mass of flames, the woman's body a tiny black dot among them. When she stepped away from the edge in horror, Jim stood on the path next to her, smiling and offering his hand.

CHAPTER 16

By the next morning, the dream had faded, replaced by the memory of last night's park bench. "My, don't you seem happy today!" Louise said as Katie floated down the office hallway the following morning. "It's nice to see that smile on your face."

"I…I'm just, um…happy it's finally spring!" Katie blushed as she hurried toward her office. She had almost reached safety when Chris stepped out of his own office and started toward her. She smiled at him as he approached, blushing even harder as he scrutinized her face. Could he tell something was up?

She braced herself for a knowing glance or a smart remark, but instead he simply looked past her and walked by without a word.

Good Lord! How long could he pout about their last conversation? Who knew he could be so huffy? Besides, what difference did it make now that the clinic was off the table? He had no more competition for his theater group.

Whatever. She lifted her head high. She had Jim on her side and they'd find some other way to help Jorge. The thought of it made her smile all the more.

She slid into her chair and brought up her computer screen, the beginnings of a hum in her throat. But her smile vanished and hum turned to gulp as she checked her email. A message from Guy Porter screamed at her from the inbox. The subject line simply read: "Program Staff Conduct." Her hand shook slightly as she clicked her mouse. He'd never emailed her before. Why now?

She held her breath as her eyes tore through the short message. Then she exhaled as she read back through it again. Only she and Chris, the two program officers, were listed as recipients, she noticed, no one else. At least Louise wouldn't see it. It read:

Dear program staff,

I understand that some of you may have a strong personal interest in some of the proposals you are bringing or have brought before the Foundation Board. As a trustee, I strongly caution you against connecting any personal feelings to our grant-making work. There are plenty of opportunities to find professional inspiration and satisfaction in your work with us. If you can't find them here, I suggest you consider seeking such fulfillment elsewhere.

Sincerely, Guy Porter

She pushed her chair back from the screen, both hands scrambling up toward her hair to find a soothing strand. Her heart pounded all the way up to her temples, and her foot tap-tap-tapped against the desk drawer. Well, that explained Chris' mood! What the hell should they make of this? Was Porter warning her off any further involvement with the clinic? Was he telling Chris to withdraw the gay theater proposal from consideration? Wait! Did he think she had some kind of personal relationship with *Jorge* that made her so inspired by the clinic proposal? Had he found about her and Jim?

"What the hell?" she muttered under her breath as she scanned the short message yet again. Her right hand reached for her desk phone to call Jim, but she stopped herself. No, she had promised not to let Porter's bullying get between them. She couldn't call him now. Maybe she'd mention it later.

But she *would* go find Chris to get his take on it.

She flew down the hall to his office, but found it empty. She circled through the break room. No Chris. She checked the staff conference room and the boardroom. He wasn't there either. Finally, she made her way to the front of the office and the lavish reception area. Her eyes, as always, were drawn to the overstuffed Chippendale chairs and the oil portraits of

Joseph Hartwell that were guaranteed to make visiting grant-seekers feel intimidated.

"Monica, did you happen to see Chris leave?"

The young, greyhound-sleek receptionist gave her an efficient nod. "Yes, he said he was going downstairs to Starbucks. Shall I tell him you're looking for him?"

"No need. I think I'll grab a coffee, too."

She couldn't get to the elevator fast enough. Chris never took a coffee break. He rarely left the office at all unless it was for a meeting. He must be just as upset as she was by that email. She stepped into an empty elevator, her heel tapping and fingers spinning through her hair as it ticked down floor by floor. 4…3…2…1…finally!

She pushed past a crowd of late arrivals and into the building's gleaming lobby. She'd been impressed by its marble columns and terrazzo floors since her first day of work, but now their cold, hard facades made her want to keep moving.

She made a beeline for the Starbucks that drew hundreds of caffeine-starved customers from up and down Peachtree Street. To avoid the bustling main entrance, she headed for the store's back doorway. Used mostly by building workers, this entryway was tucked into a corner behind the elevator bays beside a potted plant that was almost as tall as she was and wide enough to hide the entire corner from the rest of the lobby. Katie was halfway around the plant when she stopped short at the sound of Chris' voice.

"No, I can't!" He sounded on the verge of tears. Then there was a pause, and she craned her head around the plant just enough to see him, pacing by the back entrance to Starbuck's, cell phone clutched in a fierce grip at his ear. She ducked back behind the plant just in time as he swung around toward her. He didn't see her, but she saw that his face was flushed. She cocked her ear to listen.

"And I just said I *can't*! I've already put too much on the line for you! I've done everything you've asked me to! Jesus, I even ended a *life* because of you! And now I get this email? When I…" He paused a moment, muttering to himself.

"But...but...*No*, that's enough. I'm not the only one who lit that fire. You're just as much to blame as I am..."

Katie couldn't restrain herself and risked another peek around the plant.

"I've done all I'm going to do. The next move is yours!" Chris slammed his thumb onto the phone's face, abruptly ending the call.

She was transfixed. This was a side of Chris she had never seen, never believed possible. He was usually so poised, so confident. Now he appeared overwhelmed with anxiety. She watched him pace back and forth for another minute, mumbling to himself and shaking his head over and over. Then he stopped, just like that, and stared at a spot on the ground for another full minute, biting the thumbnail on his left hand while his right arm clamped over his stomach.

She wanted to reach out to him, to pretend she hadn't been spying on him just now. Maybe, if she stayed low, she could make it to a nearby column and then emerge normally, as if she were actually on her way to get a coffee. But something stopped her.

I even ended a life because of you!

The words burned into her brain, even as her knees began to buckle. She eyed the nearest column. It could cover an exit as well as a fake entrance. She was just about to inch toward it when Chris' head snapped up and he began to stride to the plant.

Katie dove in the opposite direction, almost tripping over her own foot in the process. She was positive Chris had heard her, but he continued past, crossing in front of the elevators and out a side door onto 14th Street without looking back.

She sank to the ground in the space behind the plant, legs shaking. No. It couldn't be. *I'm not the only one who lit that fire. I even ended a life because of you!* Who was Chris talking to? And what else could he be talking about other than the clinic fire?

It simply wasn't possible. Not Chris. No matter how hard she tried, she couldn't imagine Chris striking a match to burn down a building. Not unless he was under some terrible life-or-death threat. Not unless someone was blackmailing him. Who was on the other end of that conversation?

She glanced up as the rear entrance to Starbucks opened and a middle-aged man in a suit exited the store, to-go cup in one hand and phone in the other. He never saw Katie, barely moved his eyes from his phone's screen, but she let out a breath as he passed by. She felt suddenly invisible, which is what life must be like for the people Jorge served. That thought brought her squarely back to Angel, the woman who lost her life in the fire. No one was going to help her. Katie certainly couldn't.

But she could find out more about Chris. She set her jaw as she lifted herself off the terrazzo and brushed off her skirt. If he had a hand in that fire, she wanted to know about it.

CHAPTER 17

Back in her office, Katie mulled over what she knew. If Chris was involved in the fire, he appeared to feel terrible about it. The email from Porter prompted his worrying phone call, and whoever was on the phone with Chris had upset him. Could it have been Porter? She couldn't picture the two of them conspiring. In fact, she couldn't picture Porter saying more than two words to Chris if the two of them wound up trapped in an elevator. And if that email was meant to be a message directed at Chris, why had she been included?

Okay, so if Chris wasn't talking to Porter, maybe it was someone else connected to the clinic? Jim said Jorge wasn't a suspect, but did he have a reason to see it burned down? She couldn't imagine Jorge involved in a crime like that, either.

She resisted the urge to call Jim. Instead, she clenched her fingers into a fist before they reached the phone. His trial was consuming all his time and energy, and she didn't want to bother him. They'd have plenty of time to discuss what she'd overheard later. Besides, she knew Chris much better than Jim did. She could find out more by herself. She just needed the opportunity.

She was just reaching for a strand of hair to twirl when the phone on her desk jangled her out of her musings. She snatched the handset before the second ring.

"Hey girl! Where ya been hiding?" Rita's peppy voice seemed out of place in the midst of Katie's brooding.

"Oh…hi yourself. I've been…well…it's been a crazy few days."

"I need to hear all about it, and here's what we're gonna do. No argument. I just happen to have scored two tickets for the Art League Ball at the High tomorrow night. You'll be my escort. So get your best up-do workin' and meet me there at 7:30. Got it?"

"I don't know. How did you get tickets?" The Art League was one of Atlanta's most elite circles. Their annual fundraising gala at the High Museum of Art raised hundreds of thousands of dollars. It was the see-and-be-seen event of the year, assuming one was in the mood to be seen. The tickets were exceedingly valuable…and expensive.

"I won them in a lottery. I found them on the street. What does it matter?"

"Rita…"

"Okay, okay. The firm's a sponsor. These tickets were for a partner who had a death in the family and isn't in town. Did you miss the part where I said no argument? We're going. I will see you there."

"Okay. I'll be there."

Since Jim would be wrapped up in trial preparations all weekend, she might as well keep herself occupied. Even if she couldn't talk to Rita about Chris, she could and would tell her all about the park bench conversation. Of course, Rita would probably know the second she saw her face…

***

At 3:30 Friday afternoon, Katie wrapped up a meeting downtown and decided to call it a day, head home early and relax with her thoughts before heading out to meet Rita. She'd had no luck connecting with Chris. He stayed shut up in his office most of Thursday and called in sick on Friday. She swallowed a lump in her throat. She just *had* to know whether or not he was involved. If he was, she suddenly realized, she'd have to turn him in. Her heart ached with the thought of it. She and Chris had their differences, but she respected him, and he'd been a good friend and ally on the foundation staff.

She drove through the downtown streets toward her carriage house, then realized that she was only a couple of blocks from the site of the clinic. Why not take a quick detour to see what was left of the building and what kind of activity, if any, had been going on? Who knew? Maybe she'd find something, anything, that might give her a clue as to Chris's connection to the fire.

She zigzagged through the city blocks surrounding the clinic site. It was only a quarter mile off Peachtree Street, the main drag, and yet it was worlds away. The high-rises of glass, chrome and marble hadn't yet made it these few blocks west. Here and there, edgy young companies had put stakes in the ground in the form of converted lofts or garages, but there were plenty of boarded-up old storefronts, crumbling warehouses and weedy lots still in evidence. But it was easy for Katie to see the gleaming towers of Peachtree Street holding up the late afternoon skyline and imagine their relentless advance across the urban wasteland. Even the breeze that tossed a fast-food wrapper across her windshield seemed to be moving out of the way. It would all be redeveloped eventually. Maybe in that respect, the fire was just as well, since development and the ensuing property tax hikes would price the clinic out of the neighborhood anyway.

But not just as well that someone had died. She frowned to herself.

She turned the corner onto the street where the clinic lay in ruins, then braked to a stop. Had she gone the wrong way? She glanced up and down the street. No, this was the correct street, but in place of the burned remains of the clinic and its roughshod surroundings, there was now a huge gaping hole, spanning the entire block, surrounded by a chain link fence.

Signs were anchored to the chain link every twenty feet: "Private Property. No Trespassing." Katie parked next to the fence, got out of her car and peered down into the hole. She could see a parked bulldozer, bundles of concrete pipe and iron rebar—obviously the beginnings of a new high-rise.

Damn, they didn't waste any time. Only a couple of weeks. Any chance of finding a clue about Chris was gone now. She scanned the fence around the site, looking for that inevitable two-story tall sign boasting the amenities and design of the emerging colossus. She spotted it, all the way on the other side of the block, facing away from her, toward the Peachtree Street corridor. *Might as well check it out.*

She glanced at her watch. Plenty of time to get home and get ready for a fancy night out with Rita. She stepped around the perimeter of the fence, heading for the opposite end of the block. Most likely, it would boast high-end condos, anchored by first-floor retail. She sighed. Didn't anyone ever think outside the large, expensive box? The only other questions that dawdled in her mind were how big and how ugly?

Then another question bubbled up. How could the clinic property have transferred so quickly after the fire? Jorge hadn't said anything about selling it, although Katie hadn't talked to him much since the fire. Jim hadn't mentioned it either. If he were helping Jorge pro-bono on the insurance claim for the fire, wouldn't he know if the property had been sold? Wouldn't he have told her? Was it a confidentiality thing or had it just slipped his mind?

Jim had asked all those questions about the property's value when he was helping out with Jorge's grant proposal. Maybe that had triggered the idea for a sale?

A scattering of empty beer bottles, plastic bags and cigarette butts lay across the sidewalk, the remnants of those who lived or who liked to party on the fringes. The new tenants, she knew, wouldn't put up with garbage like this. This "dump" was a vestige of bygone days in this neighborhood. She sidestepped the garbage and rounded the corner, looking up to read the construction sign. Sure enough, an illustration of a gleaming high-rise greeted her. *Peachtree Ridgeline*, the sign proclaimed. *Atlanta's ultimate live-work-play environment.*

The rendering showed happy people (all white and upwardly mobile) living, working and playing in the shadow of the new building. Their faces shined almost as brightly as the behemoth construction itself. A flagship hotel, a trendy coffee shop and several boutiques and restaurants already boasted tenancy. A rooftop pool for condo owners and hotel guests provided the icing on the cake.

She rolled her eyes at the too-perfect people in the gleaming artist's sketch of the behemoth to come. These buildings popped up like mushrooms throughout the city. Even though most sat half empty, it seemed they made plenty of money for the people who built them.

She looked for the developer's name and found it: Phoenix Partners. It wasn't a company she'd heard of before, but that didn't mean anything. She knew from conversations with Rita, who worked as a paralegal in a huge real estate law firm, that developers traded partners and corporate identities as fast as they traded wives and girlfriends. She made a mental note to ask Rita about Phoenix Partners that evening. Whoever they were, if they made a killing on Peachtree Ridgeline, maybe they'd be willing to partner with the Hartwell Foundation on an affordable housing development down the road.

A wind kicked up as Katie studied the sign and grey clouds began to roll in. She hurried back to her car and dove into the jigsaw-puzzle navigation required to negotiate the streets to get home. During a long wait at a stoplight, she placed a quick call to Jorge to congratulate him—or commiserate with him—on the sale of his building and see what his plans were for a new location. She got Jorge's voicemail and marveled at how his voice could sound so smoky and compelling even in a simple outbound greeting.

"Hi Jorge, it's Katie. Look, I'm sorry I've been so far out of the loop with what's going on with the clinic. Let's talk soon and maybe I can connect you to some people who can help. And for that matter…"—she smiled broadly as a new thought hit her—"I'd like to help as well. I know you're swamped right now, but just send me something, *anything*, before the proposal deadline next Friday, and I'll do whatever I can, okay?"

So what if Jim couldn't help out? So what if maybe she was pushing her program officer boundaries a little bit by dangling that offer in front of Jorge? She could, she *would*, bring this issue back in front of the board, in front of Porter, all by herself. And this time, she wouldn't sit there like an inanimate rock if he attacked her. If it came down to it, she would give as good as she got.

Realizing she was still in mid-message, she continued. "Oh, um, and I want to make sure you're not beating yourself up about Angel. I've heard some things…well, let's just say I'm absolutely sure it's not your fault. I'll fill you in when I can."

She pressed the "end" button and dropped her phone back in her purse. Jorge was probably still at work…somewhere in the city. He seemed married to the clinic. Katie smirked. Maybe she should introduce Jorge to Rita. *That* would be an interesting relationship. Traffic started moving again, and with it, her thoughts strayed from Rita and Jorge and Chris to Jim and the promise of the following weekend's romantic getaway. Was she really ready to get that involved again? "Oh yeah," she said aloud to her grinning reflection in the rearview mirror. "I'm ready."

CHAPTER 18

So far, so good. The girl hasn't been asking too many questions, according to the boss. But she still looks like she's thinking hard about something. She visited the burn site, but she could have just been curious. People like to see some kind of physical resolution after a fire, either rebuilding or starting over. She spent some time there, studying the pictures on the sign. She didn't look like she approved, but I hope she understands the inevitable and lets it drop.

For her own well-being, she better not be thinking too hard about that fire. It has nothing to do with her. I found out who she is from the boss, and she seems like a nice enough lady. She works at the foundation. Gives money away for a living. What a job. You'd think you'd be the most popular person in town with a job like that, but it doesn't appear to be that way.

The boss has taken an interest in her. She lives all alone. Has a nice little carriage house apartment. It's hard to see into since it's on the second floor, but the landlords are gone most of the time, and their alarm system is a joke. She seems comfortable enough with just a cat for company. My wife would never have survived that way, God rest her soul. She always needed a man around. But this girl, she does a lot by herself. Not many friends that I've seen. Works all the time. Exercises regularly. If a guy can break through that rock, he'd find a real gem, I'm thinking.

Maybe she's just been preoccupied when I've seen her. Her brow is furrowed a lot. She's always thinking.

She should marry, settle down, raise a good family. But then again, maybe that's not what she needs. Seems like she's pretty good at taking care of herself.

I could take care of her if I wasn't so old. Don't get me wrong; everything still works in that department, and I'll admit she's got a nice body. I've seen her when she gets out of the shower or changes clothes. I'm not a pervert; it's just part of my job. Besides, she's young enough to be my daughter, and I prefer women a little more seasoned.

Anyway, like I said, she seems like a nice girl, and I hope she leaves the whole fire thing alone. I'd hate for something bad to happen to her. I'd hate for the boss to change his mind. It wouldn't be a job I'd enjoy.

CHAPTER 19

The High Museum was illuminated like a thousand Christmas trees. Countless small white lights festooned the walkway leading to the main entrance and twinkled on topiaries and chandeliers imported into the grand, glass-topped atrium just for this occasion. The building itself was ultra-modern—clad in white enamel, aluminum and glass, with multiple curves and planes clamoring for attention. It held its own on Peachtree Street in the north end of Midtown, like a futuristic spaceship between a turn-of-the-century church and the 1960s-era Arts Center that housed the city's symphony and premier theater troupe.

Katie checked the shoulder straps of her simple black sheath cocktail dress as she waited outside the front entrance for Rita. Thank God for basic black. It barely made the grade amid the full-length couture gowns that swept by her, but at least she wouldn't stand out like a sore thumb. She reached up to triple-check the security of her "diamond" earrings—a sparkly splash of rhinestones from a yard sale. They felt unusually heavy hanging there, exposed by the absence of her dark tresses, which were caught up in a loose bun. From her ears, her fingers moved to the base of her throat, fluttering over the simple silver strand upon which she'd strung another basic rhinestone brooch as a pendant. All in all, she thought she'd cleaned up well.

Katie caught sight of Rita, resplendent in an iridescent eggplant-colored number with a plunging neckline and, she saw as Rita swiveled to wave her fingers at an admirer, no back at all. The rich color stood in vivid contrast to the mass of shining red curls that piled on the top of Rita's head and flowed down her neck. So much for not standing out.

Rita swooped down on her with a perfumed hug, engulfing Katie in a soft gardenia embrace that said: *I am here now and you are not doing this alone*. Katie wanted to hang on like a lifeline, but she settled for a quick squeeze in return.

Rita ignored the looks of appreciation thrown her way by a throng of tuxedoed men and a scant handful of equally confident and coiffed women. "Look at you! Who knew you could be so classy and sexy at the same time?"

There was no need to return the compliment; they both knew Rita exuded class and sex constantly, but Katie said, "Wow! You look amazing!"

"Thanks!" Rita beamed. "It's fun to play dress up sometimes, ya know? And since this is probably the very best hunting ground I'll ever see, I decided to pull out the big guns." At this, she stood up straight and thrust out her chest. There was no mistaking her meaning.

A laughed bubbled up from Katie's abdomen, releasing the week's tension into the ether. "Just so I don't have to hunt with you. I think I'm about to bag some big game of my own." She gave Rita a Groucho Marx eyebrow wag.

Rita cocked an eyebrow as she slipped her elbow through Katie's and steered her toward the museum's front entrance. "Oh reeeally? Do tell, sister!"

Katie filled in the details as best she could while they waited in line at the bar. It was hard to make herself heard above the hundreds of voices and a live jazz band echoing throughout the atrium's four open stories. Still, her friend cooed and exclaimed at all the appropriate moments.

Armed with glasses of champagne, they navigated their way through the tightly packed, festive crowd to find a good vantage point for people-watching. She noticed several of Atlanta's elite among the press of bodies. The president of a local cable conglomerate laughed as he patted a state senator on the back. A fast-food mogul and his wife perused the buffet with keen interest. Board members from the city's leading hospitals and universities rubbed shoulders with the leaders of internationally known businesses. Rita gave her a quick poke in the ribs to point out the owner of the city's baseball team chatting up a perky television weather girl. There were also hundreds of up-and-comers and wannabes sipping, talking and joking among the crowd—many of them men whose eyes followed Rita.

"So, what about you?" Katie all but yelled over the noise of the crowd. "Seeing anyone new since we last went out?"

Rita shook her head. "Sadly, no. I haven't really wanted to see anyone since Mr. Jacksonville dumped me. Just haven't been in the mood. I'm convinced now that all developers suck."

"Guess he kind of got to you, huh?"

Rita blew a puff of air at an errant curl and surveyed the crowd. "You could say that."

Time to change the subject. "Hey, speaking of developers who suck, have you ever heard of a group called Phoenix Partners? They're building one of those new multi-use buildings downtown where the clinic used to be."

"Not off the top of my head. We have so many developer clients, it's impossible to remember them all. But for you? I'll look it up next week."

"That'd be great. I just like to know who the power players are so I can tap into their philanthropic side—if they have one."

"Speaking of philanthropic sides, don't look now, but here comes the city's biggest philanthropic *back*side. Looks like he's playing the husband tonight."

Katie groaned even before she turned to look. Why didn't she think of this before? Porter's wife Constance was the chair of the Art League. Of *course* he'd be here. She turned to see the "couple" headed directly her way, greeting partygoers by name as they went. The crowd seemed to part as if for royalty, so they had no chance to duck aside. She steeled her spine and placed as much of a smile as she could muster on her face, ready for another round of scathing public criticism.

"Why how about this? If it isn't Miss Nelson!" Porter gave her a fake smile as his eyes fell upon her, replaced by a look of sheer admiration as he took in Rita at her side. "And out with a very beautiful friend, I must say."

Constance Porter, as if sensing that her spouse was straying from his husbandly role, stopped a step in front of Porter and turned to assess the situation. She smiled a tight smile at Katie and an even tighter one at Rita. "Guy, please introduce me to your friends," she said with icy politeness.

Guy glanced at his wife with cold eyes and a plastic smile before turning back and practically drooling over Rita. "My dear, this is Miss Nelson, one of our fine program officers at the foundation." He waved halfheartedly in Katie's direction. "And I've not yet had the pleasure of meeting Miss…?" He raised an eyebrow and held out a beefy hand to Rita.

"Devereaux. I'm visiting Katie from New Orleans," Rita responded, adopting a Louisiana drawl as well as a haughty glare to match Mrs. Porter's.

Porter was oblivious. "Ah, the land of Mardi Gras! I bet you are front and center in every parade, Miss Devereaux."

"Actually, my family prefers to engage with our community through charity. Mardi Gras seems only to appeal to those with no sense of decency." She looked down her button nose at Porter.

Out of the corner of her eye, Katie saw Constance shoot Rita a curious look. It was all she could do to keep from laughing, yet she held her breath as she watched her friend pretend to be someone completely different. With her elegant look and confident presence, Rita fit the bill perfectly.

"Ah yes, I know just what you mean," Porter replied, adopting a more formal and serious tone himself. Constance, apparently satisfied that there was no danger here, moved ahead a few paces to engage other guests. "I do a bit of philanthropy myself as a trustee of the Hartwell Foundation." He seemed to suddenly remember that Katie was there. "You know, where Miss Nelson here does such a fine job?"

"Yes, I think perhaps she's mentioned you," said Rita.

Katie suppressed a smirk.

Just then, a fair-haired young man with bright red cheeks came up and wrapped an arm around Rita from behind. "Rita

O'Brien! I haven't seen you in a year. You look absolutely fabulous. Remind me why we stopped seeing one another?"

Rita, caught off guard, stumbled in her response. "I…uh…Gavin, hi! I've been traveling some…" Her words faded as she shot Katie an apologetic look. Gavin, whoever he was, pulled her toward another group of friends.

Katie turned around to see Porter staring after Rita, realizing that he'd been had. A flush of crimson flared from his shirt collar, then slowly crept up his neck and face as he pinned Katie on the spot with a steely glare.

"Well now, Miss Nelson," he said, grabbing her arm just above the elbow and pulling her closer to speak into her ear. "I'm going to assume that your friend just has an unusual way of flirting, because I will tell you right here and now, that the one thing I will *not* stand for is a lack of loyalty when it comes to business. And the foundation most *definitely* is my business. Do you understand what I'm saying to you?"

He pulled back and glared into her eyes. Katie noticed tiny beads of sweat forming on his brow before he leaned in again.

"I thought perhaps my email made it clear, but if not, I will spell it out for you. No one—and I mean *no one*, including you—gets anywhere in this town without loyalty. It's what makes people successful, what makes the wheels turn, what makes or breaks even smart people like you. I need to know that you are loyal to the foundation and that you will behave accordingly, or else I will see you fired. Do we understand each other?"

Her heart was about to explode, but Katie managed to nod a small yes as Porter glared at her again.

His demeanor softened as he loosed his grip on her upper arm, trailing the back of his fingers down her lower arm before letting go. She gave an involuntary shiver. "We follow a code in this city. Remember that and you'll go places, a sharp thing like you."

She swallowed hard as Constance Porter reappeared at her husband's side. She gave Katie a look of cool appraisal, but did not speak to her. Instead, she placed a hand on her husband's shoulder. "Guy, the Wenchels are here. You must come say hello." And with that, she guided Porter away without a backward glance.

Katie shuddered and squeezed her eyes closed. The touch of Porter's fingers on her arm felt like swamp ooze. She wanted to find a restroom and wash that arm thoroughly. That thought unfroze her muscles and she found she could move again. She searched for restroom signs along the perimeter of the atrium. As she made her way through the throng, Rita caught up with her.

"I'm so sorry," she said between breaths. "I don't know what came over me. And then that clod Gavin…" She rolled her eyes. "Anyway, I shouldn't have done that. I hope he wasn't too nasty."

"No. I…I'm okay."

"What did he say to you?"

"Just something about loyalty. About a code." Her own breath was coming easier now, and with Rita beside her as a social protector, she felt anger rising in her throat. *Oh no! Please, no tears. Not now.* She brushed ahead into the ladies room and took some deep breaths as she washed her hands up to the elbows. It was so much quieter in there—the heavy door muffled the music and voices—that she mumbled as she stared at herself in the mirror. "I think he may have been half-hitting on me, the way he touched my arm." Another involuntary shudder worked its way down her back.

"Humph," Rita said, throwing an arm around Katie's shoulders. "Fucking pig." She stared at Katie's reflection. "He's just trying to intimidate you. Don't you take any crap from that bastard."

Katie shrugged. "It's not like I normally run into him outside of board meetings. Why would he want to intimidate me?"

"That's just the kind of pig he is. You're a threat. You want to do things differently. He wants them to stay the same, with him in the catbird seat."

Katie stared at their reflections another moment. If *she* was a threat to Porter, then she almost felt sorry for him. It must be exhausting to be that afraid of change.

"I'm fine now, honest." She gave Rita a smile to prove it as she suppressed another shiver. "And you're right, it's probably just his warped way of telling me to stop pushing the envelope. But how ridiculous! It's not like it's *my* money. Or his!" As they headed for the exit, she steeled herself to rejoin the well-dressed hordes.

"No, it's not," Rita said. "But it should be yours. You could run rings around those stuffy assholes on the board when it comes to making real change happen in this town. Especially Porter. He's a dick on legs."

Her tone made Katie stop. "Do you *know* Porter?"

"Are you kidding? There's not a paralegal in North Georgia he hasn't hit on. The man's got a reputation as big as his ego. Actually, I was surprised he didn't recognize me, since we've attended the same meetings before. One time, he was leaving our office after a deposition, and he grabbed the ass of one of my coworkers in the elevator. She told him to step off, and then he had the gall to hand her his card 'in case she ever wanted to help him with his briefs.' How lame a pick-up line can you possibly use?"

"Ugh," said Katie, disgusted. "I can't wait for the day his board term ends, but that could be decades from now. I wonder which of us will last longer."

"That man puts the 'ass' in 'jackass.'"

When they returned to the atrium, the band had left the stage and the crowd had stopped milling around. The museum's executive director was in the process of introducing and thanking various bigwigs. Katie stood, shifting her weight from one uncomfortable foot to the other. Her strappy heels were cute, but not made for an evening of standing. Rita squirmed impatiently next to her.

The director continued, "And now, we're going to do something a little off the cuff. I'd like to introduce the husband of our chairwoman, Guy Porter, who has asked to say a few words before we get back to our celebration."

Porter took the podium to a smattering of polite applause. Katie and Rita exchanged inquisitive looks.

"Thank ya'll," Porter said, flashing a winning smile around the room. "I promise I won't be long. First off, although I'm the one here at the podium, we all know who's really responsible for this evening, and that's my lovely wife Constance." He motioned grandly to the right of the stage, where Constance stood with a painful smile. "Let's give her a round of applause."

The crowd obliged, and Porter had to wave his hands to regain their attention.

"Now, I just want to let you know that being here tonight got me thinking. What is it that makes this community, this city, so darn great? And then it came to me. A strong community is an awful lot like a strong marriage. And you know, when you got a strong marriage, you may not always agree. You may not always see eye to eye. Hell, you may even behave badly toward one another from time to time."

At this, a few men in the audience cheered and hooted before being shushed by irate wives. Next to Katie, Rita let out a snort.

"But what you do have, what makes you strong, is *loyalty*."

There was that word again. Was Porter still trying to tell her something, or had he simply inspired himself with his own words?

"You know that no matter what happens, you look out for one another. You do what it takes to keep things going. That's the way we are here in Atlanta. And that's why we have such great testaments to our shared loyalty. Testaments like this beautiful building here." He gestured to the top of the atrium, pulling the audience's gaze upwards. "Testaments like our wonderful symphony hall and theater next door." Now he guided all heads to the right. "Testaments like our traditions of giving and supporting the things that make this city great."

He had them now, and cheers broke out around the room. He silenced them with one more wave of his hand.

"So I just want to thank ya'll, all ya'll, for remaining loyal to our city, loyal to one another and loyal to the legacy of support and caring we've built right here in our community."

More applause.

"Okay, that's all I came to say. Ya'll carry on having fun now and don't let me hear about it tomorrow morning!"

The crowd gave a polite chuckle and then resumed its pre-speech decibel level.

Katie looked pointedly at Rita. "Well, if nothing else, his little speech to me gave him some fodder for the mic. I'm sorry, but I want to get out of here. Will you kill me if I leave?"

"Not at all, sister. I'm right behind you. This is not the kind of evening I expected. Even if I did meet someone, I'd never be able to catch his name!"

They walked out the front entrance and started down the long walkway to the street. Halfway down, Katie stopped.

"Rita, can I ask you something?"

"Of course, sugar, anything. But only if you want to hear the truth."

"If you knew someone, someone you liked and respected, had maybe done something horrible, what would you do?"

Rita was silent for a moment. "Well, I guess it would depend."

"On what?"

"On who did whatever it is you're talking about."

"I…I really can't say."

"Then, not to quote the jackass, but I guess it would depend on where your loyalty lies."

CHAPTER 20

Katie spent the rest of the weekend agonizing over what to do about Chris. She marched into the foundation's office on Monday determined to find out more.

A thick stack of new grant proposals on her desktop greeted her. The deadline for proposals was fast approaching. By the end of the week, she and Chris would be inundated with requests. She secretly hoped Jorge had gotten her message last Friday and would include his own in the pile.

She sucked in her cheeks and tapped her foot as she looked at the mound of paper that demanded her attention. Her heart simply wasn't in it, yet she shuffled over to her chair. Her plan for coaxing information from Chris would have to wait, but since he most likely had a similar-sized stack on his desk, he wouldn't be going anywhere soon.

She picked up the first proposal, but then smacked it back down on top of the pile. Honestly, what was the point? Porter shot down her last great idea. He and his buddies on the board were just going to keep sticking to the safe bets. Not even Jim could change that. They were never going to take a chance and fund something new and different.

"Arrrgh! I need a vacation." She groaned.

"Uh-oh, did we just find our stack of new proposals?"

She jumped when she saw Chris hovering at her door with a cup of coffee in each hand. He looked exhausted, but wore a small, apologetic smile as he offered her a cup.

"Looks like maybe you could use one of these."

"Thanks." She smiled back, taking a small sip from the steaming cup. An awkward silence filled the room as she took another swallow.

Chris returned to her doorway, where he leaned back against the wall, rather than continuing down the hall, so maybe he wanted something from her. Maybe she could get him talking about that phone conversation sooner than she'd hoped.

"Ah, just what I needed. Thanks. Is your stack that high?" She shrugged a shoulder toward the pile on her desk.

"Give or take, but remember, it's what's *inside* that matters."

"I'm not so sure. I think I'm a little gun-shy after what happened the last go-round. I don't even want to look at them right now."

"Look, the best way to get over that injury is to just jump right back on the horse. Find the next proposal you think Porter will hate, and you'll know it's something worth fighting for. Only this time, maybe we can present it together."

She laughed, and a dribble of coffee ran down her chin. She and Chris both knew that Porter was highly sensitive to Chris's "minority" status and would never attack him the same way he attacked her. She wasn't sure if Porter knew about Chris's sexual orientation, but he definitely looked uncomfortable when Chris presented in board meetings.

What if Chris couldn't present anything because he was in jail? The laugh dried up in her throat as she wiped her chin with a tissue.

"Maybe I'm just a little burned out." She paused. *Time to give Chris an opening.* "Plus, I can't stop thinking about that woman who died in the fire." She eyed him closely and saw some color drain from his face.

"I know what you mean, but there's nothing you could have done about it. It was horrible; it was unjust. But your best response is to keep fighting the good fight. She probably wasn't the only homeless person who died for no good reason that night. But we can do something here to help improve the circumstances so it doesn't happen again."

He paused a minute, then gave her a teasing smile. "Now that you mention it, you have seemed kind of distracted lately. I was hoping it was a new boyfriend or something."

"I...I...well, yes, I guess that's true, too." Her pulse quickened. *Did he know about Jim?*

Seeing her blush, Chris backed off.

"It's okay. You don't have to share a thing if you don't want to. Sometimes it's fun to keep it to yourself."

"No, no. It's funny. I was going to say the same thing about you, about being distracted, I mean."

Now it was his turn to squirm, but instead of blushing, he just looked sad. He stared at her without a word for a moment, and she read a clear message—*don't ask*—in his eyes. He seemed in pain and her heart went out to him. Everything seemed off balance.

She put both palms flat on her desk to steady herself. "Okay, so obviously we both need a little break. Why don't we leave early today; maybe go somewhere for a drink?"

He looked relieved to change the subject. "Do something different?"

"Exactly."

"I know just the place." The inkling of a grin touched the corners of his mouth. "I guarantee its somewhere you've never been."

"Okay, you're on."

"Perfect. You let me know when you're ready to go."

"I've got a call at 4:00, but I could go as soon as I'm done. Shouldn't take more than thirty minutes."

"It's a date!" Chris smiled, a real smile this time, and left her office.

Maybe tonight she could get him to come clean.

***

At 5:00, Katie drove through the Midtown streets as Chris pointed the way from the passenger seat. Since he lived near the office, he rarely drove, and she was happy to chauffeur.

"There. Turn right." He pointed to a parking lot behind a large gray, two-story building that looked like it had seen better days. "Backstreet," the sign said over what looked to be the rear entrance.

"Oh!" she exclaimed. "Backstreet? Really?" It was Atlanta's most legendary gay bar. Even Katie had heard about it.

"Don't worry. They let straight women in." He chuckled. "And it's the perfect place to make sure that no one else in philanthropy will overhear us if we say disrespectful things about the Hartwell Foundation."

"Ha! Good point."

She parked in a space that looked like it would remain well lit after the sun went down and locked the doors when they left.

Chris sniggered again. "Paranoid?"

Katie gave a nervous shake of her head for an answer, causing him to laugh out loud.

The club's door was narrow, and it led them into a tight, dimly lit passageway that fed into the lobby of the main entrance: a large, though equally dim, empty space with staircases on either side. It made Katie think that this must have been a theater lobby at one time. She had expected a huge room filled with throngs of men dancing to loud disco music, but instead Hank Williams played softly over hidden speakers. She cast a quizzical look at Chris.

"It's country western night on Mondays. An older crowd, at least until later."

He led her up a flight of stairs and into a small lounge. On their way to a table in the back, they passed an open pair of double doors that led to a mezzanine balcony overlooking a huge dance floor. A few men in cowboy hats and jeans were setting up a PA on the floor below.

"They'll teach you how to do the Cotton-Eye Joe at 6:00 if you're interested."

She laughed.

They found a small table near one of the club's few windows and ordered two beers.

"Okay, so you've spent the last few years of your life doing a good job at 'doing good' and now the thrill is gone. What's up?" Chris asked.

She hesitated. They were supposed to talk about *him*, not her. On the other hand, maybe if she opened up a little, he would too. She pushed out a deep breath, then let her words fly. "I don't know. Like I said before, maybe I'm just burned out, or maybe Porter's got me beaten down. And not really just him—the whole board. We get some great proposals, but we always have to stick to the same old stuff. That frustrates the hell out of me. Doesn't it you?"

"It used to. Not as much now that I've figured out the secret."

"What secret?" She wanted to steer their conversation toward the phone call, but she couldn't pass up this line of conversation.

"Well, look at your clinic proposal, for example. That was completely brand-new territory, and your gut maybe should have told you going in that it was too far beyond the comfort level of our trustees."

"But it was a good idea. It deserved funding."

"I'm not saying it didn't. But you came at it head-on and missed another way in."

"Enlighten me." She balled her hands into fists under the table to keep resentment from creeping into her voice.

"Well, remember that little grant we made to the zoo last year?"

"The one to expand their outreach? Yeah, I remember."

"You may recall that there was a list of organizations the zoo was going to partner with as a part of that grant, right?"

"Uh-huh."

"Well, one of them, as it turns out, was the Rainbow Theater. They've approached me about the possibility of getting a grant for years, but I knew there was no way it would ever get funded on its own. So when the zoo people told me they wanted to find potential partners for their expanded programs, I dropped the theater's name into the conversation."

Katie opened her mouth to protest his actions as manipulating the process, but he raised a finger to silence her.

"Uh-uh. I did not imply that I wanted this organization to be included or that the likelihood of funding was in any way connected to their involvement. I just planted the seed for the idea, and as it happened, the zoo people ran with it."

"Okay, fine. So Rainbow got the benefit of the funds from the foundation, but that's not a big shift in priorities or a move away from the conservative."

"Not a big shift, but a small one. Now our trustees have seen the Rainbow Theater name in partnership with a large organization they already know. So they won't be completely blindsided when the proposal from Rainbow shows up on the table in May."

"Humph," Katie snorted. "I guess that explains why you wanted me to pull the clinic out before."

"Yeah, I owe you an apology for that. I was out of line, but you can see how much time and strategy I had invested, right?"

"I guess." She scowled. "It doesn't matter anyway, does it? Thanks to the fire."

"I wish they would find out who did it." He gave her a sympathetic look that made her stomach lurch. How could he look that way if he had been involved?

"Sure you mean that?"

"What? Of course I do."

"It's just that I overheard you last week, talking on your cell phone by Starbucks. You mentioned the fire…and some other stuff."

The second the words left her mouth, she wished she had squelched them.

His jaw slackened and his eyes grew round and laced with pain. Instead of an accomplished professional, he looked like a beaten child. She thought he'd burst into tears right then and there. In fact, water brimmed in his eyes and he grew pale. He swallowed hard and shook his head. "You had no right," he whispered.

"Look." She reached a hand across the table. "If you're in some kind of trouble…"

"I'm not! It's…it's…personal."

"But I could help…"

"Katie." He looked into her eyes, pleading. "You can't help, and I can't talk about it. Let's just leave it at that."

"Okay, okay. I'm sorry." She searched his face, but he turned to look out the window. So she sat there, miserable, as the minutes ticked by and Chris worked to collect himself. Now she felt the heat rising in her own face. She felt torn. On one hand, she was angry with herself. Why had she pushed? On the other hand, she was still curious. What could make him so uncomfortable?

"Hey, Chris!" a voice called from across the room. She looked up to see two men approach their table. The one who had called out looked like any other young professional male in Atlanta. Dark suit, short sandy-blonde hair, clean-cut appearance. A young attorney or investment banker, she decided. His slightly taller companion had delicate features and a more effeminate manner—or maybe the club skewed her perception. He wore jeans and light gray sweater that highlighted his light gray eyes and dark black hair. Like Chris, he appeared to be of Hispanic descent.

"Hey, Kurt," said Chris, regaining his composure and standing up to shake the blonde man's hand. "What's up?"

"Just stopped by for a drink after work. This is Marco," Kurt added, gesturing at his companion.

Chris introduced Katie, and the four sat down at the table.

"Kurt lives in my building," Chris explained to her. Turning to his friends, he added, "Katie and I work together."

"Where?"

"The Hartwell Foundation." Chris shot Katie a quick glance. Introducing their workplace into a conversation could be tantamount to painting targets on their faces that said, "Get money here." She knew there was always a chance that someone would try to tell them about the great nonprofit they worked for or volunteered at or donated to every year that was *so* deserving of support. Worse, sometimes someone who was angry about having been turned down for a grant cornered her to vent. It was one of the reasons she rarely ventured out socially, even to a party with friends.

Kurt looked unimpressed, but she saw Marco's face light up in recognition and braced herself for the onslaught. *I'll let Chris field this one.*

But rather than suggest ways of spending the foundation's money, Marco was effusive with praise: "Oh! I know the Hartwell Foundation! In fact, I'm glad to be able to thank you both in person. I'm a part-time tech at Viva Latina. Dr. Ramirez told us that you guys were going to pay for an entire new building for us. That's absolutely fabulous! Thank you so much! The fire really devastated our spirits—and that poor chica!—but you've helped out beyond our wildest dreams."

Katie struggled to stifle her incredulity and keep her face impassive. A quick glance at Chris showed that he shared her surprise. He shot her a look as if to say, *Did you know about this?* She gave the slightest of nods no.

Just as she started to respond, Chris cut her off. "It's awesome that someone's helping to pay for your building, but I think maybe you've confused the Hartwell Foundation with someone else." That was Chris, ever the diplomat.

"No, no, no!" shouted Marco. "Not 'helping to pay'—totally *paying*. Like, for the whole thing. And it's definitely you guys because I remember when Dr. Ramirez said your name, I thought '*Hart*well Foundation, like they have a *heart* and do *well* with it.' I use word association stuff like that all the time to keep up with patient's names."

"Dr. *Ramirez* told you about this?" Now Katie was certain that Marco was confused. The young man blushed.

"Well…okay, it's not exactly like he told us. I just was looking on his desk for a time sheet, and I just happened to see the letter from you guys that talked about the grant and said that it was supposed to be anonymous—"

"Yeah," Kurt said, "Like you probably just 'happened' to see it by opening a closed file or a locked drawer or something."

Marco frowned at Kurt.

"What? Like you're not the snoopiest person you know?" Kurt asked.

Marco feigned umbrage for a moment, then giggled and grinned. "Yeah, I really am good at finding out stuff. I should be like a private detective or something. But I promise I won't blow the anonymous thing for you guys," he said, winking at Katie and Chris.

"That's good to know." She jumped in to cover their ignorance about what must be a *very* large grant. "I'm so glad that you'll have a new space. Where will it be?"

"I don't think that's decided yet," said Marco. "Or at least, I haven't heard about the location."

"You mean you haven't eavesdropped enough," Kurt said.

Marco ignored him. "But seriously, after all this—and what that girl went through—we're just happy to be able to start over."

"Did you know the woman in the fire? Angel?" Katie asked.

"No, but I heard from her cousin—he cleans our building—well, used to clean it anyway. He said she just wanted a place to stay. She wanted to go to the clinic anyway. Some female thing. She hadn't been in the country very long. Her cousin said she got attacked by some guy. He tried to rape her when she was helping his company clean a building in Midtown somewhere. It's sick."

"That's awful!" Katie gulped. The poor woman! Alone in a new country, hoping to start a new life, and instead of all that, she gets assaulted and then murdered. Jorge hadn't mentioned any of this. Neither had Jim. Maybe they didn't know, or maybe they just wanted to spare her the unpleasant details.

"No one knows who attacked her?" she asked Marco.

"Doubtful. Angel didn't speak English, and she was an illegal. Who's she going to tell?" Marco added with a snort. "It happens more than you think."

"Do the police know?"

Marco looked at her again with a condescending expression and reached out to pat her hand. "No, sweetie. We're talking about illegals. Who's going talk to the cops if it means you may get sent back?"

She clenched her jaw, caught between resentment at Marco's tone and embarrassment at sounding so naive.

Chris came to her rescue. "Well, you won't have to worry about that any more. Good luck to you."

"Oh yes!" Marco's face lit up. "There's a lot more. We'll be able to—"

"Look, I know you're excited, but I came here to get away from work talk." Kurt stood up and signaled to Marco. "Let's go learn to two-step."

"Buy me a drink first, cowboy." Marco placed his hand on Kurt's arm.

"Sure thing. Molotov cocktail?"

"Dude, that's not even funny." Marco looked disgusted. He turned his back on Kurt and swaggered to the bar.

"Crazy about me." Kurt winked to Katie and Chris before following Marco.

"What's in a Molotov cocktail?" Katie asked the now pink-faced Chris.

"Um, it's not a drink." He reddened even more. "He was referring to something, uh, explosive, below the waistline."

"Ugh!" She made a face as Kurt and Marco, beers in hand, left the room.

It was a little surreal, watching two men walk away together to go cowboy-style dancing, but not as surreal as hearing from a complete stranger about a major grant from the Hartwell Foundation that she knew nothing about and wouldn't have believed.

"You didn't know anything about this?" she asked, just to double-check.

He shook his head and leaned back in his chair. "I think Marco is confused about his philanthropic benefactors. You know Porter would never let a grant like that happen."

"True enough." But she wasn't so sure. Something wasn't quite right in the whole equation, but she couldn't put her finger on it. Chris might be able to help her figure it out, but she preferred to discuss it with Jim over the weekend.

Ah, the weekend. It was forever from now, and suddenly she didn't want to wait a second longer. She said good night to Chris and found her way out to the parking lot, where she stopped to give Jim a call. She hung up when his voicemail answered. No sense in bugging him.

As she reached into her purse for her keys, she realized she'd neglected to pay for her beer, sticking Chris with the tab. She headed back into the bar and up the stairs, glancing into the double doors she had passed earlier. Curiosity drew her inside to the mezzanine balcony. Down below, she saw dozens of faux cowboys, all in pairs and all bouncing around the room to the beat of a live country western band. The lead singer was dressed in drag as a very convincing Loretta Lynn. She watched as the men all swirled in unison as if they were choreographed.

Her eyes wandered over the unusual scene. It was almost like watching a movie or a play. Then she noticed Chris in a corner, talking intently with a man she didn't recognize. He had on jeans, a western shirt and boots like most of the other patrons, but instead of dancing, he was thrusting what appeared to be a small piece of paper at Chris, who held up both hands in protest. The stranger kept shoving the paper into Chris' shirt pocket. Chris shook his head angrily, turned sharply on his heel and stormed through the crowd and out the door a floor below Katie's feet.

She turned as well and trotted to the stairwell, catching sight of Chris as he strode down the rear hall and into the parking lot. She raced down the hall after him and opened the door. She was about to call out to Chris when she heard a loud sob escape from him. He stopped, back toward her, and yanked the paper from his pocket, ripping it into small pieces that he flung on the ground before half-walking, half-running through the parking lot and around a corner.

Katie stood for a moment, stunned. She had never seen Chris act so angry or seem so emotionally fragile. She started toward her car, then veered to the torn bits of paper on the ground and scooped them up. She cradled them in one hand, fumbling for her keys with the other as she walked across the parking lot. Once she settled in the driver's seat, she studied the fragments in her lap. In his haste, he hadn't ripped the paper that many times, so it only took a second to piece together. It was a check from a Gregory Newcombe. Chris's name appeared in the "Pay to the order of" line in a fine, scripted hand. The amount took Katie's breath away. Chris had torn up a check for $10,000.

CHAPTER 21

Katie googled the name Gregory Newcombe as soon as she got home. It wasn't a name she recalled seeing or hearing before. Her first glance at the search results froze her hand on the mouse and she gasped. Her breath grew faster as she scanned the information that popped up on her screen. She shook her head in disbelief, mumbling, "Holy shit! No!"

Gregory Newcombe was the executive director of the Rainbow Theater. He hadn't been in that position long, but long enough to have worked with Chris on submitting the grant request for the upcoming round. Before that he worked in a large fundraising consulting firm that represented many of the organizations subsequently funded by the foundation. Earlier in his career, Katie noticed with alarm, he served as a senior campaign staffer for an unsuccessful conservative candidate who had made a news splash with his anti-immigrant messages. Even if Chris had been maneuvering for two years as he'd claimed, the timing between Gregory Newcombe's installation as leader of the theater and Chris's decision to push for funding now seemed too perfect to be a coincidence.

No, not Chris. Accepting a large check from a grantee was as inconceivable as it was unethical. Even accepting free tickets to a fundraising event was considered a strict no-no. It couldn't be! Besides, if Chris were accepting a bribe, wouldn't it come *after* the grant was awarded rather than before? And he very clearly didn't accept it, whatever it was for. The torn check scraps proved that. She placed them in a plastic sandwich bag and slid them into the drawer of her nightstand, unsure if she was keeping them to accuse Chris or protect him.

Throughout the week at work, Katie bit her tongue every time she saw her colleague. Ten grand was a lot of money to throw away—unless you either didn't need it or couldn't stomach the way you got it. He looked haunted every time they passed. He didn't necessarily go out of his way to avoid her, but he never stopped to talk, only returning her invitations and greetings with the minimum reply courtesy required.

She longed to talk to Jim about Chris, but something in Rita's comment about loyalty held her back. Where did her loyalty lie? Chris had done nothing but help her career at the foundation, at least until he asked her for that very unusual favor of withholding a grant recommendation. And yet, that was just a favor. She still had no real reason to suspect Chris of any wrongdoing. She respected him too much to cast questions on his character without more concrete proof. She also wanted to call Jim to find out more about the mysterious clinic grant. But if Chris was right and Marco was mistaken, then asking about it would only make her look foolish, as she had when she jumped to the conclusion about Porter starting the fire. Besides, Jim had made it clear that the trial was overloading him. The last thing he needed was a clingy girlfriend.

Instead, she called Jorge several times, only to get his voicemail. She left messages asking about the sale of the clinic property and checking in on the progress of the clinic's recovery. She knew from Jim that Jorge had moved to temporary quarters at a nearby Red Cross blood center, but she had heard surprisingly little else. It wasn't like Jorge not to return her calls, especially when he was no doubt about to submit another significant proposal for funding—a *real* one, not a rumor.

One advantage of working at a large charitable foundation was that people *always* returned your calls. Katie pouted when she got his voicemail for the third time. *He's got to be overwhelmed with keeping things going after the fire*, she chastised herself. But wouldn't he *want* to talk to her?

She pulled on a strand of hair as she stared at the phone. For the first time in a year, as far as the clinic was concerned, she felt left out. Everyone else seemed to be moving on, no one appeared to care anymore about the *who* and the *why* of the fire or the resulting murder. She decided to call the police herself.

"Atlanta homicide. How may I direct your call?" The receptionist sounded bored, and Katie realized she did not know the name of the detectives assigned to the clinic case.

"Um, hi. I was hoping to talk to someone about the Viva Latina clinic fire?"

"Are you reporting a fire, ma'am?"

"No, no. This happened a couple of weeks ago. It was an arson."

"You'll need to call the fire department for questions about arson, ma'am."

"But…no, someone died in that fire. I…uh, I was told that there was a murder investigation associated with it?" Katie's foot jiggled nonstop as she struggled to keep a tremor out of her voice. One by one, she wiped her sweaty palms on her skirt.

"Do you have a case number, ma'am? Or a detective's name?"

"No. I don't. I was hoping you could tell me that." She gritted her teeth.

"And are you related to the victim?"

"No."

"So may I ask what your connection to this case is, ma'am?"

"I…I…Oh, never mind!" She slammed down the receiver, nervousness replaced with a flush of anger. For some reason, she had assumed that everyone in the homicide department would be familiar with this case. Jim was right: they probably were overworked and pursuing cases that had a prayer of being solved instead of concentrating on the death of an illegal immigrant woman no one knew or cared about.

She scowled at the phone. The police weren't even aware that Angel had been attacked earlier. Yet another crime that would fall off the radar screen. It was almost as if the dead woman had never existed. But the dark-haired woman had returned to her dreams several times. She never spoke, only waited on the edge of her cliff, and if Katie moved toward her, she fell.

"Get over yourself, Kate," she said aloud, and returned to the work at hand. If everyone else could move on, so could she. Lord knows, she had plenty of other things to keep her occupied.

***

Friday morning dawned bright and sunny with the promise of warmer temperatures over the weekend. Spring redoubled its efforts with daffodils bursting amid bright green lawns and delicate white flowers on dogwood trees. Katie arose full of energy and optimism. She and Jim had agreed to play hooky to get a full extra day of their weekend together.

"I'll pick you up at 10:00," he'd said on the phone. "We'll be in Highlands by lunchtime."

Highlands was a legendary North Carolina mountain town just over the state line. Many wealthy Atlanta residents, as well as some companies, owned vacation homes in the area. She'd never visited, but had heard foundation board members and others in the philanthropic sector speak of their weekends or summers there. Highlands sounded like paradise.

She showered and dressed in jeans and a fitted T-shirt, layering a tailored white shirt over it to ward off the last of a persistent spring chill. She slipped on a pair of flats, but packed her hiking boots at the top of her bag, unsure of what the day might bring. Jim pulled into the driveway just as she set out extra food and water for Babka. She smiled as she heard him taking the steps two at a time up to her door and went to meet him at the threshold.

"Morning, Miz Nelson! Are you ready for a weekend away from everything?" he crowed, sweeping her into his arms and planting a kiss on her lips before she could answer.

"Yes. Definitely," she said, as soon as he released her. "Except I hope we're not going to be away from *that*."

"Oh, no. We'll be taking plenty of *that* along with us."

He gave Babka a quick scratch behind the ear as he leaned down to pick up her small overnight bag.

"This it?"

She nodded. "I travel light."

"Glad to hear it. Plays well into my plans." He wiggled his eyebrows at her as he bounded down the steps.

She locked up and followed him, anticipating their weekend ahead. She reviewed the contents of her suitcase—the boots, another pair of jeans and T-shirt for hiking, a denim jacket and a fleece pullover in case the mountains still held a chill in early spring, a green knit dress and wrap in case they went somewhere nice for dinner and two selections of sexy sleepwear.

At the bottom of the stairs, she stopped, stunned, her mouth forming an "o," as she watched Jim stow her suitcase under the hood of a bright red convertible coupe, the like of which she had never seen. Based on details like its metal bumper and aerodynamic shape, she guessed it was an older model car, although it looked to be in top condition. "Where did you get *that*?"

"Don't be offended, but it's Porter's. He heard I was going out of town for the weekend and assumed I'm taking a 'tasty little morsel,' to use his words, so he loaned it to me. He promised me I'd get a blow job if I drove this car." Jim grinned. "I think he even promised that would happen as I was driving up I-85. The man really is a pig, but you have to admire his conviction."

"*I* certainly don't, and I don't think I want to ride in this car, either." Katie crossed her arms across her chest.

He laughed at first, but once he saw the firm anger ignited in her eyes, he coughed into his hand and pleaded his case. "Oh, Katie, honey. I didn't *agree* with him. I know you're not that kind of woman."

Thank God he didn't say, "That kind of girl."

"Look at it my way. What a nice little victory to take Porter's very sweet little car for a weekend with a woman who is beautiful and intelligent and highly principled and willing to stand up for what she believes in—everything Porter hates—and have a great time doing it, just to spite him. When he threw me the keys, I just caught 'em. Now here I am. Or rather, here *we* are. So whaddya say? Shall we use this fabulous piece of machinery for good instead of evil?"

It was only a car. Porter was the beast, not Jim. It *would* be fun to sail up to Highlands in style. And sure, by not behaving as Porter assumed any woman would in his car, she'd be striking a small victory. "Okay, as long as we're perfectly clear that Porter's fantasies stay with Porter, and you don't make up any raunchy stories about me when you give the car back."

"No worries. He has no idea I'm taking you, anyway. Made sure of that. I'll just drop the keys with his secretary on Monday. 'Sides, my strategy with Porter is always to let him do the talkin' and keep my personal life—and my thoughts—to myself."

"Just let me get my jacket out of my suitcase." She retrieved her denim jacket and slipped into the passenger seat as he started the engine.

"Listen to that," he purred, with a wistful smile on his face. "Just so you know, this is a 1965 Chevy Corvair Corsa…"—he stroked the dashboard—"and that"—with a nod to the back of the car—"*that's* a rear-mounted, 146 horsepower, 164-cubic-inch, 'flat six,' air-cooled engine. It's what set this car apart back in the day."

"Is that important?"

"Let's just say it puts my Toyota to shame. Not the biggest engine Chevy ever put in a sports car, but in my opinion, one of the sweetest to drive."

"I never figured you for a motor head."

"Oh, Dad was into cars. I picked stuff up as a kid."

In a matter of minutes, they were cruising northeast on the interstate, gunning for the city limits. Despite the wind from the open convertible, the sun felt warm and reassuring on Katie's face. She smiled as she tilted her head back and let the wind tousle her hair. She hoped Jim was enjoying the ride as much as she was.

As they headed toward the northeastern corner of Georgia, she soaked up the gradual changes in the landscape. Within thirty minutes, the twelve lanes of Atlanta traffic fell away, and the highway became a divided four-lane road. After another half-hour, smaller roads dotted the four lanes with occasional intersections. The strip malls around Atlanta's outer fringes gave way to trees and rolling hills.

She closed her eyes, soaking up the sun's rays and the fresh air, then opened them again as the car slowed for a red light. As they came to a stop, she glanced to her right and caught a man staring at her. Or perhaps he was staring at the Corvair. Hunched over the steering wheel of a nondescript green sedan, he had close-cropped gray hair and a jaw as angular as a cinderblock. Probably in his mid-fifties. He looked tough and serious, like a Marine drill sergeant or a policeman. *Where did cops go on their days off?* He probably was interested in the car, but then again, she wasn't unattractive, was she? She flashed him a friendly smile. He looked embarrassed as Jim floored his accelerator at the green light and the Corvair leapt forward, leaving cop-man in the dust.

Her limbs and mind unwound more with every passing mile. For a moment, she pictured herself back in high school, playing hooky on a sunny spring day during senior year—her only rebellious act as a teenager. At that time, she savored the freedom of knowing she'd graduate soon with honors and had already been accepted to the college of her choice. She had nothing to lose, and the future was as bright and sunny as the day. As she remembered that feeling, even the dream image of Angel drifted far, far away.

She turned to grin at Jim.

"What?" He had to shout over the noise from the wind and the road.

"I'm just happy," she yelled back, stretching her hands up into the slipstream that flew over the convertible's windshield. "I feel like I'm back in high school!"

He smiled back and reached over to squeeze her knee. She sank back into her high-speed reverie, but continued to smirk sideways at Jim from time to time. *It was about damn time.*

A while later, larger hills rose up on either side of the road. Small towns appeared here and there with roadside restaurants and gift shops. Jim had to drop his speed, which allowed her to absorb more of their surroundings. They stopped to peek at a scenic river gorge in the small town of Toccoa, where they bought lattes at a little coffee shop. While he ordered, she perused the local headlines in a newspaper lying on the counter. A story about a local clinic reminded her about the odd conversation earlier that week at Backstreet. She hesitated to bring up the topic during this weekend escape, but her curiosity wouldn't let up. The questions continued to nag at the back of her mind. She couldn't tell Jim about Chris, but she could ask about that grant.

"Hey! No frowning this weekend." He'd sneaked up behind her with the coffees and wrapped his arm around her shoulder as he handed her one. He squinted at the paper in her hands. "Bad news?"

"No, no." She turned to him. "A story in the paper reminded me of something I heard about Viva Latina. Can I ask you a question about it?"

"Can I ever stop you?" His eyes twinkled.

She shifted under the weight of his arm. "Do you know anything about a big grant we're making to them so they can build a whole new clinic?"

He looked surprised, and she thought she saw a shadow flit across his face. "Where'd you hear that? I mean, sounds like gossip—or maybe wishful thinking."

"A friend of an acquaintance of a friend works at the clinic part-time and said he was sure about it." Saying it, she realized how silly it sounded. She looked up into his eyes, and after a pause, they both broke into laughter. "Okay, maybe it does sound far-fetched, but he'd seemed so certain."

"That and three-fifty'll buy you a latte." He took a sip of his coffee.

"He also said the woman who died had been attacked. She'd apparently been the victim of attempted rape not too long before."

Jim blanched for a moment, but then regained his composure. "Oh, Katie, that's horrible. What kind of sick person would do that?"

She shrugged and shook her head, unable to answer that question. "Do you think it's true?"

"Probably as true as the rumor about a grant."

"So you haven't heard anything about the grant?"

"Can't say I have, and I should know if we were doing something like that. Now come on," he said, squeezing her shoulders and pulling her closer to him. "We've got a weekend to enjoy."

She pulled away. "Just one more question."

He sighed.

"Did you know the clinic site has been sold? They've already dug up the whole block for a new development. Did Jorge tell you about that?"

"He told me that a developer had been interested before. Now that he had nothing to lose, he agreed to let it go. I didn't get the impression he made much on it, though."

"Why didn't you tell me?"

"Sorry. I was wrapped up at work. Jorge didn't make it sound like that big a deal. I assumed he'd tell you himself if he wanted to. Besides, my focus is on the insurance claim that hasn't been paid yet. I didn't have anything to do with any sale."

He gave Katie another squeeze. "Now, no more shop talk. From this point on, we're just two young lovers out for an adventure." He waggled his eyebrows again and she giggled.

"'Two young lovers?' Are you sure you're not gay?"

"Damn," he shot back as they hopped into the car. "You've found me out. Yes, I'm very gay, but I'm desperately hoping you can cure my affliction this weekend."

She blushed as they pulled away. "I'll be happy to try," she said under her breath.

CHAPTER 22

They continued north, passing through a few other small mountain towns, tiny hamlets and roadside tourist stands offering fresh produce and souvenirs. After about half an hour, they turned east and crossed the border into North Carolina. The road became steep and twisty, demanding a slower pace. The landscape changed dramatically as well, squeezing the road with huge moss-covered boulders and emerald-green ferns framed by delicate hemlock branches. It was as if they were driving into their own personal weekend in fairyland where magic would no doubt occur.

The drop in speed reduced the wind noise, but Katie hesitated to make conversation that could distract Jim from negotiating the curves. She watched transfixed as his right hand navigated the space between the steering wheel and the stick shift, while his feet danced between the gas, brake and clutch.

He makes it look so easy. She herself had never learned to drive a stick.

He wore a satisfied smile as he slid through the turns. "My dad would've loved this road," he said aloud.

"'Would've?' Has he…is he still living?" She recalled him speaking of his father in the past tense before, although he had never mentioned a death.

"Oh, yeah. Just meant that he never gets out to do anything fun. Works all the time, even though he loves cars. Too bad he never took the time to drive something like this. Poured his entire life into his practice."

"That *is* too bad." *And sad, too.* She hoped she would never get so focused on work—even meaningful work—that she would forget to actually *live.* She resolved, again, to enjoy this weekend to the absolute fullest.

The air became cooler as they climbed, sending refreshing gusts under the collar of her jacket. Ancient hemlocks and big, leafy rhododendrons bordered the road, changing the bright sun to dappled shade. While spring had blossomed in the city, up here it was still in the early, delicate stages. Every now and then, small clusters of trillium, golden ragwort or trout lilies flashed delightful colors as the car sped by.

The sun neared the top of the sky when they arrived in Highlands. The town had one main road with several tributaries. While only a few square blocks, it boasted several cute shops offering home furnishings, antiques, tasteful gifts and clothing.

They parked along Main Street, in front of a boutique that flaunted the names of Versace, Burberry, Dolce and others in the windows. Katie didn't spy a typical tourist T-shirt or fudge shop anywhere. Highlands was a far cry from some of the other towns they had driven through.

"Thought we might walk around for a minute to stretch our legs," Jim said. "Then we can either find a café for lunch or get a picnic and go for a hike." He pointed up the street. "There's a grocery store just a couple of blocks that way."

At the mention of lunch, her stomach rumbled. "Let's have lunch here somewhere and then go hike. I'm starving."

"Buck's Coffee is pretty good." He nodded to a place across the street. "They have sandwiches and salads and other stuff, or we can do something a little fancier."

"No doubt, but low-key sounds good to me. And you can learn a lot about a place from a coffee shop."

As they crossed the street, Katie looked at the license plates of the cars parked along either side. Georgia—specifically Atlanta's Fulton and DeKalb Counties—and various Florida plates dominated, with an occasional South Carolina, Tennessee or Louisiana car in the mix. "Not many folks here from points north, are there?"

He gave a little snort. "Not too many people who aren't from Atlanta or Florida."

"But where are all the North Carolina tags? What about the people who actually *live* here?"

"They're all parked around back. They *work* here."

He held the door to Buck's Coffee Café open for her, and she stepped in, welcomed by the creak of wide and worn hardwood floorboards beneath her feet. Long and narrow, the café extended straight back before her. The smell of freshly baked bread and a hint of fresh garlic wafted from the back, causing her stomach to let out a small growl. Paintings from local artists adorned the walls, guiding her from the sunny front windows back to a long, heavy wooden bar with a warm walnut finish. It looked as though it could have been imported from a British pub. They made their way back past couches and armchairs intermingled with café tables for two or four. As she walked along the length of the bar, she studied a glass-fronted case containing a tantalizing selection of baked goods and pastries, as well as gourmet sandwiches. Her mouth watered as she scanned the giant chalkboard hanging above with the menu and daily specials.

They each ordered a sandwich and found a table near the bright front windows tucked underneath a large acrylic painting of a black bear.

"So how did this town get to be so ritzy when the others we passed seemed so much more blue-collar?" she asked.

"Ah, Miz Nelson, time for a history lesson?" He grinned and rubbed his palms together.

She smiled. That mock-formality was now one of their "things," a signature of their personal interplay. She relished it...and everything about Jim.

"Highlands here is different for a couple of reasons. First, 'cause of its roots. Created in 1875—I think that's right—by two businessmen from Kansas. The legend is that they took a map and drew one line from New York to New Orleans, and another from Chicago to Savannah. They thought that wherever those lines crossed would become a big trading crossroads, so they set about building a town that would live up to that expectation. The fact that this place happened to be 4,000 feet up a mountain and not so easy to get to kinda spoiled their plans. But the fact that it's spectacularly beautiful certainly didn't hurt. Luckily, people valued the natural beauty here and have taken good care of it, mostly, which of course makes it more expensive."

"Geez! Did you study this place in school or something?"

"Nah, brochure by the cash register." They both laughed. "Remember that country club we passed on the way up here?"

She nodded.

"Started by Bobby Jones in the '30s. *That's* what really put this town on the map, sealed the deal for it becoming a resort area. Only about 1,000 folks live here year round. But in 'the season…'"—here he made air quotes with his fingers and stuck out his chin, adapting his best Northeastern blue-blood yachtsman accent—"there can be ten times as many."

"Huh." She gazed at the young man behind the counter and wondered how he fit into the Highlands scene. Was he enjoying a summer job, flirting with wealthy women and garnering large tips before heading off to some other place? Or did he grow up here, the great-great-grandson of someone who helped to build the town? If you lived here year 'round but weren't wealthy, was it the love of its natural beauty and charm that kept you going? Or did you learn early on from watching the summer people that money didn't buy happiness? And what about philanthropy? Did the people who came here only part of the year do their part to help those who remained here for the winter? Or were there any poor people here at all? What about…

"Katie? You still with me?" Jim put his hand on her arm.

"Oh, I'm sorry. I was just kinda taking it all in. How come you know so much about this place?"

"Uh, hello? Big Atlanta law firm? Exceedingly wealthy partners? This is the go-to place for those boys. Sometimes when they're feelin' generous, they bring along the little fish like me. Mostly for golf, though, so I'm really happy to be here with you instead. We have to do some hiking. Fantastic waterfalls around here, not to mention the views."

"As long as you don't try to drag me onto a golf course, I'm game for just about anything."

"Anything?" He gave her a knowing smile, and she laughed as the barista brought their food.

She savored her smoked salmon sandwich, basking in the happiness of this little mountain town and her newfound love. What could be better? All the worries of her everyday life faded away. It was good to let go sometimes.

Once they finished their lunch, Jim and Katie bought café mochas to go and wandered the streets of Highlands. As they strolled hand in hand, she noticed the dark green sedan that she'd seen on the road from Atlanta and smiled. *Even the police get to enjoy a vacation now and then. Maybe he's meeting someone special up here.*

At the corner of Main Street and South 4th stood the Old Edwards Inn, a historic hotel that appeared to have expanded to include a collection of rustic-looking buildings spanning an entire block of Main Street. Katie saw a plaque for the National Register of Historic Places, as well as one signifying that the inn was ranked highly by Condé Naste. The façade was a classic mix of red brick and stone. The slate roof and multi-paned windows gave the building a European feel.

"Is that where we're staying?" she asked, looking up at the inn's cozy balconies perched above the street. It'd be fun to sit up there with a glass of wine and watch the people below.

"Nope," he replied with a sly smile. "We're staying somewhere a little more, um, *private*—but it's a surprise."

They continued to explore the town, and before she knew it, her watch read 4:30 and the afternoon sun started to wane. She could feel her stomach rumbling again.

"Whoops! Guess we won't be hiking today. Gettin' close to wine and snack time," he said, reading her mind. "We're stayin' in a place with a kitchen, so I thought I'd cook for us tonight."

"You know I'm not going to turn that down!"

"Smart girl. Let's hit the grocery store down that way." He pointed over his shoulder. "Why don't we just take the car so we don't have to carry all the bags back?"

She agreed, so they climbed in and drove the short three blocks to the Mountain Fresh Grocery. As they pulled into the parking lot, Katie's cell phone rang.

She glanced at the incoming number. Rita. Maybe she should answer, even though she was technically on vacation. "Okay if I wait out here while you shop?" she asked as Jim stepped out of the car.

"Absolutely. Just be sure you say nice things about me."

"No question." She answered the call with a smile as she watched Jim walk into the grocery store.

"Hello?" But all she heard was static on the other end of the line. "Hello? Rita? Can you hear me?"

Nothing. She ended the call and looked at her reception bars. One would assume that this place would be a high-priority for the cellular companies, but her phone indicated otherwise. Perhaps she'd have better luck later when they reached wherever they were going to spend the night.

In the meantime, she entertained herself by watching people make their way in and out of the grocery store. Here was a petite, bronzed and ponytailed woman who practically needed a ladder to climb down from her monster SUV—with Atlanta tags, naturally. There was a white-haired grandfather in golf attire with two beaming blonde cherubs in tow who must be grandchildren. They talked nonstop of ice cream flavors.

An elderly couple pulled into the parking lot in a Jaguar and emerged in tennis clothes. They ignored her, focusing on one another. The man put his hand on the woman's elbow, and she smiled up at him as they crossed the parking lot. Were they married? Having an affair? Childhood sweet-hearts?

She started to daydream about growing old with Jim—would they still be that much in love?—when a woman's sharp voice made her snap to attention.

"Don't get too comfortable in that seat, lady. The guy driving that car has a dick the size of a Vienna sausage and the attention span of a four-year-old."

Stunned, Katie turned her head to a young woman standing nearby. "Excuse me?"

The woman wore cutoff jeans, a generic tank top and flip-flops. It was clear she had a good figure. She'd twisted her blonde hair loosely behind her head, although several strands had worked their way loose into straight wisps. She held several plastic grocery bags in each hand. A clump of keys peeked out from her front pocket.

She glared at Katie for a minute, saying nothing. Then her face softened. "Look, all I'm sayin' is that I been there in that seat where you're settin'. Don't make no big plans."

With that, she turned on her heel and hurried across the parking lot, slinging her groceries into the back of a small, gray pickup truck with North Carolina plates. She backed out of her parking space without looking behind her and tore out of the lot.

"What that was about?" Jim said as he walked up to the driver's side of the car.

"I'm not sure. I think maybe she thought I was someone else."

But no, the woman had been talking about the driver of the car, not about Katie. Had she been talking about Jim? She really didn't seem like his type at all, from what Katie could tell—but then, she'd been wrong about men before, hadn't she? The woman could have been talking about Porter, since it was his car. But still…

"So, how long have you been coming up here?" she asked.

"Not very long. Got my first invitation last year, but always just for golf with the guys. Never had a reason to come up here on my own."

"That woman in the truck seemed to think she knew you." She scanned his face for a reaction.

"Not likely." He shook his head. Then he added, "You know, some guys at the firm go after the local ladies when they come up here, but that's not my scene. I doubt I'd even recognize any of them. What'd that girl look like?"

"Oh, you know. Blonde, pretty, all the right curves, the kind of girl men notice."

"Nope, no one I know, unfortunately." He paused for a beat, searching her face. Then a look of delighted incredulity spread across his face. "Hey now, you're not jealous are you?" He laughed. "Miz Nelson, does that mean that you are, perhaps, quite into me?"

"Maybe." She let out a breath of relief and felt a knot that had been tightening in her stomach relax. "It depends on what you're cooking me for dinner tonight."

"Well, then, I'd better get busy!"

***

Jim guided the Corvair through a couple of quick turns, and they were soon winding up another mountain road. Like the road that led to Highlands, hemlocks and rhododendrons crowded along the shoulder. Katie caught glimpses of large houses tucked behind the foliage.

Katie was enjoying the ride and the scenery when Jim turned off the blacktop and onto a surprisingly smooth, well-manicured gravel driveway buttressed by thick forest. They passed a small but well-kept two-story garage on their left, but didn't stop. Up ahead, the driveway bent slightly to the right, and a clearing peeked through the trees. Although the surrounding woods looked nearly primordial, the driveway and the house she could now glimpse spoke of money and calculated order. They drove around the turn, and she drew a sharp breath. "Oh! It's beautiful!"

The house that appeared in the clearing—under majestic hemlocks, tulip poplars and oaks—wasn't an exceptionally large structure by Atlanta standards, but the weathered stone and cedar shingle siding on its exterior gave it the feel of a respected and venerable sage. From its two-storied main structure, single-story wings with steeply-pitched roofs extended from either side. Bright windows reflected the spring forest and the sky beyond. Riots of pink rhododendrons hugged the corners of the house and large, smooth boulders emerged here and there along its sides. In some cases, it was difficult to tell where the rock face of the house stopped and the stony ground began. Amid the rhododendron, vines of Virginia creeper crawled slowly up the shingles, as if to reclaim them into the soil.

On closer inspection, Katie noticed that this appearance of timelessness was actually well calculated and carefully tended. The creeper vines were well clear of the house's wood-paned windows. A layer of mulch surrounded the rhododendron and rock beds. And the wooden shingles, while weathered enough to create character, showed no signs of mildew or water damage.

Jim navigated the circular drive and parked in front of a large portico with a high peaked roof held up by whole tree trunks, stripped of bark and polished smooth as silk. A bumpy railing made from interwoven branches bordered each side of the portico, ushering visitors toward a massive front door hewn from solid oak.

She waited while he opened the hood of the convertible, then grabbed her share of luggage and grocery bags. She gazed up at the beams supporting the portico roof as he shook out a jumble of keys and found one for the front door.

"Whose house is this?" she asked.

"This weekend, it's ours," he said with a face full of pride. Seeing that she wasn't satisfied with his answer, he continued. "Actually, it belongs to the firm. Partners usually keep it booked up, but this weekend they're all tied up with that celebrity golf tournament in town. I got the jump on it before any of the other minions." He grinned. It must have been quite a feat, considering the size of the firm.

"It's impressive," she said, as he opened the door and stood aside for her.

"Just wait. You ain't seen nothin' yet."

She stepped through a short hallway with a darkened room off to either side, then into a great room with a heavy stone fireplace at one end. A balcony hovered above on three sides, but the great room alone took her breath away. The house's back wall was composed almost entirely of windows, two stories high, framing a spectacular view of the mountains beyond. A deck wrapped around the back in either direction, beckoning visitors to come, sit and be enthralled with the glory of the surroundings. The evening sun, setting just off to the right through a translucent curtain of clouds, bathed the entire scene in a smoky purple light, tinged around the edges with a luminous golden glow.

"Whoa. I thought you only got sunsets like that at the beach," she whispered, awestruck.

"Yeah, this is a special place," he said, placing his hand on Katie's shoulder. She turned to kiss him, and the warmth of the sun flooded throughout her body. It did indeed have the feel of sacred ground.

He kissed her back with tender passion and then took a small step back. "I'll open the wine and get some cheese so we can sit outside to watch the sunset—unless you're ready for dinner?"

She shook her head. "I think the sunset sounds perfect."

Together, they watched the sun go down and evening climb up to the ridges beyond. They spoke when it suited them and enjoyed comfortable silence in the space between. She breathed the spring air deeply and giggled out loud at some of his childhood stories.

When the last of the sunlight disappeared, Jim looked pointedly at her. "Guess it's time to get cooking. Tonight, we're having local trout, fresh from the stream, roasted new potatoes and asparagus. Sound good?"

"Are you kidding? What can I do to help?"

"Just grab a stool, and I'll let you know if I need a hand." He led the way into a state-of-the-art kitchen that took up the house's entire east wing. "If you'd like, wander around and choose your sleeping quarters. There are two down and five up."

"*My* sleeping quarters?"

"*Our* sleeping quarters?"

"Ours, yes. Most definitely." She marveled at how easy and natural it felt to want to share everything with him. As if they had known each other for years.

"Just checking." He chuckled from the kitchen as she slipped back into the great room to explore the house. Now that it was dark outside, she could concentrate more on the massive main room. The size of a swimming pool, it boasted a combination of oversized leather furniture and a few no doubt very expensive "shabby chic" pieces in hunting-motif prints. One seating group clustered around a fireplace that towered over the opposite side of the room from the kitchen. Two other conversation areas were built around coffee tables and ottomans in the center and near side of the room, where a large and heavy wall of cabinetry no doubt housed an impressive selection of entertainment technology.

The room off the hallway to her left as she'd walked in proved to be a dining room. Across from that, a large office. At the other end of the great room, a hallway opened up to the right of the fireplace, leading to a large master bedroom suite at the back of the house and a smaller bedroom and bath at the front.

She found a stairway that wrapped around behind the fireplace and followed it up to the second floor. She found three bedrooms that opened onto the balcony, each with its own bath, and down a hallway that ran above the one on the first floor, another office and another front bedroom.

While all the bedrooms were well appointed, she couldn't help but feel that they lacked charm. *Definitely feels like a boys' club.* Six bedrooms down, one to go. Maybe the last would be lucky seven? She opened the door on the back western corner of the house.

"Oh!" The sound escaped with a breath. This room was so different from the others! Colorful floral fabrics made it bright and airy where the other rooms were heavy and dark. It even felt more lived in, more a home and less a hotel-room or hunting lodge. Perhaps the women partners of the firm stayed here. But wait; *were* there any women partners at Kinsey & McMillan? She didn't know.

Then she noticed a set of glass double doors that led to a private balcony overlooking the same view as the first-floor deck. Two Adirondack chairs had settled there, as if the house had arranged the space itself to better serve her. She could imagine the cozy comfort that awaited them as they curled up with morning coffee there tomorrow. She wouldn't be surprised if a cartoon bluebird lit upon her finger as she sat.

She made her way back downstairs, pulled by the wonderful aroma of cooking. "I found our spot. Shall I take the bags up?"

"I can help." Jim turned toward her with a skillet in one hand, a colander in the other and a towel hanging precariously over his shoulder.

She laughed. "You appear to have your hands full. I can manage." She retreated to get the bags before he could argue.

Back upstairs, she placed the two suitcases side by side at the foot of the bed and just stood there, contemplating them for a moment. Two bags: the symbol of a shared journey. She and Jim.

Did her loyalty lay there, with Jim and their relationship? Maybe. They weren't completely there yet, but they were on their way. It would be such a relief to be able to tell him everything that had happened lately, from Porter's email to Chris's destroyed check and talk of the fire. She had promised to keep work out of this weekend, though, and she would honor that promise. Besides, she could always share it all with Rita.

Rita! She pulled out her cell phone, but the signal was even weaker than in town. No bars. Maybe she'd find a better signal tomorrow on their mountaintop hike. She turned the phone off to preserve its battery before heading back downstairs. The aroma that wafted toward her was as enticing as the thought of what would come after.

CHAPTER 23

Once again, Jim didn't disappoint in the kitchen. He'd pan-fried the fresh trout in just enough butter to make it crisp on the outside. He'd roasted the potatoes and asparagus together in the oven, releasing deep buttery flavors from each.

As they ate, they talked about what it would be like to afford such a house and live nestled in the mountains. When the dark clouds that had cast the purple glow during the sunset began to deliver rain, Jim ducked out to put the top up on the convertible while Katie soaked in the luxurious feel of pampered relaxation. It would be heavenly to lie together and listen to the rain all night.

"So, how long has it been?"

His voice interrupted her reverie, causing her to blush. How long had it been? Not since Michael, actually, but that really wasn't something she wanted to discuss. "What?"

"How long has it been since you, you know, were able just to kick back and relax like this? Just seems like you work hard all the time."

Oh. How long since *that.*

"I can't really remember, but you're one to talk, mister. How many hours did you put into that big trial just in the past week?"

"S'okay. I know how to work hard and relax hard…er…if that's possible." He blushed, the innuendo obviously unintended.

After dinner, she insisted on washing the dishes, which he dried and put away. Again, conversation was light. They speculated about the rain, now coming down in earnest, and whether they'd have to change their plans to go hiking tomorrow. An occasional lightning flash, followed by a distant clap of thunder, punctuated their concern.

As he put the last dish away and poured the last of the wine into their glasses, she felt herself stiffen. She pushed away from his embrace and stepped to the window, her back to him. It wasn't that she didn't want to sleep with him—she did, very much. But all of the sudden, it was *time*, and for some reason, she felt more nervous than she had been her first time, way back in college.

What the hell is wrong with me?

As if sensing her discomfort, he put down his glass and wrapped her in a strong embrace from behind, placing his face against the side of hers so he could whisper into her ear. "I want you to know, Miz Nelson, that I've never brought anyone here before. I think it's incredibly special. I think *you're* incredibly special, and I can't wait to show you just how much."

She couldn't help herself. She giggled.

He took a step back and studied her, his brow furrowed and his lips thin.

"I'm sorry," she said, reaching for his hand. "I'm just nervous. I'm not used to guys who say things like that."

For a moment, there was no sound but the storm growing outside. Then in a gentle voice, he said, "Look. You know me. What you see is what you get, and I say what I mean." He paused and looked down into her eyes before adding, "And I meant what I just said."

Katie's heart gathered in her throat, and she glided into his embrace. She placed her palms on either side of his face and gave him a long, deep kiss as an apology. "I meant that, too," she whispered and led him upstairs to the room she had chosen.

She'd planned to ask him about this room—why it was so different from the rest—but she never got the chance. She'd pictured the room bathed in a golden light when they entered, maybe from candles or dimmed lamps, but as it turned out, they didn't need conversation or mood lighting. As soon as they stepped over the threshold into the darkened room, they began to explore one another with hands, lips and tongues.

His touch teased her, caressing and tickling, and she found herself feeling more aroused than she could ever remember, yet completely safe at the same time. The combination was intoxicating. She allowed herself to explore his body with a passion she had never allowed herself before.

As her clothing fell away and her senses awoke, she almost cried with longing. He gazed deeply at her as he hovered over her body, now electrified and eager.

"Now," she gasped, and he lowered himself toward her…

"What the hell are you doing here, you goddamn son of a bitch?" A woman's voice pierced the peacefulness of the house from the echoing great room below.

Katie, rocked with confusion, stared wide-eyed at Jim, whose look of shock turned to panic. He leapt from the bed, half-covering himself. "Oh, shit!" he exclaimed. "What the fuck?"

The woman's voice continued its assault. "Whichever one of these goddamn bedrooms you're in, get your ass and your townie tramp out of here now! This is *my* weekend and you know it, you sorry piece of shit!"

Jim scrambled into his clothes, zipping up his jeans and throwing his T-shirt on inside out. "Stay here," he whispered. He slunk out the door and down the hallway.

Katie felt around the floor for her jeans and shirt. She was now thankful for the lightning flashes, which provided enough visibility to help her see her way to get dressed. Her nerves crackled as the screeching turned into an indiscernible rant from the floor below. Crouched in the doorway, she strained to hear.

"Can I help you?" she heard Jim's voice at the bottom of the stairs.

Then the woman's, quieter now, but icy cold. "*Who* are *you*?"

"Oh! Mrs. Porter! I'm Jim Hunter, an associate at your husband's firm."

Mrs. Porter? Porter's wife? Katie froze. What would she tell Porter about her being with Jim?

The woman laughed, but even that had a cold edge to Katie's ears. "My husband's firm? Hardly. The only reason that bastard made partner was because he was married to me. And if I knew then what I know now, he'd be working in the mailroom." There was a short pause and then the woman's voice again. "So, Jim Hunter, what are you doing in *my* house?"

"I'm sorry," he replied. "I thought this house belonged to Kinsey & McMillan. I had it reserved for this weekend."

"Right," said the woman. Her voice changed somewhat, from a tigress to a cougar, with a predatory edge creeping into it. "Surely you're not here alone? Not an attractive young associate like you."

"Uh, no." He sounded off balance.

Katie left the safety of the bedroom for the hallway. Porter or no Porter, she would make sure this woman understood that Jim was most certainly *not* here alone.

"No, I have a friend with me," he said as she came up beside him and clasped her hand around his arm.

"Well, of course you do," said the woman, looking Katie up and down with her steely gaze. There was a flicker of recognition in her eye, quickly concealed by disdain. "Isn't young love just grand."

Mrs. Porter's Burberry raincoat was cinched tight over dark gray slacks and expensive-looking alligator heels. A simple, yet pricy gold rope necklace peeked out from under her coat collar, and a couple of understated rings glittered on her fingers, making her single, rather large diamond solitaire seem slightly out of place.

"Mrs. Porter, meet Katie Nelson. Katie, this is Mrs. Porter," said Jim, his voice even and guarded.

"I believe we've already had the pleasure," she said to Katie. She turned her attention back to Jim. "I'm sure the two of you were planning to enjoy your weekend fling here in my house, but unfortunately, that won't be the case. I believe it's time for you to take your things and get out."

"Now wait a minute, ma'am," said Jim. "I had this house reserved. It's *our* weekend."

"Ah, but it's *my* house."

"Uh, no ma'am, I believe it's the firm's house."

"Hah!" Her laugh came out more like a sneer. "Do you know anything about this house, young man? Did my sorry excuse for a husband ever tell you how my father had it built for our wedding present? Did he tell you how he sold it out from under me to pay for some stupid real estate scheme of his that went bad? Did he tell you that he hired one of his Atlanta bimbos to redecorate it like a boys' club instead of a decent home? Did he tell you that I have every right to be here whenever the hell I want?"

She seemed close to tears by the end of her rant, but she paused to gain control of herself. Control, Katie sensed, was very important to this woman. She'd appeared in countless photos from society events, in newspapers and regional magazines. Mrs. Porter's philanthropy, from what Katie could remember, consisted mostly of symphony balls and galas for the children's hospital. Very traditional ways to contribute. Katie had scoffed privately at the lack of creativity exhibited by Mrs. Porter's set, but now, seeing her here all alone and so obviously unhappy with her life, Katie grasped how important it was to her to hold onto tradition.

The room upstairs must be hers. The woman's one connection to her past and the tradition that went with it. Inadvertently, she and Jim had…had…Katie blushed despite the urgency of their situation.

"Look," Jim pleaded, "It's pouring rain outside. This is a big house. I'm sure we can all fit here for the night and work it out in the morning."

"No, *you* look. My husband and his law buddies may have taken the title of this house from me, but they know it's mine. It was mine to start with, and soon enough it will be mine again. I'm not stupid. Guy may have tricked me once, but it won't happen again. I have my own attorneys, and they're smarter than that jackass will ever be. As soon as I found out what he did with my house, I began to transfer all of our assets back to my name only. Now that's done, and now he can't put money in a church collection plate without my say-so."

Seeing the surprise on Jim's face, she continued, "Oh, he talks a good game, but your boss is as broke as they come right now, young man. Next time he gets into trouble with real estate, it can be your *firm's* problem, but it won't be mine."

She smiled, showing frosty teeth. "So, as far as I'm concerned, you're trespassing. I'll call the police if you don't leave, and you should know the chief and I go way back." She turned on her heel and strode to the kitchen without so much as a backward glance. It was apparent Mrs. Porter was used to making it clear when a conversation had ended.

"Let's just go," Katie whispered.

"No! This weekend is about *us*, not her!"

"I don't want to stay here with her anymore than she wants to stay with us. And I don't want anyone at your firm to find out we were here together. Do you? Let's not make a big deal of it. This weekend will still be about us no matter where we are."

His eyes found hers with an expression she couldn't fathom. He took one last look toward the kitchen, turned back to her, then nodded. He followed her upstairs, where they gathered their still unpacked bags.

They paused in the foyer. He dropped the bags and took a breath. They exchanged a look and then he placed a finger to his lips. She waited while he went into the kitchen. "Okay, Mrs. Porter," she heard him say, "we're leaving, if you're sure we can't work this out."

There was a quiet reply she couldn't hear and then Jim's voice again, "Okay then, ma'am. Sorry if we upset you."

After he had closed the front door behind them, they stood staring out at the downpour they now had to navigate through.

"What did she say?" Katie asked.

"She apologized, actually. Said she really needed to be alone. It was weird. She just sat there staring out the window at the rain. Seemed really sad."

"Can't really blame her for that. Look who she's married to."

"At least for now." Then he rubbed his hands together and smiled at her. "Ready to get wet?"

"Let's do it!" she cried and ran with her bag, splashing through the puddles to the car. She flung the bag into the car's back seat before jumping into the passenger's side.

He dashed around to the driver's side, duplicating her actions and landing, soaked, in the seat beside her. He started the car, and they rolled forward, energy and confidence far deflated from when they'd pulled in. The rain was so heavy, they could barely see the gravel drive in front of them. Once magical and welcoming, the house had melted into a dark, cold shadow in the rear window.

"We're never going to make it back down that road," Katie said, thinking of the winding track they'd negotiated on the way up.

"True. Can't sleep in the car in the driveway, though. Keeps raining like this, it'll soak right through the roof."

Spending the night in the car wasn't an appealing option, but it beat the prospect of sliding off the mountain from a dark, wet, winding road. Then an idea popped into her head. "What about…"

"…the garage we passed on the way in? Great minds think alike! Let's see if we can at least get that far," he said, peering through the deluge and easing the car forward.

After an eternity, the garage materialized ahead. A small lamp on a pole outside the door illuminated the front of the building, which faced the main road and away from the house.

"Maybe she won't realize we're even in here," Jim said, squinting into the rearview mirror. He pulled around to the front of the garage. The large wooden garage door was partnered with a normal-sized doorway on the far side. He maneuvered as close to that door as he could, but they were still several yards away.

"I doubt she'll really care," Katie said. "She got what she wanted; she won that battle. We're just collateral. Wrong place, wrong time."

"You are wise, Miz Nelson. Now, perhaps you can use your smarts to figure out how to get us in there without getting completely soaked to the bone?"

"Just run like hell!" She sprang from the car and sprinted for all she was worth. He followed close behind.

She tried the handle of the small door, but it didn't budge. "Aaagh! It's locked!" she yelled above the noise of the rain as he caught up to her.

"Maybe I have the key!" he yelled back, fumbling in his pockets. He tried several of the keys on the ring with the Corvair's and let out a whoop when one did indeed turn the lock.

Together, they stumbled inside, searching opposite walls for a light switch. She heard a small click, and a dim, single bulb illuminated a staircase rising in front of them and another door just to the right.

"This has to go to the garage." He opened the door and peeked in. The smell of gasoline wafted out as he reached around for another light switch. "Ah, a pull chain," he said and strode into the middle of the garage to pull the string hanging from a ceiling fixture. She followed him in. The weak, watery light from a single bulb above illuminated hedge clippers, shovels and other landscaping tools, a rundown lawn mower and three two-gallon gas cans. On a higher shelf was a collection of old kerosene lamps that appeared dusty with disuse, along with a container of kerosene that appeared more contemporary. The smell made her slightly dizzy.

"I'm gonna pull the car in here," he said, trying the latch on the garage door. It swung open with a minimum of protest, revealing the heavy rain still pummeling the Corvair.

He gestured to the stairs, back through the doorway to the entry. "Why don't you go see what's upstairs? Maybe there's a blanket or something."

She shook her head, grateful for the fresh air that washed in through the open doorway, replacing the heady smell of gas and kerosene. "That's okay. I'll wait for you."

Jim dashed through the rain and dove into the Corvair. He maneuvered it into the garage. She pulled the door closed as soon as he killed the engine.

"That's better," he said, emerging from the vehicle. "Now I won't lie awake all night wondering if the roof sprang a leak." He reached above the car to pull the light string. In the dim light, he guided her back to the entry vestibule.

"What about the bags?" she asked.

"They can wait."

They climbed the stairs to another door—this one unlocked—and peered into the single room above the garage. She had expected a dusty storage area, but what she saw as he flipped the light switch was far from it. It was haphazardly furnished, but clean. A daybed stood on one side, a desk in the middle, bookcases on the other side. A single window at one end of the room looked out onto the glow of the outdoor lamp, while the window at the other end showed nothing but inky darkness.

"Well, this is…" Jim began, just as a bright flash of lightning and an enormous crack of thunder startled them both. The overhead lights flickered and went out. "…dark," he finished.

"I don't suppose there's a flashlight around somewhere?"

She felt his hand on her arm, turning her toward him, then sliding around her waist.

"Now Miz Nelson, what would we possibly need with a flashlight? What could we do in the light that we can't do in the dark?" His husky tone sent a ripple of electricity down her spine.

Lightning flashed again, its brilliance illuminating his face. His eyes, full of desire, locked onto hers.

He was right. What else could they possibly want to do other than take advantage of the dark? She took it as a sign, a blessing of their time together.

"Now, where were we before we were so rudely interrupted?" he whispered into her ear as he began to work her T-shirt slowly over her head.

"Right about here," she said, surprised by how quickly the longing surged within her at his touch. She reached for the snap of his jeans as his hands found her breasts.

She lifted her face and found his in the dark, kissing him with a passion that pulled at her very core. They stumbled to the daybed and found their way back to the place they had left off. This time, there were no interruptions. No nervous giggles. No hesitation. Not the first time, nor the second. There was only him, and for the moment at least, that was more than enough.

CHAPTER 24

Katie awoke the next morning to the soothing sound of dew dripping on a leafy carpet. She remembered the storm and wondered if the roof of the garage had sprung a leak. When she opened her eyes, she noticed that Jim had opened the windows at either end of the room. Beyond the windows, a thick fog wrapped the trees and enveloped the garage. The fog gave her the illusion of drifting alone inside a cloud tethered to the mountainside…

Where was Jim? She wanted to curl up in front of a fireplace by his side. She wanted to sprawl beside him on the floor with a large order of Chinese take-out. She wanted to squeeze up next to him as they strolled on a mountain path or on the beach or… *Where was he, anyway?*

The thud of a car door shutting drew her attention to the front window. She wrapped herself in the daybed comforter and padded across the floor. Down below, she heard Jim pull their bags from the backseat of the Corvair. He had opened the garage door, and sound traveled up to her through the mist. He hummed to himself, a tune she didn't recognize, but it sounded folksy, mountainy.

He must really love it up here. She listened to him in silence, enjoying the chance to eavesdrop into his private world. Her mind began to wander, imagining that they had a small house of their own somewhere up here. She pretended they had just arrived for a weekend together. It was so easy to picture that she chastised herself. *We're just getting started here. Who knows what will happen?*

She stepped back from the window when she heard him open the door at the bottom of the steps. She trundled to the opposite window and peered through the fog for any signs of life from the big house, but she couldn't see anything beyond the vague outline of trees. Good. There was no way Mrs. Porter could see the garage, either.

"Good morning!" he said as he burst through the door at the top of the stairs. "Did you sleep well?"

"Wonderfully." She smiled as he placed the bags on the floor and came over to kiss her. "I wonder about *her*, though," she added, nodding toward the back window and the big house.

"Oh, I doubt she's even awake. It's only 6:30."

"Do you always wake up with this much energy?"

Jim had dressed (although in yesterday's clothes) and looked like he had at least thrown some water on his face. "Yep, 'specially when I'm in the company of the beautiful damsel I rescued from the horrible storm."

"You rescued *me*? I think it was a mutual thing, buddy."

"Amen to that!" He hugged her. "May it always be that way."

They stood wrapped together for a moment longer, then he released her. "Got your bag, and there's a decent little bathroom through that door there if you wanna shower or somethin'." He pointed to a little door opposite the daybed.

She pulled herself up for a quick kiss, got her bag and stepped into the bathroom. It was simple, but clean and perfectly adequate for a much-needed shower. After she emerged, clean and freshly dressed in hiking attire, Jim took his turn. While he showered, she examined the room. Jim had already made up the daybed, so she perused the bookshelves. Old law books, a few architecture tomes and a handful of paperback novels—nothing especially striking. The desk in the center of the room was clear of papers. A piece of thick glass lay across it, protecting the beautiful inlaid wood top underneath. A leather cup held a few pens, and a matching sorter for letters stood empty.

All in all, it was incredibly tidy for a room that likely wasn't used often. Maybe the maid service for the house cleaned this space as well. She pictured some lowly law clerk, invited for a weekend at the house, made to spend the entire time here, locked above the garage, generating billable hours at the desk. The thought made her chuckle.

She wandered back to the rear window to check that their cloud curtain was still intact. Against the back wall, she caught sight of some scribbled writing on a number of cardboard boxes stacked randomly against a corner. *1918–1924* read the one on top, written by a scrawling hand in pencil.

Were these old law documents? Deeds or trusts? Letters? She popped open the top box and found it divided into twelve sections, much like a case of wine, but the box instead held ten wide-mouth glass bottles. She pulled one out and held it up to the light. It had a thin layer of dust, knocked aside in places. She made out an embossed stamp on one side of the bottle just below where the neck began to narrow, and she shifted it in the light to read it.

"T.L. Jones Dairy Farm, Black Mountain, NC. One quart," she read aloud.

"What's that?" Jim asked as he emerged from the bathroom, vigorously toweling his hair dry.

"A really cool old milk bottle. There are boxes of them here." She pointed to the stack. "Well, at least that's what's in *this* box."

"That *is* pretty cool." He came up behind her and looked at the seal over her shoulder, then reached into the box and pulled out another. "This one's from a different place," he said. "And so's this one," lifting out yet another.

"Look how thick the glass is; it's kind of wavy, almost like it's made from two different layers. It's more like a work of art than something you'd put milk in."

"Why don't you keep one? It'd make a nice vase, maybe be a little souvenir of, you know, our first night together." He squeezed her elbow.

"I couldn't. It doesn't belong to us. We just happened to crash here for the night and…"

"Well, if it's here, it belongs to the firm, and I know for a fact that none of the partners would even notice it's missing. And as a representative of the firm, Miz Nelson, I say you may have it. Not only *may* you, but I *insist!*" He pressed the bottle into her hands.

"Well, okay, since you put it that way." She gave him a quick peck on the cheek. "It *is* a unique souvenir."

"Exactly why you should take it." A sudden rumbling noise emanated from his midsection. "Either there's another storm coming, or we'd better get to town and get some breakfast."

She laughed, then blushed as her own stomach gurgled at the prospect of food. She tucked the milk bottle into her bag and descended the stairs. After a few moments, she heard him coming downing the stairs behind her.

On the drive down the mountain, they approached a road crew in the final stages of clearing a downed tree. "That explains the power outage," she said, pointing to a dead electrical cable lying by the road.

"Yep. Glad we didn't try to drive down this road last night."

They both were quiet for a moment. Things might have turned out very differently if they'd tried to get to town instead of seeking refuge in the garage. As they continued past, the fog lifted, pulling her spirits in the same direction. She simply couldn't stay unhappy in Jim's company, driving on a beautiful mountain road in a vintage Corvair while the weather hinted at the promise of a warm, sunny day. From the smile that grew on his face, it was clear he felt the same.

He navigated the winding road to town and parked on Main Street, right in front of an old drugstore. The façade didn't strike her as all that attractive, relative to the cute boutiques and adorable restaurants that dotted the street. She shot him a questioning look.

"The real beauty of this place lies within," he assured her. "In just a few minutes, I'm sure you'll agree that 460 is indeed a magic number."

"460?"

He pointed to the store's address as he held the door open for her.

Café 460, tucked inside the drugstore, turned out to be a 1960s-era soda fountain, complete with a row of worn vinyl booths and a long galley kitchen. It was bustling at breakfast time.

"Figured we deserved some comfort food after last night. Lots of butter and bacon grease." He rubbed his belly as they slid into the only open booth at the end of the row.

Katie watched the other diners. Almost all were men wearing tradesmen's clothes, T-shirts or denim work shirts with rolled up sleeves, jeans and work boots to a man. They spoke with familiarity to the two waitresses and the single cook who manned the kitchen, installed behind a long Formica counter with vintage chrome stools upholstered in red.

"Jenny workin' today?" she heard a man at the near end of the counter ask a waitress who refilled his coffee.

"Nah, she's got her grandbaby today. She'll be a'spoilin' him 'til dark."

"Lordy, we're all gonna have to look at more pitchurs next week then," said the customer with a chuckle.

"Ain't that the truth," his neighbor at the counter said.

Katie saw several other patrons nodding in agreement.

We are real outsiders here. She watched their waitress' demeanor change from laughing to reserved as she approached their table. She was polite enough as she took their order, but she didn't smile or make any small talk as she had at the other tables.

Had the waitress grown up here? What was it like? Katie wanted to ask, but she couldn't bring herself to. She had driven up from a large city, had spent the night in a palace—well, almost—and would leave after breakfast in a bright red sports car for a day of fun activity and an evening of cozy intimacy…while this woman finished a long shift and headed back to—what?

Katie imagined the waitress going home to a trailer or a nondescript ranch house tucked away from view. Maybe she picked up a toddler at her mother's on the way and then went home to cook and wait on an out-of-work husband.

That was a cruel stereotype, wasn't it? She could just as well live in a charming and well-kept cottage, maybe one passed down through generations with a long and loving history. Perhaps her husband worked as a carpenter or an artist or a schoolteacher. Maybe they spent their evenings reading books aloud to their attentive, curious children, or shared stories from their youth.

Katie studied the waitress's face as she made her way back to them.

She looked to be about Katie's age, but seemed years older in her manner. She carried two heavy white coffee mugs in one hand, spoons and plastic creamer containers in the other, and she made it look easy. She swept a practiced eye across each table she passed, on the lookout for problems or orders. She caught Katie staring at her and gave her a tight smile before averting her gaze. "Food's comin' right up, folks," she said as she laid the coffees on the table. Then she turned to the next table.

Katie looked down at her steaming coffee and bit her lower lip. Her hand snaked up to her ponytail, tossing it over the front of her shoulder, where her fingers got busy. Why should she feel so awkward? Maybe she felt out of place because she wasn't really sure what her place *was*. She wasn't as wealthy as others in her day-to-day work life, but she was by no means poor. Instead, she just bumped around in that no-man's-land of "middle class." In her work, she focused so much on the haves and have-nots, she realized, that she didn't have much time to consider the "have enoughs."

"What's wrong?" Jim asked.

"Oh, nothing. I was just wondering why the waitress never smiles at us."

"Maybe it's because of her teeth."

"Her *what*?"

"Her teeth. Dental care can be expensive and hard to find in rural areas like this. A lot of people get self-conscious about their teeth if they're, you know, unhealthy."

"How on earth do you know this?"

He shrugged. "Dunno. Guess I read it in a foundation proposal or an article or a brochure or something. It just kind of stuck with me."

She studied the waitress again, watching how she talked with her fellow server. Sure enough, she thought she spied a gap where a tooth used to be. "You'd think with all the money that vacations here," she said to Jim, "someone might have noticed before and created a clinic." Her fingers twirled faster around the ponytail's end.

"Maybe. Or maybe the visitors just think the locals are unfriendly."

"Touché."

The waitress brought their breakfasts and refilled their coffees. Katie dove into her plate, savoring the scrambled eggs, hash browns, toast and bacon. It wasn't the kind of breakfast she had often, and she relished every bite.

In between mouthfuls, Jim told her about the hike he had planned for the day. "I thought we'd go to Whiteside Mountain," he offered. "The view is stunning, and Peregrine falcons are supposed to nest there this time of year. I've never seen one, but it's worth a shot. Wanna try?"

She agreed. Hiking along a mountain trail with Jim at her side sounded like the perfect activity. They could explore new ground together, literally and figuratively, just like she'd envisioned.

"Before we set out, though, I wanna make sure I can get us a room for tonight. I kinda don't want to sleep out on the trail." He left a generous twenty for breakfast and they sauntered out, rubbing their stomachs.

As he headed up the block to find a hotel room, Katie strolled in the opposite direction, toward a picturesque church with freshly painted white clapboard siding. The early morning fog had completely burned off by now, and fresh sunlight streamed down, bringing everything into crisp focus. "The Episcopal Church of the Incarnation," read the sign in front. An explosion of spring blooms reached toward heaven, barely contained by the white picket fence surrounding the church.

Their beds bordered a small walkway that led to the peaked front door.

The scene made her think of the English countryside, and she allowed herself to fantasize briefly about what it would be like to be married here, surrounded by the beauty of the mountains in this quaint little chapel. She turned when she heard Jim calling to her, and she headed back up the block toward him.

"We lucked out!" His voice rang with excitement. "Got us a room at the Old Edwards." He gestured up the street to the same hotel that she'd noticed when they first arrived.

"Won't that be really expensive?"

"Of course, but we deserve something special after what we went through last night. I'm pretty sure that no one will kick us out this time." He grinned and wiggled his eyebrows at her. "Only thing, though, our room won't be ready until this afternoon. How 'bout we get some picnic supplies and go for that hike?"

After a quick stop at the grocery store, they headed east on yet another beautiful, winding mountain highway. It was only a short drive before they turned onto another, smaller winding road that led past more enormous houses. This time, in the bright sunshine, Katie could see that some of the houses on the left side of the road were perched on the edge of the mountain, suspended in vast and breathtaking views.

After about a mile, they pulled into a long gravel parking lot that created a half-moon around the Whiteside Mountain trailhead. They gathered their supplies and wandered across the parking lot to read the Forest Service signs. The trail was a short two-mile loop, according to the map, but it was steep and rocky in many places.

Jim shouldered the backpack containing their picnic and water bottles, flashed Katie a thumps-up and a smile and headed up the trail. She followed close behind.

She had to hike more slowly than her normal walking pace, negotiating the football-sized rocks that jutted up from the trail bed. She concentrated on the path for the first half hour.

They met a few other hikers, an older couple moving at an even slower pace than Katie's and a young woman working her way down in the opposite direction, chasing an unleashed dog that had sprinted gleefully past them moments before.

"I can see why so many people want getaways up here," she said, pausing to catch her breath and enjoy the view.

"Just wait. It gets even better."

Eventually, the trail became smooth and the soil sandy. As they neared what appeared to be the summit, Katie noticed that the path led into a clearing of tall grass. They followed the trail through the clearing, where it opened up onto two observation points, surrounded by wooden safety fences. One faced east, the other south.

"Oh, wow!" she said as she leaned on the rail and breathed it all in. "It's amazing."

Jim stood next to her in silent agreement.

Scanning the view to the east and south, she could follow the waves of smaller ridges that ran zigzag across the valley floor between the perimeters of taller mountains. In the middle, snaking left to right, ran the river that had carved a path over millions of years to carry rainwater from these peaks to the sea. A two-lane highway wound through the trees, sometimes next to the river and sometimes not. A light wind breezed through the valley, rushing up to fill her ears and ruffle her hair, carrying the scent of fresh evergreen growth and moist earth after last night's rain.

"It's like looking off the end of the earth," she whispered.

"Yep. I bet, back before the skies got so smoggy and hazy, you could see Atlanta from here."

"Right now, it's kind of hard to remember what Atlanta looks like."

"That's a good thing. Coming here helps me put things in perspective. It's like I can look down on myself and my life in Atlanta and see where I'd like to change things."

"What are you thinking you'd like to change now?"

"Spending more time with you comes to mind at the moment." He leaned down and gave her a deep and lingering kiss, pressing her back into the solid wooden fencepost with a hunger that felt beyond the physical.

He's sad about something. This realization piqued her curiosity, but she decided not to press. It would come in time.

"We should keep going or we'll never get off this mountain," he said, clearing his throat. He cracked open a water bottle and handed it to her. Then he opened one for himself.

"We had to have hiked close to a mile on the way up," she said. "Surely the walk down won't take long?"

"Oh, we're not headed down yet." He smiled. "This path follows the cliff for a good half mile or so first, and we need to find a picnic spot somewhere. And if you think this is cool"—he swept his hand across the view before them—"just wait. The view gets better and better, but you wanna watch your step, because it *will* distract you."

"We'll just see about that." She stepped past him, and he bowed his head, sweeping his arm wide, inviting her forward along the trail. "You're so gallant!" she said.

"What, because I care about you and don't want you to get hurt?"

"Sure, that and the picnic and planning all of this. It's just not what I'm used to."

"Are you kidding? You should always be treated like this."

"Ha! You need to teach your fellow men some lessons then. The last one I dated stopped planning anything romantic the second we got engaged. Well, at least, anything romantic with *me*." She frowned at herself. *Why did I bring Michael into this? It will spoil everything.*

"You were engaged?"

"Mistakenly." Her voice hardened.

Jim grabbed her hand from behind and whirled her around to face him. "Whoever he was, he was a complete idiot. And while I'd like to beat the crap out of him for treating you badly, I'm also glad he did." He smirked, looking down at the path for a moment. "Does that make me as bad as him?"

"You could never be him." She smiled and turned back up the trail, wanting to leave all thoughts of Michael behind.

"If it makes you feel any better, I haven't had the best luck with women either." His boots tramped along the path behind her.

'Other than learning how to cook in law school?"

"Well, yeah, but just going to cooking school would've been a lot less dramatic. I'm not good with a lot of drama."

She bit her lip, thinking of her outburst at dinner two weeks before. *That* bit of drama had ended well, but she could completely understand how ongoing hysterics would turn off a laid-back, easygoing guy like Jim.

"I hope you don't consider me a drama queen."

"You? Oh no. You're more the down-to-earth, no-nonsense type. You call it like you see it. I respect that. That, and the very fine view I have swinging up the trail in front of me at the moment."

"Jim!" She blushed more fuchsia than the rhododendron blooms they'd passed on the trail, glancing behind them to make sure no one was in earshot. She giggled to see the color rising in his face as well. "Easy there, mister. I thought there was another view up here you wanted to see."

"And so there is."

"Maybe you'd better go first then."

"Hmm. Maybe so." He gave her a squeeze as he stepped past her.

The trail continued along the southern face of the mountain, delivering breathtaking views of the valley and the vastness beyond. There were larger rocks to scramble over, and in many places, a tightly strung cable fence was the only thing separating the hikers from a long, steep plunge down the cliff. After a bit, the trail moved back from the precipice, weaving in and out between stands of trees and outcrops where eons of wind and water had carved rows of natural benches. Jim insisted that the outcrops were ideal for picnics, but the first one was already occupied by a single hiker, a young man with a bushy beard, a red bandana wrapped around dirty-blonde dreadlocks and a long-sleeved shirt tied around his waist. Next to him sat a large daypack, with water bottles and climbing ropes hooked to the outside. He gave them a friendly wave.

"Dude, if you're looking for a rockin' picnic spot, there's another clearing like this one just past those trees." He pointed down the trail in the direction they were headed.

"Are you actually going to climb down *that*?" Katie asked, pointing to the cliff's edge with wide eyes.

"Not today, dudes. The falcons are there!" He made wings with his arms and swayed as if coasting on a thermal current. "Totally awesome!"

"Did you see one?" She shaded her eyes with her hand and looked out into the air.

"Not yet. I figure the hikers are totally bummin' them out at the moment. But if you, like, sit still and stay quiet over there, I bet one'll show up soon. They fuckin' love the thermals up here, man! Ooh, sorry. Language." He grinned.

She grinned back as Jim thanked him and they proceeded to the next clearing, one blissfully free of other people. A phenomenal panoramic view greeted them, along with a warm breeze that rushed up the rock face.

As Katie perched on the rocks and gazed in wonder, Jim pulled cheese, apples, hummus, crackers and two enormous chocolate chip cookies out of the daypack he'd been carrying, followed by a large bottle of sparking water.

They ate in pleasant silence for a while, and then she asked, "Why did you pick philanthropy? I mean, what made you want to get involved with the foundation?"

"Well, like I said before, I wanted to make a difference. That, plus Porter kind of pushed me into it. But there's another reason. Guess I kind of wanted to make Dad proud of me. Let him see that I was following in his footsteps, sort of."

"But you're already a lawyer like he is; what more does he need?"

"Talkin' more from an ethical or moral standpoint than a career one. To my dad, serving other people was the most important thing in the world. For the longest time, I didn't agree. In college, and in law school, I was only focused on earning money."

"What changed?"

"Dad got sick. Cancer. We thought he was going to die. He almost did. Watching that kinda shook me up, I guess."

"That makes sense. Are you two close now?"

He stared at the ground a moment before answering. "Not really. He got frustrated with my focus on making money, and I haven't really convinced him I've changed yet." He paused. "Maybe I should take you to meet them sometime."

"I'd like that." The separation from his father might explain that sense of sadness. Maybe she could find a way to help him repair it. Then she asked, "What about Porter? What made him want to be on the board?"

"Ha! That's easy. He likes power and money. Being on the foundation board makes people think he has both of those in spades. Even if his wife *has* cut him off."

Katie pondered this. The thought of Porter using his seat on the board as a personal stepping-stone repulsed her, but it was completely plausible, given what she knew about the man. But had he ever actually used his position for personal financial gain? That would be unethical to say the least and illegal in almost any case. It would also cause massive problems for the foundation with the IRS. Then again, that's why there was a full board of trustees, not just a handful. They'd keep Porter from doing anything illegal. Wouldn't they?

She was about to ask Jim about this, but he asked a question of his own.

"So what about you? Do you see yourself in the foundation world forever?"

"Maybe, if I can keep from getting completely frustrated by the fact that it moves so slowly and is so hesitant about making changes and trying new things."

He laughed. "Well, my grandfather was a pretty traditional kind of guy when it came to entrepreneurial thinking. You're not exactly with the leading edge here."

"I know." She sighed. "And I really *do* like my job. But down the road, I'd like to go somewhere where they aren't afraid to take some risks."

"I know what you mean. I've dreamt of leaving Kinsey & McMillan to start my own firm. I'd be able to take the kinds of cases the big firms don't want, but that make a big difference for the little guys."

"Like your work with Jorge?"

"Yeah, I guess. It was fun while it lasted, but as far as I can tell, that's kind of coming to an end. Once the cops clear him for good, I'm pretty sure his insurance company will pay up."

"He must be busy fundraising for a new place right now. In fact, I expect to see a big request from him next week, right before the application deadline hits." *Especially since that rumor about the Hartwell Foundation funding him is untrue.*

"Okay, this sounds too much like shop talk. Why don't you go enjoy the view while I clean up? Down by the cable railing over there, you might be able to see the side of the cliff where the falcons are supposed to be."

He insisted he didn't need help, so she complied with his suggestion. She scampered down to the railing that ran along the cliff's edge, the gravel she kicked with her boots clattering over the rocky face. The railing was composed of two wire cables secured by metal fence posts anchored to the rock every ten feet or so. A thin wire strand looped between the two cables to hold them loosely together. She tested the top railing, then leaned over it to take a good look around. Not a bird in sight. Just a…

Oh! A black flash swooped by the edge of the cliff, just below her feet. A falcon! It flapped away from the rock face and wheeled to make another pass. She leaned out farther, the top safety cable hugging her waist, to see how close the bird would fly in front of her. Was it afraid of her? Should she be afraid of it?

Jim will want to see this. Without turning around for fear that *she* would miss it, she called out his name as loudly as she dared to avoid spooking the bird.

Just as the falcon dove toward the cliff, she felt a hard push between her shoulder blades. Her call turned into a scream as she felt herself flip over the railing headfirst.

CHAPTER 25

She grappled for a cable, a post, anything to keep from rocketing down the mountain. A fireball of panic surged in her chest. It blocked her throat, stifling a second scream. Her body jolted as her boot got caught between the top cable and the loose wire. A shot of pain raced from her ankle to her head. She bounced once, like a bungee jumper, and scrambled to grab the lower cable. She held on tight, surprised at her own strength. Her fingernails dug into her palms as she tightened her grip.

"Katie!"

Suspended upside down, she watched Jim, eyes wide, drop to his stomach on the rocks and reach under the cables for her.

"Don't look down. I've got you."

"Holy shit! Dude! Are you okay?" The dreadlocked hiker scrambled down the rocks to where Katie hung from both cables. Her arms were beginning to shake with fear and fatigue. The young man whipped a climbing rope off his pack and wrapped one end around the closest fencepost with lighting speed.

"Okay. Hold tight, I'm gonna share this cable with you."

Before Katie realized what was happening, he slid toward her and threw a knee over the lower cable near her hands. The cable bounced slightly and she gasped, her fingers beginning to lose their grip. The next thing she knew, the free end of the hiker's climbing rope was cinched around her ribcage so tightly she could barely breathe, and he was supporting her weight with one muscled arm, the other hanging like a monkey from the cable. His long dreads hung in her face, obscuring her view of the drop beneath her.

"Okay dude, I've got her. Work her leg free from that top cable." Jim jumped to do as instructed.

"Now pull her legs over this bottom cable and grab that rope."

Jim unhooked Katie's boot and pulled her legs back to the safe side of the railing. Panic returned for an instant as the hiker released his grip, but then his sharp pull on the climbing rope tugged her away from the edge to safety. As it pulled her backwards, she scrambled with it, like a crab, up the slope of the rocks.

She sat panting, rubbing her sore ankle. What had just happened? How…? Who had pushed her?

She stared at Jim. He crouched next to her, grabbing for her hands, rubbing her back. He was breathing as hard as she was, clearly worried. *No one else had been there, but there was no way…*

"Are you okay? Are you okay?" He kept asking until she nodded her head.

She willed her breathing to slow down.

"Dude, what happened?" the hiker asked.

Jim's eyes filled with tears. "Oh, Katie, oh, honey, I almost killed you! I was coming down to see…and I…I tripped. On that." He pointed to a rock that jutted up at an odd angle from the edge of one of the rocky tiers. "And I fell *right into you*! I'm *so* sorry." He grabbed his head with his hands and let out a moan. "Oh my God! I almost killed you!"

She reached out to him and he collapsed into her. She cradled his head in her arms. "No, no. Don't say that. I'm okay. I'm okay. See? I'm all here." She fought to keep the tremor out of her voice as the reality of it sank in. He had nearly killed her, even if it was an accident.

"Hey dude. Take it easy. It's okay. She's fine. She's fine. It's all good." The hiker squatted a short distance away, hands on his knees, peering at them.

Katie lifted her cheek from Jim's head to look at him and tears filled her eyes. "Thank you. You saved my life. I don't know…"

They all sat, frozen for a moment, the sound of their breathing the only noise.

"Aw hey, it's all good. Just one of those things. He would've pulled you free if I didn't." The hiker jutted his chin at Jim. "Don't let it kill your buzz, man."

"I'm glad you came along when you did." Jim's voice sounded more normal now. "I don't know if I could've…Thank you."

"Dude, no worries. I climb these rocks, like, all the time when the falcons aren't here. There's actually a ledge like 20 feet down, so she wouldn't have gone too far."

Katie responded to his grin with a blank look. If his remark was meant to reassure her, it didn't help much.

"C'mon, dudes! It's done. It's all good. It's still a fuckin' awesome day! Just get up and keep movin'! You can, like, tell this story to your grandkids!" He jumped up, threw his arms wide, tilted his head back and let out a loud, "WooooHOO!"

Katie laughed despite her state of shock. "So much for not scaring the falcons."

"Oh shit, dude! Now I gotta wait some more." He searched the sky for a minute, then grinned at them. "Or maybe that sounded like some kind of badass falcon mating call!"

"No, seriously. How can we thank you?" Jim didn't appear ready to join in the hiker's playful mood. "Can I give you a reward? Buy you some dinner? What's your name anyway?"

"Lennon. Like John, but that's my first name. And no dude, I don't need anything. Just helpin' out, ya know? Besides, I gotta get back to Asheville as soon as I get off this rock. There's a killer band playin' tonight."

"No really, I'd like to do something."

"No way, bro'. Just take care of that lady. You need help getting down?"

Jim helped Katie to her feet. She tested her ankle. While it was sore and a bit tender, it wasn't broken.

"Sure we can't do something to thank you?" she asked Lennon, who now was ruffling through the pockets on his backpack. "At least get you something for the road?"

"Nah, I'm all good." He pulled out a plastic baggie of trail mix. "I'm just gonna hang up here a while longer and reee-lax."

They said goodbye, then Jim shouldered the backpack and Katie followed him down the trail, his hand reaching behind and grasping hers tightly until she protested.

"Reee-lax, Jim. I'm not going to fall again. We're not on the cliff anymore." She pointed to the hemlocks that surrounded them. Even the slope of the return trail was mild compared to their earlier ascent.

"Sorry, but I almost lost you up there. I think I have a right to hang on now." Far from comforting, his tone sounded angry.

She stopped and shot him a quizzical look.

He glared back for a moment, breathing hard, then looked up toward the treetops and rubbed his neck with his hand. "I'm sorry. I don't know what's wrong with me. I shouldn't be angry. I just can't believe I was such a klutz, and it nearly…" He released a whoosh of breath.

Even though it was her life that had nearly ended, she couldn't help but feel sorry for him. He wasn't the first man she'd seen who masked guilt with anger.

"It's okay." She placed her hands on his chest. "You were scared. It was an accident, but Lennon's right. I'm okay. Let's just leave it on the mountain." She slid her hand down his arm and pulled him forward down the trail.

They walked silently, side by side. Jim appeared to be brooding, despite the occasional squeeze of his hand. Katie had no words as she relived the episode in her mind. The shock of the force pushing her. The terror of helplessness as the rock face rushed up to meet her…

But she had *survived.*

By the time the trail ended, her ankle felt almost normal.

Jim gave her a weak smile. "God you're amazing."

"Yep. Death-defying even. And don't you forget it." Her own words echoed in her head as her boots reclaimed the gravel of the parking lot, a flat and neatly contained haven of safety surrounded by a solid barrier of crossties and thick walls of vegetation. She actually did defy death up there. She had been on the edge—over it, in fact—and lived to tell about it. A shot of adrenaline zinged through her and she suddenly felt as if she could do anything.

Awestruck by her own sense of power, she felt the urge for action. She wanted to do something crazy, like wrestle a bear or get in a bar fight or pull Jim back into the woods and make love like a wild beast.

"I just can't get over how lucky you are…we are." Jim reached for her but she turned away.

She didn't want to think about being lucky. The feelings of helplessness and fear seemed petty compared to the fact that she'd *survived.*

She scanned the parking lot and saw restrooms at the other end. Escape! "I'm just going down there for a minute."

Her strides felt like giant steps across the parking lot. Cheating death made you feel larger than life, and it felt great—much like that day years ago at the seaside with her father. Now, just like then, she knew if she had wings she would surely leave the ground.

In contrast to the bright, sunny parking lot, the women's restroom offered only the dimmest of lighting and a dank, musty smell like a cave. Her adrenaline high stopped in mid-flight. She held her breath as she walked to a sink to splash water on her face. The icy cold smacked her with a jolt of reality. As she straightened up, the raw skin scraped by the cable on her abdomen screamed, and the face she saw in the mirror shocked her. Instead of looking like an all-powerful being who had just conquered death, her face looked raw—wide-eyed and pale, with wild hair and a long smudge of dirt down the left cheek.

Who was she kidding? She *was* damn lucky to be alive. She felt tears welling in her eyes as she relived the accident. Again, she felt the force of that push between her shoulders and the sting of the wire cable as it bit into her waist. Lifting her shirt, she saw the red line across her midsection that would darken to a bruise by the next day. And her eyes—her eyes in the mirror were the same eyes as the woman in her dream. That woman, that Angel, had not been so lucky.

The tears began to fall in earnest. Katie swallowed hard. *It's okay*, she told herself. She was okay. She would be fine. Jim had saved her, hadn't he? Before the hiker got to them, it was Jim who reached for her. And now he felt so bad about it. There was no way it could have been anything but an accident.

But maybe this accident happened for a reason. Maybe it was a sign that they weren't meant to be together. She stared at her face a bit longer, then pulled herself together. She dried her eyes, washed her face and smiled at her reflection. The face that smiled back looked passably composed. It nodded to her in approval. She dried her hands and left the restroom.

"Hey there, good lookin'. You heading into town?" She could feel the sly grin on Jim's face even though the sunlight temporarily blinded her. He had pulled the Corvair around to the door to scoop her up. "Got a really nice hotel room, and I could use some company."

She managed a laugh as she slipped into the car next to him. Driving past the trail entrance, the once-inviting, shaded opening in the trees now looked like the gaping maw of a dark and forbidden bottomless pit. She clutched the seat tightly as the convertible wound back down the mountain toward Highlands.

CHAPTER 26

On the way back into town, Katie's stomach began to lurch with every turn.

"Jim, can you pull over? I think I'm going to be sick." She covered her mouth to help fight an upsurge of bile.

"Hang on." Jim slipped her a worried glance. "There's a place right up here…"

He slowed around one last bend, and then roared to a stop in a packed-earth parking lot of a rustic house with an "Antiques" sign poking out by the side of the road. A couple of parked cars waited out front, while an older couple struggled to put what looked like an old chandelier into the trunk of one of them. They raised their heads at the sound of Jim's tires pulling so abruptly off the road, then returned to their task.

Katie opened the door of the Corvair and stood on shaking legs, savoring the solid feel of the ground. Jim hurried to her side and rubbed her back while she took several deep breaths. After a few minutes, her stomach returned to its accustomed place and her muscles loosened.

"So…maybe not quite over it yet?" He squeezed her shoulder and pulled her to him.

"Maybe not, but I'm better now. Can we hang out here for a minute before we go on?" She nodded toward the antique store. It was inviting, and in the back of her mind, she imagined finding some small treasure that would end up being extremely valuable one day. Silly, she knew, but it would help take her mind off the accident.

Jim agreed, and together, they entered and began to poke through the various displays. She pointed out a complete chest of silver with a patina that made it almost too pretty to ever think of polishing. He ran his hands lovingly over an ancient roll-top desk, saying, "Somethin' like this would look great in my office some day."

"Hey, look!" She swept her arm to a row of antique bottles. Several looked exactly like the ones they had discovered that morning. They each picked up various bottles and turned them in the light, reading the embossed names of dairies in the glass.

"Whoa, this one is $150," she said, noticing the price tag.

"This one's $185." He picked out the most expensive of the bunch. "Wonder what yours would go for?"

"I wonder if we shouldn't go put it back where we found it."

"Nah, not going back there as long as *she's* still around. 'Sides, if it becomes an issue—which it never will—I'll handle it." He placed the milk bottle back on the shelf. "Now, don't get too excited about that price. Remember, this is Highlands. Same bottle in any other mountain town would probably be half as much."

"I see you're interested in milk bottles." A round little man with glasses and a balding head appeared out of nowhere. He wore a cardigan over a button-down shirt, suspenders visible when he turned. He blended right into the shop's surroundings.

"Just curious," said Katie, smiling at him. "I have one and was wondering what it was worth."

"That depends on what kind you're talking about. The ones like that one you're holding, where the words are all stamped or embossed into the glass—those are from the 1930s or before, so they're worth a little more. Around the mid '30s, the dairies started to make their labels with a paint-on technique, like the ones up there." He pointed to a shelf with a row bottles sporting red, blue or black lettering rather than the clear stamp that Katie's bottle had.

"Every now and then you come across a really rare one, and they can fetch close to $1,000, but I don't have any of those right now. Er…but they're all very collectible." He gestured toward the rows they had just examined.

"Why don't I get yours out of the car?" Jim asked. "We could have it appraised by this gentleman, just for fun."

"Okay…" It was sweet, the way he was trying to help take her mind off the mountain.

When he returned, milk bottle in hand, the storekeeper's eyes lit up. "Ah! That there's a fine sample. This dairy, if I recall, was smaller than most, so there aren't quite as many of these around. I'd sell it here for about $300. In fact, I sold one very much like this not two months ago. It was purchased as part of a mixed case." He peered at the bottle more closely. "You didn't by chance purchase this from a collector, did you?"

"Uh, no." Katie's brow furrowed.

Seeing her confusion, the storekeeper added, "I ask, uh, because a man driving a car very much like that one…"—he pointed to the Corvair, visible through the shop window—"…was in here a couple of months ago. He bought an entire case, including one like this. Said they were for his wife. She's apparently a collector."

That did it. Katie's mind leapt from the accident and snapped to attention. "What did he look like?"

"Big fella. Kinda loud but pleasant enough. I gave him a good price, since he said it was for a gift. I'd be upset if he just bought them to resell, though. I would have upped my price, sure."

Porter? Katie raised her eyebrows at Jim, who shrugged.

"I think he was more interested in telling me about his car than in learning about milk bottles," the storekeeper admitted. "But he seemed to think his wife would be happy with them."

Katie frowned and knit her brows closer. *Porter, definitely, considering the car, but Porter would never consider a gift just to please his wife, would he?*

"I also have some interesting estate jewelry pieces, if you're in the market for those," the storekeeper said, looking at Katie's left hand and then at Jim.

"Um, not just now," she said before a blush could creep up her neck, "but what can you tell us about that roll-top desk?"

While the storekeeper and Jim discussed the desk, Katie roamed through the shop, her mind elsewhere. *Why on earth would Porter buy a case of milk bottles, if indeed it was Porter who bought them?*

As their conversation wound down, the shopkeeper insisted on wrapping her bottle in bubble wrap and putting it in a bag bearing his shop's name.

"You don't want that rolling around loose, do you?" he asked with a smile. "You come back and see me now, you hear?" He waved to them and then turned to greet another couple who were just entering the store.

Jim placed the bag under the hood with the luggage. They climbed into the Corvair, and he guided them back onto the road. "Well, this car certainly gets its share of attention, huh?"

"For sure. Why would Porter buy his wife a case of old milk bottles?"

"I'm not convinced it was Porter. There are lots of big, loud, wealthy guys up here. And I'm not the only person in the firm he's lent this car to. I know the McMillans' house is full of antique stuff. He's a big guy. Could have been him."

Katie was skeptical, but Jim had a point. Someday, maybe, he'd take her to one of the firm's legendary parties hosted by the McMillans or another senior partner at one of their Buckhead mansions. They'd spy the milk bottles displayed on some gazillion-dollar antique sideboard or bookcase and share a knowing glance.

But for now, he was taking her to a romantic old hotel and for a romantic dinner. *And afterward, well, there was always that to look forward to as well. No more thinking about Porter—and not one more thought about what had happened on the mountain. She was here. It was past. Jim was the present and possibly the future.* She encouraged the deep green of the roadside forest to envelop her senses as they drove along the winding roads.

After parking in front of the Old Edwards, Jim took her hand as they walked through the inn's double oak doors. Rather than the grand, sweeping lobbies of Atlanta's high-flying hotels, the Old Edwards lobby was small and cozy, covered in warm oak paneling and lit by intimate sconces. Wavy glass windows ornamented with plantation shutters let in light and street views. They approached the concierge desk and seating area just inside the door.

A host in a suit and tie welcomed them. "May I offer you a complimentary glass of champagne as you check in?"

Katie and Jim exchanged a look. "Of course!"

As he took care of the arrangements, she settled on an upholstered chair of rich brocade with her flute of champagne and took in the features of the lobby. Protecting the wide-board wood floors were an array of oriental rugs, worn with authentic use, treasures from someone's estate. A narrow staircase rose up behind the bar, with turned spindles and a solid, smooth handrail. An unobtrusive check-in desk waited up another short flight of stairs. Folk music floated to her from hidden speakers.

On a red lacquered Chinese coffee table in front of her chair, she found an assortment of old guest registers from the inn, dating back to the late 1940s and early '50s. She flipped through a few pages, noting that even then, guests from Atlanta dominated the register. She imagined how nice it would have been, after a long and loud motorcar ride, to arrive and check into an oasis like this.

Jim came to join her as the bellman shouldered their bags. She followed them down a hallway, flute in hand. They made their way through the inn's lounge, where the rich paneled walls, oil paintings, fresh flowers and tufted upholstery chairs begged Katie to linger for a glass of wine or better yet, a cosmopolitan. Just beyond the bar, the hallway emptied into a library. What caught her eyes more than the rows of old books were the rich, buttery draperies with a bright floral motif that framed the windows and an enormous floral display that leaped from a center table. She always thought of libraries as dark, but this one was positively sunny, even in the waning afternoon light. A large antique sofa and chairs were clustered around a sizable stone fireplace, with a baby grand piano at the ready in the far corner. If their room was anything like this, she would never, ever leave it.

From the library, they walked through a private stone terrace tucked between the inn's original building and a relatively new spa building. It reminded her of a narrow passage in a European town, a warren made of different buildings and wings, archways and slate roofs above. She could almost hear Italian or French folk music just around the corner.

"Are we there yet?" she asked.

Jim and the bellman laughed. They continued across the terrace and into the original inn, up a narrow flight of stairs and down a hallway, where they arrived, at last, at their room.

The bellman set down their bags and cleared his throat. "Okay, so this building used to be the entire inn. Now it just has a few of our guest rooms up here and the restaurant down below." He pointed down to his feet. "But don't worry. There's good soundproofing, so you shouldn't hear any noise from *them*." He showed them the room's amenities, then opened the door to their private balcony that overlooked the bustle of Main Street.

"Any questions for me, folks?" the bellman asked, but Katie left the reply, and the tip, to Jim. Instead, she stepped out onto the balcony and noted—in addition to the white wicker chairs and bright red geraniums—a hefty wooden railing. There would be no more falling today.

"Hi there…" Jim's voice was soft in her ear as he slipped up behind her and slid his arms around her waist. "How ya feelin'?"

"Better all the time." She turned to kiss him and felt the grit of dried sweat on the back of her neck. A wave of exhaustion spread over her and she dropped her head onto his shoulder.

"We have a little time before dinner. Want to take a nap?" He stroked her hair with one hand and held her close with the other.

"No. I'd never wake up. What I really need is a good hot soak."

"At the risk of sounding ungallant, why don't I pop in there first, and then you can have all the time you need. I'll meet you at the bar after."

"That sounds perfect, and after dinner, I'll show you how much I appreciate it."

"It won't be nearly as much as I appreciate having *you*, after what happened today and..."

"Stop it. I'm already over it, see?" She pulled back and smiled at him. "Now go take your shower so I can get in there and get all dolled up for dinner."

While he showered, she stood on the balcony, a few feet back from the rail, and allowed her gaze to roam at will over the shoppers and strollers below. It looked idyllic, almost too good to be true. The charming surroundings and the prospect of a deliciously romantic evening were a welcome relief after the day's near disaster.

But her feelings would not give way to contentment. She rubbed her hand over her waist, where the cable had scraped her. She battled to push the feeling of that shove between her shoulders out of her mind. Jim was obviously so upset that he couldn't have—*wouldn't* have—pushed her. The aftermath of the shock was playing tricks on her psyche. He loved her.

Her gaze wandered to the Corvair, parked in a space along Main Street, and then she froze. A man who looked somehow familiar stood next to the car, studying its interior. He was a burly fellow with close-cropped graying hair. Had she seen him before?

The man paused and glanced around at the passersby.

Was he planning to steal something? Their bags were inside the room. Only the glass milk bottle remained locked in the car. What would he want with that? How would he even know it was there? Maybe he wanted to steal the car itself!

As she watched, the man stepped away from the Corvair, looking around as if he were lost or searching for his family. He raised his gaze to the balconies of the hotel across the street, then turned his eyes in her direction, toward the Old Edwards.

She inched back away from the railing. She wanted to dart inside, but she didn't dare to call attention to herself.

The man spotted her right away, and to her surprise, he smiled and raised his hand in greeting.

She returned a half-hearted wave and shivered. Even from a distance, his smile looked cold and calculating. Then she remembered him: he was the man in the green sedan, the vacationing cop who had stared at the Corvair, or maybe at her, at that stoplight on the way up to Highlands.

The man didn't linger; he turned on his heel and strolled down the block, away from the inn, as if he hadn't a care in the world.

When Jim emerged from the shower, dressed in soft chocolate brown trousers and a cream-colored button down shirt, she ran to him, craving the feel of his protective arms around her. "What's this all about?" he asked.

She told him about the encounter.

He frowned, but gave her another hug for reassurance. "Look, the guy saw a hot car and then an even hotter girl, and it made him smile—or ogle. He's harmless."

"It's still creepy."

"Lots of people come up here from Atlanta. And even if you don't enjoy it, there are lots of men who'd want to stare at you. Like me. You're beautiful, Katie."

She felt the color flush in her cheeks, but her reaction had as much to do with his compliment as with her annoyance at his somewhat condescending tone.

Fortunately, he must have sensed her displeasure because he added, "Look, I'm sure you're safe here. This is a five-star inn. They're used to providing security for their guests. I'll go have the car valet-parked right now. How 'bout you take your time up here, and I'll meet you in the lounge when you're done? Dinner reservations are for 7:30, so you've got plenty of time."

She checked the clock. It was only 6:00. She agreed and kissed him to tell him so.

Grabbing the car keys and a room key card, he said, "Just don't keep me waiting too long." He wagged a finger at her before shutting the door.

She sauntered into the bathroom to fill the tub, marveling at the wonderful warmth of the heated basket-weave tiles on her bare feet. "It's the little things," she said aloud as she added bubble bath to the water.

When she slid into the bath, the raw slash across her middle stung at first, but then faded as she felt her spine melt. She luxuriated in the sheer decadence of the hotel and her surroundings. *I could* so *get used to this.* But nagging thoughts refused to let her relax completely. She gritted her teeth. *Okay, I'll make myself think about something else. What about the waitress from this morning? What about the locals? Do they ever get treated like this?* The thoughts mingled with the noise of the water and the tiny popping of the bubbles and, just for now, tuned out the day's earlier trauma. She was just fine, and what promised to be an incredibly romantic night lay ahead of her.

She turned the faucet off and lay back, inhaling the scent of lavender. It was so quiet, she thought she could hear the voices of people out on the street, faint and far away. She closed her eyes and let the warm water and bubbles work their magic.

Then she heard a noise that wasn't so far away: the door to their room opened. Jim must have forgotten something, but he didn't call out to her.

"Jim? What did you forget?" Her voice shattered the silence.

The noise from the bedroom ceased, but Jim didn't respond.

"Jim?" Her heartbeat quickened. "Who's there?" Her heart was racing now.

No one answered.

She cocked her ears, deliberating what to do. If it wasn't Jim, whoever it was made absolutely no noise. Now that he—or she?—knew she was in the bathroom, what would he do next? Did he mean to sneak up on her? She pictured the man from the street hiding in a closet or behind the draperies.

If someone *were* after her, why not just come get her while she was in the bath and vulnerable? Her eyes darted around the strange bathroom, searching for a place to hide or a weapon or…Oh no, naked and sudsy was *not* the way she wanted to be confronted! She slipped out of the tub as silently as she could and wrapped a towel from the heated rack around her body. The warmth reassured her. Hair dripping, she padded across the tile and put her ear against the door. Nothing.

Should she crack the door and peek out or swing it open to surprise whoever waited in the room? She opted for surprise. She counted to three, her lips forming the silent words, then swung the door open with a loud, "What do you want?"

But there was no one in the room—no one hiding behind the curtains or on the balcony or under the bed. Her face reddened when she noticed the crisply turned-down bed linens and matching decoratively wrapped chocolate truffles on each pillow.

"Great. I was attacked by the maid," she said to the empty room, feeling her muscles unclench as she returned to the bathroom. "Get a grip, Kate." She stared at the luxurious tub still full of bubbles. Should she or shouldn't she? She pulled the plug, then stepped into the shower for a quick rinse. So much for luxury.

While she pulled her knit dress from her suitcase, she checked to see if anything looked in disarray. It was impossible to tell. She finished dressing and made sure she had her key card before she went to go meet Jim. She found it in her purse, along with all her other belongings.

Paranoid much? Her imagination, she had to admit, got the best of her. First the mountain and now this. She shook her head, smiling at her own insecurity. Jim would never have pushed her on purpose. It had been terrifying, and she still shuddered as she remembered the feeling—but it wasn't his fault.

There. Done. *But of course, I'll still let him make it up to me.* Her smile broadened into a grin.

She closed their door and headed down the hallway. She hadn't paid much attention to the direction they came during the tour. How did she get back to the bar? She headed to one end of the hallway and followed a flight of stairs down one level. That should put her on the right floor, at least.

Opening a door onto the interior courtyard, she recognized one building as the new spa. To the right was the passage leading to the library, she remembered, and that connected to the bar. In the library, a soft melody from the baby grand in the corner welcomed her. She stopped to smile at the piano player, an older man with thick glasses. She savored the warmth from the room's generous fireplace and checked her appearance in the large gilded mirror opposite. Satisfied, she peeked around the corner into the bar to locate Jim.

He was seated in one of the cozy wingback chairs near the far wall, gesturing and talking with a man seated opposite him. When he caught sight of her, his face lit up and he beckoned her over. As he rose to greet her, so did his companion, turning to face her.

If she had been holding a glass, she would have dropped it. The man chatting with him was the man from the street, no mistake. He gripped a sweaty tumbler with thick fingers on a hand that looked as if it could break a tree limb without assistance. He smiled at her, warmer this time, and offered his hand as Jim introduced him.

"This is Fred Harmon. He sells Jaguars and Range Rovers in Atlanta, but I've learned that he's really a vintage Chevy man at heart. Fred, meet Katie Nelson."

Fred caught her eye. "We almost met before," he said in a friendly midwestern accent. "It's a real pleasure to finally meet you."

Katie stifled a snort.

He noticed her reaction. "I'm sure you must think I'm stalking you, but I swear…"

"Why would she think that?" asked Jim.

Fred turned to him and grinned sheepishly. "I saw her on your balcony this afternoon while I was admiring your car. I must have stared a little. I'm sorry."

She gave him a stiff smile and said, "It's all right."

"Fred's confessed that he's quite attracted to the Corvair," Jim said.

"But only because the lady was clearly taken," Fred said.

Katie resisted rolling her eyes and looked to Jim for answers.

"He first noticed the car on the way up. After running into us—and it—again, he wanted to talk engines."

There was an awkward pause as Katie struggled for something to say. It still didn't compute in her head. This man, here with Jim—had she mistaken his earlier look from the sidewalk?

"Well, I better be going," Fred said. "You two no doubt have dinner plans, and I need to meet some of my buddies." He clapped Jim on the shoulder. "Thanks for the carburetor tip. It made my weekend. It was nice to meet you." He turned to Katie. "Nice to meet you, too, little lady. Sorry if I startled you earlier."

"No, you didn't. I mean, it's okay. Nice to meet you, too."

Fred held her gaze for a ghost of a second, his lip turned up on one side in a friendly smirk. Then he left.

Jim wrapped his arms around her. "You look fantastic."

She returned his hug. "It's good to see you too." She peeked over his shoulder toward the exit. "That guy creeps me out a little, but at least now I know who he is."

"See?" Jim looked at her. "A little too much like a car salesman, but harmless. And he definitely won't be joining us for dinner." He circled his arm around her waist. "Shall we head to the restaurant?"

Madison's, the Old Edwards's highly praised restaurant, boasted a strong connection with local farmers and a conscientious effort to purchase as many local ingredients as possible. The inn even had its own farm.

Jim, foodie that he was, fidgeted like a hound dog before the hunt at the prospect of a meal from a renowned chef and kitchen. Katie was just downright hungry.

They entered the cozy dining room and were shown to a booth nestled in the corner, overlooking the inn's outdoor wine bar. The multi-paned casement windows along the restaurant's wall were open, allowing the soothing sound of a gurgling waterfall to waft in. Flickering lanterns filled the space with a warm glow, and Katie settled into the booth's deeply cushioned seat with a sigh of contentment.

A tall man in a suit appeared and introduced himself as their "wine navigator."

Wine navigator? She shot Jim a glance, but found that he was already scanning the wine list with an air of appreciation.

He stopped and grinned at her, an expression of awe in his eyes. "Some of these are incredible. Expensive, but incredible!" He winked at her, and then ordered a bottle of something she'd never heard of.

She gazed at the menu, stomach growling. Everything sounded fabulous. The menu even listed the names of the farms and farmers who supplied the chef. She was pleased to know that the business of this upscale inn was directly tied to people who—as farmers—had to be locals, living here year-round. Maybe there was more give and take than she'd realized.

As she perused the menu, she felt rather than saw the waitress approach. She happened to look up just as the woman arrived.

"Good evening," the waitress said. "I'm Christy, and I'll be your…Oh!" She stopped when she met Katie's eyes.

Christy was the young woman who had spoken to her yesterday in the grocery store parking lot. Tonight, she looked completely different. Her hair, piled up loosely the day before, was slicked back and sophisticated. Even her voice was different, the mountain accent subdued. The two women exchanged a look, both embarrassed and unsure of what to say next.

Jim looked from one to the other. "Have…have you two met before?"

"I…I'm sorry about yesterday," Christy said, looking from Katie to Jim and back again.

"It's okay," Katie answered. "Don't mention it." While Christy was obviously flustered, Katie admired her for her manners.

"It's just that…the car you were in…I know someone with a car like that. Or at least, I used to." She paused, looking rueful. "It was my mistake."

Katie wondered if the mistake she was referring to was speaking out in the parking lot or what she most likely had done with Porter…if it was Porter. "No problem," she said, wanting to give the poor girl some sympathy. "You were just trying to give me some sound advice."

Christy let out a breath. "Yeah. When you make a mistake, you want to help others avoid it, ya know? Anyway, it was a long time ago. Christmastime. I've already moved on." She tossed her head as if shaking off a bad memory, and her voice regained its all-business polish. "I see that you've found our specials for tonight. What questions can I answer for you about the menu?"

Jim asked a quick question about the champagne sauce, which Christy handled. When the waitress left them to their choices, he turned to Katie. "What was that all about?"

"That's the girl I told you about yesterday. She came up to me in the grocery store parking lot. She recognized the car and might have been one of Porter's 'girlfriends.'"

"Oh Lord. I wish I'd never brought that stupid car up here. It's like he's following us around. I really, really, really just wanted to get *away*, with just *you*."

"I know, I know. Next time, we're bringing my Honda. There definitely aren't any stories following *that* car around."

She pretended to focus on the menu, but secretly, she marveled at the lifestyle Porter led. What kind of person carried on so brash and loud while knowing he was actually so powerless and basically penniless? All in all, Katie mused,

Porter must be terrified deep down of something. But what? Being poor? Being alone? That could explain all of the bravado. She had almost began to feel sorry for him when Jim's voice cut through her thoughts and brought her back to the here and now.

"Lost in the menu, or someplace else?"

"I'm sorry. I'll stop. I'd rather focus on you anyway."

"Glad to hear it," but he looked a little doubtful. "I'm right here, and I'm focusing on you, too. Especially after today…" He reached across the table for her hand.

She dropped her eyes. Why was she obsessing about a man she despised when the one she loved was right across the table? She squeezed his hand and met his gaze. "It was an accident. I'm perfectly fine, and you are not a bad person." She smiled across the table at him.

Over dinner, she and Jim toyed with the idea of owning their own mountain getaway. They discussed their plans for the future. They joked about Jim opening a firm here in Highlands to focus on issues that only the super-wealthy would care about, such as whether to leave massive fortunes to disappointing children or beloved cats, or who owned the air rights above the eighteenth green. They invented a local foundation to fund ridiculous causes such as buying Jimmy Choo heels for those making less than $100,000 a year or sending poor mountain children to private boarding schools in Switzerland.

The conversation eventually turned toward more serious topics, like what it must be like to be a native in a place like Highlands, where "outsiders" overwhelm your community, yet your entire economic livelihood depended upon them.

"It may seem like the locals are an indigenous tribe that's been overrun by a colonial empire," he said, "but Highlands has been a resort community for generations. To me, it's no different than a South Carolina mill town or a fishing village in Maine. Tourism has always been the industry that drives the local economy. It's what people grow up knowing."

She frowned. Maybe it was what people knew, but was it right? "A local foundation could make a huge difference. Someone to support the community of year-round inhabitants, someone to make sure they had a real ownership stake in what happens here. Otherwise, it seems to me, they're just vulnerable to the will of outsiders."

"There *is* a small community foundation here, run out of a larger foundation up in Asheville. You run into the same thing you find with the local economy. All the money, and I'd guess much of the control, comes from 'outsiders,' as you put it."

"So just like us, the people who live here are stuck using other people's money to change their world." A new sense of kinship with the locals kindled in her mind.

"So true." He raised his glass. "To meaningful work."

"To meaningful work." She clinked his glass with hers and took a sip. "And while we're at it, to us and tonight," she added.

"To us and tonight," he echoed, staring into her eyes. "Let's get the check."

Back in their room, he took his time with her, caressing every inch of her body with his fingertips and tongue. He worked his way down her belly until he stopped short with an "Oh!"

"What? What's wrong?" She lifted herself up on her elbows.

Jim caressed the darkening horizontal bruise across her midsection and looked at her with sad, soulful eyes. "Oh Katie, I'm *so* sorry!"

"Hey, it's nothing. I've had bruises before. I'll have them again. I honestly don't even feel it. See? Look." She proved it by flipping him over and reciprocating his actions, getting to know every curve and sinew of his lean frame.

"Love you, Katie," he whispered later in her ear as she snuggled against him.

"I love you, too. Thanks for saving my life," she whispered back before falling into a dreamless sleep.

CHAPTER 27

Sometimes, the best way to keep an eye on someone is to get right out in the open.

I decided to let her see me after I lost them that first night. I had them in the big house in the evening, but in the morning, they weren't there. I never lose people for long, but the boss told me to stay close to them, in case he needed me.

I still think she doesn't know anything. She may suspect, but she's got no proof, and I don't think she's the kind to do anything without serious proof. She likes to unravel the puzzle, I think, but there's one key piece she'll never have.

Once I realized I'd lost them in the morning, I had to find them fast, before the boss found out, but that wasn't hard, thanks to the car. They must have slept at some no-tell motel on the outskirts of town. I understand why they left the big house. She showed up. I would have left, too.

They had breakfast in a diner, went hiking, bought something at an antiques store. When they checked into their fancy hotel, I checked out their car. Nothing there. That's when she saw me, standing there like an idiot. Up on a balcony, she looked like her mind was a million miles away. She looked good up there, and I couldn't help but smile when I thought about what she might be doing up in that room. She didn't like me looking at her, though, so I left and she went back inside.

That's one thing about her being so young. She feels too special to be admired by the likes of me. Maybe she should. But an older woman would have understood where I was coming from. She would've owned the moment. She would've stood there and let me look. Maybe she would have smiled back.

When the girl was in the bathroom, I checked her luggage, just standard procedure. It wasn't hard to get into their room. I got lucky because the maid was doing turndowns. I didn't even have to work the lock. I just made like I was about to open the door from the outside when the maid came out. It's amazing what a smile can do in the right situation. I like that most of the world is still so trusting. It makes my job a whole lot easier.

When she heard me, I couldn't stay. But I did what I went there to do. There was nothing in her suitcase.

After that, I went to the bar to check on things. When she came down, the girl was surprised to see me—she clearly didn't trust me—but she was polite. In truth, I was glad to see she was suspicious. I'm glad to know she's got good instincts and can take care of herself. I'd hate to think of someone taking advantage of her.

I also hate to think of what I'd have to do, though, if she decides to pursue the mystery of the fire on her own. I still don't know what she knows—just that she's not talking about it. I hope it stays that way.

I left them alone shortly after she came down. I made sure she didn't see me any more. Once is enough.

CHAPTER 28

Morning arrived gently, feathers of sunshine tickling Katie's face. Her eyelids fluttered open to see a pale yellow glow washing the walls and the bed covers, where she lay tucked under the comforting weight of Jim's arm. He still slept, his face turned toward hers, his breathing soft and slow. She took advantage of the moment to study his face, the curve of his mouth, the way his hair fell, the rich brown of his eyelashes.

As if he sensed her gazing at him, he opened his eyes and pulled her close with a soft "good morning." She smiled, snuggling into his embrace. No, he definitely wasn't Michael. This weekend had taken them into a new place, a place that had turned out to be a bad one in the past. But this time, it was different. She knew that Jim had meant what he had said and knew that she did as well. For the first time in a long time, she trusted her instincts.

They stayed in bed until 9:30, extraordinarily late for her, and then had a late breakfast in the Old Edwards dining room. They lingered over fresh-roasted coffee, hand-squeezed juice, yogurt with fresh berries and delicate crepes while Katie contemplated the striking difference between this breakfast and yesterday's. It was as if in the space of 24 hours, she'd been a part of two completely different worlds. At the moment, she couldn't quite figure out which world she and Jim would fit into best, given the choice.

"I always thought I'd enjoy being wealthy," Jim said, as if reading her thoughts. "I could get used to living like this."

"Me too. I was just wondering if I'd get *too* used to it and forget to do any good with my money."

"You kidding? You of all people would be the one giving it all away and rallying people to the cause. I'd have to put the brakes on so we wouldn't end up in the poorhouse."

"Hmmm, maybe." Perhaps it was best that they were only staying for one night.

After breakfast, they packed up and headed out for one last day of adventure before the drive back to Atlanta. Jim drove them northwest to hike past a series of waterfalls—"No cliffs," he'd promised.

The waterfall hike culminated in another phenomenal 360-degree view from the clearing at the summit of Wayah Bald. The trees ringing the summit were short and gnarled by the wind, keeping the panorama unblocked.

She peered south, toward Atlanta, and thought she saw a wisp of smoke rising from somewhere beyond the hills. *Something else on fire*, she thought, remembering the clinic. That seemed like a million years ago in a different universe.

They enjoyed one last lunch in Highlands before hitting the road back to Atlanta. The outdoor café perched atop an embankment a few feet above the sidewalk. The café belonged to another, smaller historic inn, painted in crisp white and accented with bright red geraniums popping from multiple planters and hanging baskets. Black wrought-iron tables in the shade of deep red umbrellas offered them a place to relax. As a bonus, Katie could survey the activity up and down Main Street.

From here, Highlands did indeed look like a perfect, sleepy little mountain town. She could understand why so many Atlantans were drawn here. It was hard to imagine anyone down on the street having a care. Then she remembered the waitress from the Old Edwards. She certainly had a care or two, thanks to Porter.

Something the waitress said gave Katie pause. What was it? Oh yes—she hadn't seen Porter since Christmas. Did that mean he hadn't been to Highlands since then? If so, he was lying about being here the weekend of the fire. Or maybe Porter was here, as the man in the antique store had suggested, and had just moved on to a new woman. Or maybe it was someone else who had purchased the case of milk bottles. It was all so confusing.

"Something on the menu troubling you?" Jim asked.

"No, I was just—oh, never mind. I was getting lost in my own head. What are you ordering?"

He decided on a Black Angus burger, while she opted for grilled trout over a crisp salad. They people-watched during lunch, entertaining one another with stories made up about the passersby. A woman with huge hair and hot pink lipstick was a CIA agent deep undercover as a hair stylist, hoping to take down a black market hair dryer ring. A man with a bright red scarf walking the poodle and arguing into his cell phone was a famous Hollywood director going incognito in what he considered the boondocks. And of course, the four mid-50s women who drove by in the Lexus were members of the same Atlanta bridge club, up here to pick out new vacation homes as Christmas presents. All too soon, the afternoon sun made it clear that it was time to head home.

"It seems a shame to have to go back." She sighed as he turned the car southward. "It's so beautiful and peaceful up here."

"No argument here. But I know I'm taking the very best part of this weekend back with me." He reached over and patted her knee before gripping the stick shift to negotiate the winding road down the mountain. She tilted back her head in the wind and enjoyed the last couple of hours of freedom before the real world reclaimed them both.

As they entered the Atlanta city limits, she finally remembered to turn on her cell phone. It had been off now for nearly two days straight. It was a ritual of re-entry to power up and check her messages. Two voicemails and a text from Rita that simply said, "Call me."

The woman was relentless in the quest for gossip. She smiled to herself. There would be plenty to share later, but right now she just wanted to savor the last little bit of the fabulous weekend. As long as she was alone with Jim, everything else could wait. She gave his hand a squeeze as they exited the freeway and headed toward her neighborhood. After he'd pulled into her driveway and helped carry her bag upstairs, he asked, "Shall I stay?"

"I'd love it, but I've got to get my head around going back to work tomorrow, and I won't be able to do that if you're here." She gave him a kiss. "Besides, I kind of want a little time to myself so I can revel in just how wonderful this weekend has been, and how wonderful *you* are."

"Okay, but I will see you again very, very soon, right?"

"Absolutely. Let's talk tomorrow and make dinner plans."

Once he left, she unpacked and fed Babka, who loudly protested her absence while weaving between her feet. She placed the souvenir milk bottle on the coffee table in her living room. Tomorrow, she'd buy some cut flowers to put into it.

Then she took a long, hot shower, made herself some soup and snuggled with the cat on the couch. She looked over a pile of grant applications she'd brought home on Thursday night. The submission deadline for this grant cycle had been Friday, and for some reason, she'd thought she might get a head start on the pile over the weekend. Turns out, she'd not only forgotten to take the stack of papers, she had completely forgotten that they existed.

"Babka, I had such a good time," she said. "I think we may have a little more company around here from now on." The cat purred in agreement.

She flipped through the stack to see if there was anything new and interesting, but instead noticed something missing. Where was an application from Jorge? She thought for sure he would put in a request to help Viva Latina get back on its feet. He must have waited until the last minute again. Jorge always turned in his requests on the last possible day. She'd have to wait until she got back to the office to see what he submitted.

She jumped in surprise as the phone rang, startling Babka, who leapt to the ground with an angry yowl.

"Rita," she said to the cat, looking at the caller ID. "I don't think I have the energy for that."

She let the call go into voicemail. Rita would grill her about every detail of the weekend, and she wasn't ready to share the experience with anyone else just yet. She'd meet Rita for a drink in a few days and satisfy her friend's curiosity. For now, she just wanted to enjoy the feeling of being in love by herself.

"Come on, fat kitty. It's time to sleep," she said, padding off to her bed.

This time, she dreamed that she and Jim were at the lunch counter at Café 460. Only this time, the waitress had dark hair and a Latina face. She wore a nametag that said Angel, but she said nothing, only hovered by their table and stared at Katie, waiting…

CHAPTER 29

On Monday morning, Katie awoke unnerved by her dream. She rushed through her morning routine, resolved to work through the new Viva Latina proposal that had to be waiting for her there. She wanted desperately for Angel's death to lead to something positive.

The stack of new proposals she found on her desk didn't faze her. In fact, quite the opposite. This last batch of proposals meant an end to weeks of phone inquiries and discussions with grant-seekers. For the next few days, she could hole up in her office and let the receptionist verify that, "Yes, we did receive your request; yes, we are in our initial review process right now," when people called. While Katie didn't mind talking with grant-seekers—enjoyed it, in fact—she still wanted quiet time to give the Viva Latina proposal the attention it deserved. She hadn't forgotten her promise to Jorge, even if it was just on a voicemail. She would do everything she could to help him this time around. And, she realized, doing it on her own would help keep work issues out of her relationship with Jim. It was a win-win, love and more professional satisfaction. Now all she needed was that proposal…

She searched through the stack, but found nothing from Viva Latina. *Maybe it had mistakenly gone to Chris?*

She walked down the hall, straightened her shoulders and knocked on his doorframe. He had been so reclusive lately that his open door proffered an open invitation. "Hi there. Did you have a good weekend?"

"It was okay. You?"

"It was okay." She tried hard to keep her smile contained, but she could do nothing to stop a blush.

"Well I guess *so*," he replied. "What did you *do*, exactly?" Chris was all smiles today.

She was dying to spill the beans, to share how wonderful the weekend had been. But she didn't. She couldn't. She and Jim had agreed to keep their relationship private for at least a little while longer, and she didn't want to be viewed as the girl who slept with the boss, especially by Chris, who she knew already had his suspicions. He apparently had plenty of secrets. She could keep hers.

"Nothing special," she said, trying to make her voice sound as casual as possible.

Thankfully, Chris just nodded and didn't press her.

"Did you happen to get a request from Viva Latina? I was expecting one, but it didn't show up on my desk."

"No…I didn't." Chris looked uncomfortable. "But Louise wanted to speak with you about that. I told her I'd tell you when you came in."

"What about?" She bit her lower lip and reached for a strand of hair. Had she done something wrong? She didn't think so. Had something else horrible happened to the clinic? Or to Jorge? Was that why he hadn't returned her calls?

"She can tell you. It's nothing bad." Chris's face told a different story. "Just go talk to her."

Concern building with each step, she walked down the hall to Louise's corner office. It was formally appointed, with a large oak desk and a small conference table surrounded by upholstered chairs. Gold-framed paintings of French gardens hung on the walls with Louise's diplomas, and the shelves on the credenza behind her desk were dotted with glass statues, sculptures and plaques—all honors bestowed on Louise or the Foundation itself by grateful grantees. But there wasn't one family photo or personal memento in sight. Louise was wedded to her job.

"Katie, good morning. Please come in," said Louise, rising and pointing to a chair at the conference table. She wasn't exactly a warm person, but as a foundation leader, in Katie's opinion, she exhibited focus and wisdom, and she worked very effectively with the board.

"Chris said you wanted to see me?" Katie asked, taking a seat.

"Yes. I wanted to let you know that we'll be working with a smaller grant budget this cycle. You'll need to keep that in mind as you evaluate your proposals."

"How much smaller?"

"About $10 million."

Katie felt the look of dismay escape before she could mask it, but Louise jumped to her rescue. "Don't look distressed. It's a good thing, one I think you'll particularly appreciate. In a special executive session about a week ago, the board decided to give $10 million to Viva Latina to build a brand new clinic, a state-of-the-art facility. It will allow them to double their capacity. Isn't that wonderful?"

Katie's jaw fell to the floor, and she struggled to say something, to make any sound in response. Finally, she managed, "A week ago? But how…? Why didn't…? How come no one said anything?"

"The board wanted this gift to be anonymous—no publicity, no fuss, just a quiet gift. Even the staff was only to be told on a need-to-know basis. I'm telling you and Chris today only because you need to know why our grant-making budget will be different this time around. So you can adjust your work accordingly."

"*When* did this happen?"

"A week ago Friday. They met in the evening."

A week ago Friday. Katie struggled to maintain her composure as her mind raced backward through the previous week. A week ago Friday, she'd been out with Rita, assuming Jim was hard at work. But instead he had been at a board meeting—and then lied to her about it.

She turned her attention back to Louise. "The whole board was there?"

Louise gave her an odd look. "Yes. They were all there."

She wanted to ask more, much more, but they were questions for Jim, not Louise. "But why did they decide to do this? At least one of the board members was so vehemently against the proposal last time."

"I'm not sure what the other board members said to him, since it was all behind closed doors, but the majority must have been in favor," A reserved smile spread across Louise's lips. "I thought you'd be delighted."

Katie forced a smile onto her face to erase the shock that surely must be sitting there. "I am. I'm delighted. Well, that explains why I had no proposal from Jorge! This is great news. Thanks for telling me."

"Here's a copy of the grant documentation," Louise said, sliding a thin folder across to her. "Since you brought the first Viva Latina proposal to the table, I thought you'd like to be responsible for overseeing this one. Also, the board wants a recommendation from staff as to the most effective way to allocate the remaining grant funds for this cycle. You and Chris and I can meet about that after you've reviewed all the new proposals."

Katie couldn't get out of Louise's office fast enough. She stormed down the hall, head spinning. Jim knew! He *knew*, and he told her nothing about this. In fact, he had outright lied. How could he hide this from her? How could he just let her think that Jorge was still struggling?

With great effort, she stopped herself from slamming her office door, but then she slammed down into her chair, trying to make sense of it all. She flipped open the folder Louise had given her and reviewed the short grant document inside. Because it originated from a closed-door, executive session of the board, the document only held the basics of the grant, but it was just as Louise had described, $10 million for a new building, payable immediately, to be kept anonymous.

She jumped out of her chair and paced behind her desk, both hands wildly scrabbling through the ends of her hair, pulling it so tight it almost hurt. A blinding wave of hot anger careened through her mind. She trusted Jim, but he kept this from her. What did that say about them? What did it mean about the weekend?

Hot tears sprang from her eyes, and she pressed her forehead against the cool glass of a window in an effort to calm down and regain control. She forced herself to breathe. He must have an explanation. She should talk to him about it. She would call, and he would explain. Still, better wait until she was home before picking up the phone. Just in case he…he…

Her train of thought derailed as her brain began to process what she'd been absently watching down below. Even from her 14th-floor perch, she recognized Chris on the sidewalk below from the bright blue oxford and khakis she'd seen him wearing only moments ago. He was talking to a man she didn't recognize, but from the way Chris leaned away and the man leaned forward, she guessed it wasn't a comfortable exchange.

Without thinking, Katie swept out of her office and down the hall to the elevators. She punched the elevator call button again and again as she wrapped her fingers around her hair and tapped her foot. Even after it arrived, she continued wrapping and tapping down all fourteen stories to the lobby.

Unless they moved while she was in the elevator, Chris and his companion should be visible from Starbucks. She hurried through the café's back door, around the tables to the front windows. Bingo! Chris was still engaged in the heated exchange, but the man had his back turned to her. Chris pointed a finger at the man's face, then crossed his arms in front of his chest when a couple of passersby glanced their way. Katie pressed herself against the edge of a service counter at the end of the windowsill so Chris wouldn't see her if he bothered to look her way.

His companion shook his head and held up his hands, backing away. Then he turned and Katie's eyebrow rose as she saw his face. It was the same man from Backstreet, Gregory Newcombe, the executive director of the Rainbow Theater. The writer of the $10,000 personal check. If Chris was taking bribes from him, neither of them looked very happy about it.

CHAPTER 30

She waited until Chris left—in a huff—before she sneaked back. When she got to her office, she found a voicemail from Rita. "Stop ignoring me. I know you're smitten and all, but I did that research you asked me to do, and I wanted to give you the results. Call me back already!"

Katie closed her office door before dialing Rita's number.

"It's about damn time, girl. How was the weekend?" Rita was always one to get straight to the point.

"It was really nice…I think."

"Uh-oh, that sounds like 'He's a really nice person, but a loser in bed.'"

"No, no! That definitely isn't a problem." Rita's glib tone grated on her nerves.

"Whoa. Okay. I was just kidding there, sister. What's up?"

"Nothing. It was really nice, really special. He's a great guy. It's just that…" She paused. She couldn't explain it, especially not over the phone. She couldn't explain Jim's betrayal, and not just because she wasn't allowed to tell anyone about the grant.

"Kind of a morning-after thing? I know what that's like, honey. But don't you worry. It's hard going from a great time back into reality without questioning everything. It'll all come clear. Just take a deep breath. Sometimes it helps *not* to talk about it, so you can tell me just to shut up."

"Um, yeah. That's it exactly. Thanks for understanding."

"I just think you deserve to be happy, with whoever makes you that way. Don't settle for one thing less!"

"I know. Thanks. Now shut up about it, okay?" They both giggled. "What about your weekend?"

"Funny you should ask. I finally got to research that Phoenix Partners property you asked me about on Friday. Turns out it's being developed by a partnership between a builder out of Florida called Dominick Russo and a local company called S&P Properties, which was created less than a year ago by Malcolm Sutter, one of the biggest developers here in town, and two partners at Kinsey & McMillan. someone named Warren Sanford and your very own Guy Porter."

Katie's breath caught in her throat for a moment. "Go on."

"All that's public record, but here's the fun part. Remember my developer man who moved to Jacksonville? Well, his name is Todd, and it turns out maybe he can't live without me so much. He came up this weekend and was sooo nice, if you know what I mean."

"Mmm hmm." *Get to the point already.*

"While he was here, I mentioned that Phoenix property, and he told me that the word on the street was that the development was about to be hit by some major financial problems because they were so delayed on construction because they couldn't get the complete parcel. Some little place wouldn't sell to them. Although it just happened to burn down, they may already be in arrears with financing, and if they don't find some cash soon, it's bye-bye, building. Todd says the sharks are already circling."

Katie froze. That was Porter's project. Porter needed the land that the clinic had been on. Porter needed money. Porter, Porter, Porter. Her head was swimming.

"Todd also told me that Sutter apparently has no sense of humor wherever finances are concerned, and that he's burned partners in the past who didn't live up to their end of the bargain. Glad I'm not mixed up in stuff like that. Sutter's a powerful guy. He could totally ruin someone if he wanted to."

Katie swallowed hard. *Porter was Sutter's partner. No doubt Sutter was putting pressure on him. Porter had been in town that night. Porter had said he wasn't. He was most certainly a horrible man, but could he actually have burned down the clinic?*

Her gut twisted in a knot so tight she doubled over in her chair. *Porter most certainly could.*

But what about Jorge? Did he know? Was the foundation's ten-million-dollar grant for a new clinic nothing more than hush money to cover up Porter's arson? Did the other board members know? Did Jim know?

"Hey, Katie? Are you still there? Did I say something wrong?"

"Oh, Rita, no. I just...someone just came into my office," she said, fighting the bile rising in her throat. "Can I call you back later?"

"Um, sure, okay."

"Thanks for the info. I'll call you." She hung up. *What did it all mean?* After several minutes of thought, her feet tapping feverishly on the carpet and her fingers twirling her hair, she picked up the phone and dialed Jim's office.

"Hello, beautiful. I've been thinking about you all day." His voice was warm, filled with what sounded like true affection.

She grimaced. "We need to talk."

"What's wrong?" He sounded genuinely surprised, and she took that as a good sign.

Good. Let him worry. He should be worried, after keeping that grant decision from her. But she also seriously needed to talk to him about Porter. "I'm fine, but there are some things we really need to discuss. Can you come to my place after work?"

"Sure. I was hoping you'd say that. Can I bring dinner?"

Dinner? She couldn't even think about dinner at the moment. "Fine."

"Katie, are you sure you're okay?"

"Yes. I'm fine, but we just really need to talk, okay?"

"Okay. Around 6:30?"

"Yes. See you then." She hung up, somewhat satisfied that he sounded as confused as she was. What the hell was going on? Why hadn't he trusted her with the news about Viva Latina? And if he knew about the grant, what else did he know? How much did he really know about Porter's activities?

A dividing line was emerging between them like a median on a highway. She was heading in one direction, and he in the other. She knew that the trustees could circle the wagons to keep the staff out of any discussion or decision, but that had never happened before in her time at the Hartwell Foundation.

Over the weekend, that barrier had disappeared as they'd shared thoughts, dreams and more with each other. Or so she thought. Now, here it came again. Was that barrier ever really gone? She was staff; he was a trustee. He was her boss, and therefore their relationship was not equal. It couldn't be equal outside of work either. In theory, maybe, but not in reality.

Tonight was going to be difficult. She'd have to guard against her emotions. She'd have to ask some piercing questions. She would risk derailing their relationship. But if nothing else, she would get some answers.

She slogged through the rest of her day, going through the motions, unable to concentrate. Finally, at 4:00, she made up a fake appointment so she could leave early.

As she drove to the carriage house, she couldn't shake the feeling of betrayal that grew inside her. *Jim knew. He must have known, at least about the grant. And he could very well know much more.*

Back home, she fed Babka and changed from her work clothes to shorts and a T-shirt. She tied on her running shoes and went for a jog to try to settle her mind. It didn't work.

After a quick shower, she paced as the clock inched toward 6:00. She wrestled with her feelings, betrayal versus love, love versus betrayal. At the moment, betrayal was winning. The memory of Michael slipped to the forefront like a dark shadow. Jim had kept things from her. Michael had kept things from her, too. It was happening again. "At least I caught it sooner this time," she said aloud.

But her thoughts wouldn't be still. *Jim is not Michael.*

But there's really no difference when you get down to it, is there? Dishonesty is dishonesty. Walk away now.

Her cell phone rang, disrupting her internal debate. She saw Jim's number and answered.

"Katie, I'm sorry, but I can't make it tonight," he said. "Jorge has been taken in for questioning about the arson, and I need to make sure my friend can be there to represent him."

"What? I thought the arson investigation was pretty much closed?"

"Me too. Apparently the insurance company wasn't satisfied. One of Jorge's employees overheard him complaining about the building at some point, saying it should just burn down and be done with it. They consider that worth further inquiry, and that means the police are involved."

"Oh, no. Poor Jorge!" She put her hand to her chest. How could they suspect him? And wasn't Jim supposed to be helping him? Maybe he'd screwed Jorge over, too. But then why agree to give him that huge grant? Katie's brain spun with confusion. *What the hell was Jim up to?*

"Look, gotta run, but I'll let you know what happens."

He hung up abruptly. She stared at the phone, as if the blank screen could somehow explain everything to her.

CHAPTER 31

As promised, Jim called the next morning as Katie was driving to work. "Jorge was released. Definitely wasn't enough there to hold him, but I think he's beginning to feel the pressure."

"I can't believe they'd suspect him. I thought it was clearly a hate crime."

"I know, but I can see their point. He'd get a nice claim settlement, as well as a new clinic site. It's not out of the realm of possibility."

"I'm sorry, but that's simply not something I can believe," she snapped. "Especially coming from you."

"What's that supposed to mean?"

"It's what I wanted to talk to you about last night. But I'd prefer to discuss it in person." *So I can see your face when you respond.*

"Okay." Now he sounded hesitant. "Let's reschedule for tonight."

She agreed and hung up just as she arrived at the parking deck. Still fuming, she nearly broke a nail hammering on the elevator button. She scowled at the floor as she rode up to the 14th floor. *How dare he imply that Jorge would do something like that?*

Then, out of the blue, she remembered her conversation with Jorge after the clinic's grant request had been denied. *"There is always more than one way to accomplish a goal. Sometimes, it just requires a different approach,"* he'd said. And then, later, after the fire and Angel's death, he'd sounded so remorseful when he said, *"I should have stopped it. It should never have happened that way. It is not the way we…"*

Katie swallowed hard. Maybe Jim was right. Maybe his involvement wasn't beyond the realm of possibility. But she just couldn't accept that Jorge—the one who spent his days saving lives—might have committed two felonies. He was *so* dedicated to doing what was good.

The day dragged on as she trudged through her proposal pile. She channeled her anger into concentration, making up for the lack of progress yesterday. At 5:15, she gave up and made the drive home. Finally, at 6:30 on the dot, he knocked at her door.

"Hi," he said, stopping at the doorway. He leaned in for a kiss, but stopped when he noticed Katie's stony expression. "Let me just set these groceries down, and we'll talk."

Katie didn't say a word; she didn't trust her voice. Now that he was here, in her apartment, part of her wanted to fall into his arms and let him make sense of it all. She was upset about what had happened to Jorge. She was still furious about being kept in the dark about the foundation's grant. But she also sensed that Jim was nothing like Michael, and that there were differences between her current situation and the one in the past.

Jim returned to the living room, and she allowed him to take her hand and lead her to the couch. She sat at one end, and he sat at the opposite end—just like when they had their park bench conversation only a few short weeks ago.

"So, what's up?" he asked, his voice gentle, concerned. But did she notice the slightest tinge of condescension?

"Louise told me yesterday about the grant to Viva Latina," she said, deciding to remain as businesslike as possible. No tears. No emotion. Just stick to the facts. She could always fall apart later, after he left. "I understand it will pay for an entire new clinic."

"Yes!" Jim's face lit up. "Isn't it great? I thought you'd be thrilled."

"I would have been more thrilled if I'd heard it from you."

"I know. I wanted to tell you—hell, I was dying to tell you—but I couldn't. The board agreed no one should know until they had to know."

"Okay, fine, but how did it come about? Whose idea was it? How did you get Porter to agree? Or did he come up with it himself?" She was testing the waters here, she knew.

"Katie, I can't tell you that. It was an executive session. You know that. Can't you just be happy at the outcome?" He shook his head at her as he rubbed his palms on his thighs.

"No!" she shouted, leaping up from the couch as if it had caught on fire. Heat crept into her face, but she didn't care. "I can't be happy about the freakin' outcome if it came from someone else's wrongdoing! And I can't be happy about it if you're not going to be honest with me!"

"Whoa, wait a minute." His voice rose to echo the volume in hers. He stood and thrust his hands out, palms up, like a magician proving there was nothing up his sleeve. "When have I *not* been honest with you? Not being *allowed* to talk isn't the same as telling you something *untrue.* It's part of my responsibility as a *board member* to stick to protocol. But you *know* that." He paused, collecting himself. In a calmer tone, he added, "And who did anything wrong? What are you talking about? What is all this really about?"

"I'm not exactly sure," she said, crossing her arms in front of her chest. She paced back and forth in front of the coffee table. There were so many pieces, and so many *missing* pieces. How could she make sense of it all?

She bumped the table once, and the milk bottle souvenir, still devoid of flowers, wobbled like a bowling pin. Was it only the day before yesterday that she had placed it there? Ages had passed since then.

He steadied the bottle with a careful hand.

"I'm not sure," she repeated. "But I think it has something to do with Porter. I know it does." She whirled and looked right into his eyes. "I'm convinced he burned down Viva Latina."

"Wh-wh-what?" He looked incredulous. "What are you talking about? We've been *over* this!"

His vehement response threw her off balance and she dropped to the couch.

"Look, I know you despise the man," he continued, shouting again. "He's not my favorite either, but you can't just accuse him of something…"

She raised her palms and her voice. "Just hear me out, okay? You know I saw Porter the night of the fire, driving in Buckhead. Then he told everyone he was in Highlands for the weekend. Then that waitress, who recognized Porter's car, said she hadn't seen him since Christmas…"

"But you don't know she was talking about Porter…"

"*Then* I learned yesterday that the building going up where the clinic was is in fact one of Porter's projects, and that it's likely heading for bankruptcy." She raged on, her anger and frustration unbridled now. "You and I know that his wife is about to pull the rug out from under him. Maybe he knows it, too. And finally, there's this secret grant all of a sudden that no one bothers to tell me about"—she shot him a cutting look as she said this—"and it kind of seems like maybe it's guilt money or hush money or something."

"Katie…"

"And to top it all off, everyone seems to forget that a woman *died* in that fire!" She took a breath, then said, "But the real problem is, I can't tell you because *you* won't freakin' talk to me about any of it!"

As her words drifted to the ground between them, Jim sat for long minutes without a word, his eyes darting this way and that, his fingers drumming an erratic tattoo against his thighs, his lips moving as if he were explaining her outburst to himself.

Katie tried to be patient. She stood up to pace, then sat back down again, jiggling her foot with nervous energy. She was determined that he answer her, and she would wait for hours, if that's what it took.

Finally, he looked up at her and spoke, his words slow and careful. He seemed to take great pains to control himself. "You're making a very serious accusation, Katie. Without the facts to back it up. Arson investigators and the police think it likely was Jorge."

She opened her mouth to protest, but he held up a hand. "No, it's my turn. The fact that you saw Porter that night, if indeed it was Porter, could be a complete coincidence. The fact that he may or may not have seen that particular waitress in

Highlands doesn't mean that he wasn't seeing some other woman. Unless you've got papers to prove that the building is heading for bankruptcy, then you're relying on hearsay."

"But it all adds up…"

"No, it doesn't. Not any more than it adds up for Jorge. You don't know the whole story. *We* don't know the whole story. And you can't tell me that there's no one else who might have come out ahead if that clinic burned."

Katie blanched. There was someone else. Gregory Newcombe. The Rainbow Theater. Without Viva Latina in the mix, their chances of getting a grant would be much higher. Her heart sank to her feet. *What if Gregory Newcombe paid Chris to start the fire?* She shook her head.

"What?" Jim was watching her. "You know of someone else, don't you?"

"Yes…no…I don't know." *It couldn't be.*

"Who?"

She couldn't believe it; she wouldn't believe it, and she certainly wasn't going to tell Jim now. Instead, she raised her head and looked him straight in the eye. "I can't tell you."

He paused and swallowed hard, looking hurt and then angry. "The same goes for the Viva Latina grant…I've said all I can say."

Katie's eyes dropped. Jim maintained his ethics as a trustee, but it hit her like a knife in her heart. The divide between them was widening. Trustee and staff. Boss and employee. And because of that divide, she couldn't tell him about Chris either, regardless of how much she wanted to. She couldn't betray the trust of a fellow staff member—at least, not yet. She realized with a start where her loyalties lay. "I'm sorry," she said.

"Katie, what you're saying about Porter could be very damaging, not just to him, but to the firm and to the foundation. Lot of good things would take a hit if Porter did something like that. Yeah, he's a beast in his personal life, but that doesn't make him a criminal. Before you point a finger at him, you should think very, very carefully, especially about whatever it is you can't share."

"So what can we do to find out about him for sure?"

"*We* can't do anything," Jim said, standing up. "Look Katie, Porter's a man who has great influence on my career and on the Hartwell Foundation. As a trustee, I owe it to the foundation to get the facts straight before this goes any further. And as a part of Kinsey & McMillan, I kinda owe them as well. In fact, since Porter is a partner, even if I did find out something horrible, I couldn't share it with *you*."

"So that's it? You're just going to leave me out of it now? Tell me I can't be a part of finding out what's going on?"

"Find out about your own secret, the one *you* can't share with *me*!"

"Oh, so you're the only one allowed to keep secrets?" Her face was beet red, she knew, and tears were imminent, but she couldn't control the rising volume of her voice.

"As a trustee, I fucking *have* to!" He clenched his fist and hammered into his other palm. It made a loud smack that silenced both of them. After a moment, he let out a long breath. His next words were much softer. "But as your boyfriend, I'm asking you to trust me."

Trust him? When he was cutting her out so completely? *Oh no, not again. Never again.*

"I don't think I can consider you my boyfriend," she said, her voice just louder than a whisper.

He looked stunned. "Katie, come on. I'm asking you just to *trust* me, and you can't do that?"

Katie stayed quiet, arms folded, eyes on the floor.

"No," he said. "I guess you can't."

"How can I? When I will never know exactly what's going on, and you will always have the final say. *That* will always be a problem."

He buried his face in his hands, and Katie watched as a few stray wisps of his hair fell over his fingers. She thought about how that hair had felt soft in her hands, and how those fingers had ignited her body.

"I'm sorry," he said when he regained his voice. "I didn't realize it was such a big deal to you. If it's really my being a trustee or an attorney that's getting in the way, I can't help that."

"No," she shook her head, using every ounce of strength to fight back the tears. "You can't." She hesitated, then added, "Please. Just go. Now."

"*Katie!* What are you saying?" He was pleading. "What are we doing? Is this really what you want?"

She just nodded her head. "Please just go." She stood and walked to the door. It seemed like the most difficult walk of her life, but it couldn't be as difficult as spending her life with a man who couldn't tell her everything she needed to know.

He followed her, stammering. "I…I was gonna to ask you to…to go with me to meet…my mama this weekend. And…and instead, this is it? It's over? Already? But I…I love you…" His words trailed off.

She stood at the open door, as still and silent as a corpse, as if all the life had been sucked out of her. It took all her will power not to explode in tears, not to throw herself into his arms, not to even look into his face.

When he left, Katie felt more alone than she'd ever felt in her life. "I loved you, too," she whispered. Then she slid her back down the wall and sat on the floor. She sat there for a long, long time, tears trailing down her cheeks while her shoulders shook with her sobs.

CHAPTER 32

The rest of the week, Katie either holed up in her office or hibernated at home. She spoke only when necessary and even then, only with monosyllabic, curt answers. Since she had the excuse of reviewing proposals, everyone eventually just left her alone.

During the week, Rita called several times. She ignored them. Jim didn't call at all, for which she felt mostly grateful. Her heart softened for just a moment when she found a note on her desk one morning that said, "If you change your mind, please call me. Love, Jim."

Even the weather was gloomy and stormy. Normally, she would have welcomed it as a fitting backdrop to her mood, but instead, she found herself reliving the stormy night in Highlands. She sank deeper into an emotional swamp, wallowing in self-loathing for allowing herself to fall in love with a liar yet again. It was as if Michael hadn't just broken her heart, but left her under a curse.

Thinking of Highlands also reminded her of the creepy car salesman. What was his name? Fred Harmon. She couldn't shake the thought that he was watching her for some reason other than the love of a 1965 Corvair. She looked up the website for the luxury car dealership where Fred claimed to work. Sure enough, she found his photo. The site claimed he'd been there for nearly 10 years. According to his bio, he'd won several awards for sales and customer satisfaction. He even listed restoring vintage cars as a hobby.

"I'm an idiot," she said aloud, smacking herself on the forehead at her overreaching suspicions. He probably was a perfectly nice guy—just one who liked to leer at girls on balconies. Okay, even if he was a complete pervert, that didn't mean he was actually *following* them. And he did disappear for good once he and Jim talked cars.

Why was she so freaking paranoid? Had Michael, and now Jim, messed up her mind that badly? *Jim isn't Michael*, a voice inside her head told her. She sagged over her desk, her long hair enveloping her face.

She slogged through her proposals, but could barely concentrate on the pages—often finding as she came to the end of one, that she had no idea what it said and had to reread it from scratch.

Her brain instead wrestled with what had gone wrong with her relationship with Jim, and why. Was he really a liar, or had she simply pushed too hard for his attention, throwing aside any respect for his ethics? She didn't know, and these questions only added to her confusion. One thing was clear, however. Regardless of what he had said at the beginning of their relationship, she knew in her gut that continuing to work at the Hartwell Foundation wasn't an option. Seeing him at board meetings, knowing his eyes were reviewing her work—she would always be under a shadow now.

She let herself imagine a new job at a different foundation, some place with priorities that reflected her own. Not that there were so many to choose from, but Atlanta had its share. The challenge was finding a suitable opening. In the foundation world, staff turnover was rare. Giving away charitable dollars paid infinitely better than raising them, and the work wasn't nearly as stressful. As a result, many foundation staffers simply aged in place. She decided that she wasn't going to age in place at the Hartwell Foundation. Maybe she should switch back to the nonprofit community, go back to the trenches and struggle for a good cause. But that didn't feel right either.

On Friday afternoon, she was surprised to hear Jorge's deep voice when she answered the phone.

"Katie, how are you?" he asked.

She hesitated. Should she put on a bright, cheery tone and pretend that everything was fine?

The pause gave her away. She heard Jorge's deep intake of breath through the line before he spoke. "Katie, I suppose you have heard. I am sorry I have not returned your calls. Being a suspect leaves one somewhat preoccupied. You have been a great advocate for me and for the clinic, and I should not have stayed out of touch. But there is something I would like to discuss—not about me, but perhaps about *you.* Might we perhaps meet for coffee after work this evening?"

About *her*? Although his words were as formal as ever, she sensed an underlying urgency in his tone. She agreed to meet him at their usual coffee spot.

After work, she hurried to the coffee shop. Jorge was already there waiting for her. He looked exhausted. She sympathized with him; she knew how hard it was to keep the clinic going even on a good day. She couldn't imagine how tiring it must have been in the aftermath of the fire and especially now with the accusations of arson and murder. Her own shoulders sagged just thinking about it. She wanted to reach out and take his hand, but she knew that kind of interaction was off-limits.

"Thank you for coming here to meet me," he said with a weak smile. "I have missed our conversations."

"It's okay. I know you've been busy, and for what it's worth, I don't think you did it." *At least, I don't think I think you did.*

His smile broadened. "Thank you."

"And I'm happy you've sold your property and received such a big grant from us." She paused a beat before adding, "Even if I didn't know about it."

"That's what I wanted to talk to you about." His eyes turned serious, piercing. "The property sale was expected, but this grant is very strange. While I am certainly happy to have such a generous gift, something is just not right about it."

"How so?" A strange prickle ran up the back of her neck.

"The way in which it was given is simply odd. We did not ask for money. In fact, I was just going to apply for some short-term funds to keep us going while I planned out our next steps. The next thing I know, a letter from the Hartwell Foundation arrives at my office via courier. It explains that a grant has been made, and it says that I must tell no one about the source of the gift."

"Sometimes our trustees prefer to make large grants anonymously," she said, choosing her words cautiously. "The founder had a strong desire to maintain humility, and the trustees sometimes don't want a lot of publicity to open the floodgates for other requests." She frowned, staring down at her hands around the plain white cup of decaf, remembering once again that Jim had not shared any information about this grant with her.

"I understand, but then I received a phone call. It came night before last, after I returned from the police station. It was a man's voice, but not one I recognized. He said that now that I had my money, I had to make sure that I completely understood the importance of not talking. He used that phrase several times, 'not talking.' I think he meant more than talking about the grant. I think he was referring to the arson."

"Did you say anything to the police about the grant?"

"No. I said very little, thanks to my attorney. But the caller seemed concerned that I might have."

"Was it a loud voice? A deep voice?"

"No. In fact, the man was whispering. I had to strain to hear him. I suppose it could have been any number of crackpots who don't like the work we do, except for the fact that he knew about the money."

She fell silent. Very few people knew about this grant. Who would have called Jorge? Chris? Or maybe Gregory Newcombe? Or was there yet another person who knew more about what was going on with Viva Latina than she did? Color climbed up her neck to her cheeks.

"Are you okay?" His hand touched hers on the table.

So much for decorum. She turned her palm up to clasp his and looked into his deep hazel eyes. "Jorge, I think something's up, but I'm not sure exactly what it is yet. I need to be sure before I can talk about it. But I think it's best if you honor the foundation's request for anonymity as long as you can. Our whole board is potentially involved, so I have to think the funding is legitimate, even if the reasons aren't."

"I am concerned about *you*, Katie. I think everything is not well for you."

"Oh, please don't waste any time worrying about me." She waved a hand, shaking off his concern. "I'm fine. And you've been through so much. At least now with this grant, you're well taken care of."

He looked at her with immense sadness in his eyes. "No, that is not true. While I now have $10 million for a new building, which is a wonderful gift, I'll never be 'taken care of,' as you put it, until the need for that building no longer exists. If you know of a way to make sure every woman, regardless of income, can get high-quality medical care—if you know how to get that 'taken care of,' could you please let me know? And while you're at it, can you figure out a way to go back in time to keep Angel from spending that night in my building? Can you 'take care' of that, too?"

Now her blush of anger turned into one of shame. She'd been so wrapped up in her own bitterness, she'd almost forgotten that a person's life had ended so tragically. She wasn't worthy of this man's trust; he would never be so self-centered. "I'm so sorry. You're right. I didn't mean that like it sounded. I still feel horrible about her death. I…I have dreams about her. What happened to your clinic was unforgiveable. And what happened to her—first the attack, then the fire—was unconscionable."

"That is true. I only learned the details of her rape last week. She was apparently cleaning in one of the big buildings in midtown. Her cousin said he left her on one floor alone, and when he came back to get her, it had already happened. She described the man, but it could have been one of hundreds…If only I had known earlier…"

"What happened to her is *not* your fault. The best thing you can do for her, to honor her, is to keep doing what you're doing with the clinic." Her shoulders slumped again. "At least maybe our trustees finally understand the groundbreaking work you're doing. Maybe this is a sign that they're actually going to get past funding the same old stuff."

Never before had she admitted dissatisfaction with her foundation job in the presence of a grantee. It was part of the unwritten code of the foundation world, never show any chink in the armor. Her hand went to her throat, as if she'd just revealed some horrible secret and wanted to stop any more from coming forth. At the same time, a wave of relief washed over her.

Jorge eyed her for a moment, then said, "You know, fulfillment can never come from spending other people's money. The real change, the real difference, can only come from your own passion."

She nodded dumbly, struck by the rawness of her own admission and the truth of his words.

He squeezed her hand and continued. "When you concentrate only on the money—especially if it is someone else's—then you always end up being trapped. I think you are much too smart for that."

She crossed her brows, thinking how to defend herself. Other people's money had done a great deal for him. She opened her mouth to protest, but he raised a hand for silence.

"Don't misunderstand. I am not saying there is not great value in what the Hartwell Foundation has done, especially for Viva Latina. No matter what the motivation, it is a gift that will have a positive result for hundreds of women. I am talking about the effect that working at the foundation—or any foundation—might have on *you.* Although you are doing an important job, I wonder if it really suits your passion." He paused a moment, then looked right into her eyes. "I also wonder if it keeps you from discovering what might be most important in your life."

Was he talking about work or something else? Was he making a reference to her relationship with Jim or maybe one with him? She was at a loss for words and stumbled through a goodbye as he rose to leave.

"Katie, are you sure you are okay? There is nothing in all of this that is causing problems for you?" Jorge clasped her hand and look directly in her eyes.

Yes! It's all causing problems for me! "No, really Jorge, I'm fine." She masked the lie with a forced smile that she kept pinned to her face until he had walked away.

That night, Angel appeared again in her dream. Once again, she paced along the edge of a steep cliff. Katie feared she was going to fall over the edge, but when she tried to call out a warning, no sound came.

CHAPTER 33

I figured she'd check up on my story, so I made sure the dealer's website said all the right things. Even if she'd come to the dealership in person, she'd have seen me, and they would have told her, "Yeah, Fred Harmon works here."

My real name isn't important. Only the job matters. The real job.

Being a car salesman is a great cover for me. I set my own hours and have flexibility to do what's needed when I'm called. Plus no one ever probes too much into my background. Who wants to hang out with a car salesman, right?

I caught it when she hit my bio page, so I kept an eye out for her around the lot, but she never went that far. I figured that would satisfy her.

But she's still working the angles of the fire. She should have let it go by now. Instead, she had what looked like an intense meeting with that spic doctor.

The absolute worst thing is that she called the romance off. This isn't good. She was supposed to get all wrapped up in the romance and let the rest drop. With them broken up, she could discover too many loose ends. The whole thing can come unraveled.

Speaking of becoming unraveled, the boss is seriously looking over my shoulder. Calls me way too much. He told me to make a call to that spic doctor to keep him quiet. I've got no patience for that. I need a free rein to do my work. I can't wait to be finished with this job.

Now that I think about it, I should probably wrap this one up on my own. The tide has turned, and certain people aren't doing what they should. I'll clear it, of course, but then I'm going to have to shut this down.

I hope the girl will cooperate, do the right thing. I don't want this to get ugly, especially when she can avoid it.

Please, please, please cooperate. I don't want this to end badly for you.

CHAPTER 34

Damn it, Chris.

The more she thought about Jorge's story of the mysterious phone call—and the more she pondered the check Chris had torn up and his obviously tense meeting with Greg Newcombe—the more Katie realized that Chris *had to* play a pivotal part in the odd happenings. Her palms sweated as she considered this fact. After all, he had served as her mentor, so well respected on the staff and in the field. It didn't seem possible, but still, the phone call, the torn-up check and his odd request to stop working on a new grant for the clinic—all of that seemed to point in his direction. Even if he wasn't involved in the fire, he appeared to be involved in *something* suspicious. What else could it be?

She should just march into his office and talk to him. But how could she confront someone like Chris and accuse him of playing a part in a murder? He would never speak to her again, and her own reputation would be in the toilet. She needed more proof—something irrefutable—before she could point a finger. Searching Chris's office might yield just what she needed.

For two days, she watched and waited. During the busy proposal review season, neither she nor Chris spent much, if any, time away from the office during the workday. Even lunches were mostly quick dashes for takeout, and she couldn't risk being caught. Finally, on Wednesday, she pulled up the office calendar on her computer screen to see a new entry that showed Chris unavailable for three hours in the afternoon, with no reason listed.

She tried as casually as she could to verify this information as she passed Chris in the hallway that morning. "Hi, you around later? I wanted to pick your brain on a couple of proposals I've got."

Chris had become so dark and brooding lately, she almost expected him to snap at her in response, but he smiled politely. "I'm sorry. No. I have a doctor's appointment at 2:00 and I won't be back after that. Maybe tomorrow morning?"

"Sure!" She flashed him a smile far too casual to betray any disappointment.

She waited until 3:00, just to make doubly sure Chris was well clear of the building, before she entered his office. Her pulse quickened as she stood for a moment in the doorway, then she slipped through and quietly closed the door behind her. She didn't dare turn the lights on, but his office, like hers, had floor-to-ceiling windows, and the cloudy sky outside provided the light she needed to see. Like Chris himself, the office was tidy. Where Katie covered nearly every flat surface with stacks of paper during this part of the grant cycle, Chris still maintained a pristine order. No doubt he used the file drawers in his desk for actually filing documents, rather than for hiding random clutter.

His desk faced the door, a matching credenza behind it, backed against the windows. Bookcases lined the left wall, and a small, empty conference table and two chairs sat to the right. Katie tiptoed from the door around to the other side of the desk to begin her search. His computer monitor sat squarely in the middle, the screen dark. Although she had frequently bemoaned the fact that the foundation's technology still rested in the Dark Ages with its grant-making vision, on this occasion she sent a mental note of thanks to the board for not yet taking the entire grant records system online. File folders and paper forms didn't require user passwords.

Only one folder lay on the shining mahogany, and a quick flip through it showed it was a proposal from Piedmont Hospital for a new cancer wing. There was a page of notes, written neatly in Chris' impeccable handwriting, but it revealed no secrets.

Katie dipped down to open the file drawers on the right side of Chris's chair. She scanned the file tabs. There it was, the Rainbow Theater! She pulled the file and sat in Chris's leather chair to open it. Inside, she found all the usual forms and records, including the income statement and balance sheet from the theater group. She forced herself to slow her gaze and consider the numbers carefully, but there was nothing there that indicated any financial distress on the part of this nonprofit. Its numbers were solidly in the black, so it obviously wasn't hoping to use Hartwell money out of desperation.

She read through Chris's handwritten notes twice. They were thorough and professional, and they indicated nothing out of the ordinary. Then she thought of something and flipped back to one of the general internal forms they had to fill out for every grantee. There was always a question about relationships on these forms, to keep any personal connections between foundation staff and grantees completely aboveboard. If either of the program officers or Louise considered a connection too close, the proposal would move to the other program officer's portfolio.

In answer to the question, *Does anyone on the foundation staff have a personal relationship with anyone on this nonprofit's staff or board?,* Chris had written, *Yes. I know the executive director professionally.*

Was that all? The meetings Katie had witnessed had looked anything *but* professional. But then again they hadn't looked like meetings between friends either. This was intriguing, but it wasn't enough.

She refiled the folder, placing it in exactly the same spot, then slid the drawer closed and turned to check its twin on the left side of the desk. As she turned, her hand brushed the mouse on Chris' computer, and the screen flickered to life. The light drew her eyes. The screen was just as tidy as the desk. The open browser windows had all been neatly collapsed into the bottom navigation bar. One was the office email program. She could check that, but Louise could and sometimes did monitor foundation emails, so it was unlikely that Chris would use that account for anything that wasn't strictly professional. Another window showed the website for Piedmont Hospital. That made sense given the folder Chris had left on the desk. He was doing research. But the last window gave her momentary pause before she reached for the mouse. *Gmail.*

Her fingers trembled as she clicked to open the browser window. This was Chris's personal email account, and invading it felt like a more serious breach of privacy than sneaking into his office. She scanned the list of senders to Chris's inbox, her left hand finding reassurance at the ends of her hair. There it was: Gnewcombe@yahoo.com. She clicked, then frowned at the message there.

> Don't lecture me about loyalty. Yours is no better than mine. And we all know loyalty comes with a price. Name yours.

What did it mean? She studied the message, her brain working feverishly in an attempt to unravel what she read. There was that word again: *loyalty.* Loyalty was supposed to be a good thing, right? But how come every time she'd seen or heard it lately, it seemed so threatening?

Chris had not replied to this message, but she could click backward to see the conversation that led to this entry. Gnewcombe had started the conversation, she noticed, and she slid the mouse to the top of the list.

"What are you *doing*?" Chris's voice, filled with icy fury, sliced through her concentration. She gasped and her eyes darted from the screen to the doorway, where he stood, hands on either side of the frame, glaring at her. She hadn't even heard the door open! She jumped up, sending his chair slamming back into the credenza.

"Nothing…I…um…I was…" She stumbled to find an excuse as a wave of heat spiked in her face.

He stared at her, jaw clenched, breathing deeply, before finally speaking. His words were cold. "Are you *looking* for something? Could you not do me the courtesy of *asking* first?"

Katie stood speechless, paralyzed by embarrassment.

"This is very unprofessional of you. You should leave. Now." Chris gestured toward the door.

Katie sensed the slightest hint of condescension in his tone, but it was enough to change her embarrassment to anger. So what if he was the foundation's golden boy? He was the one who had been acting unprofessional, and she wanted an explanation. She set her jaw as she walked around the desk, pulling herself up to her full height to meet his eyes. "We need to talk."

If Chris was surprised, he didn't show it. "What about?"

"Something weird is going on, and I want to know what it is."

"Oh? What do you mean, something *weird*?" His tone remained detached, but his eyes flashed a momentary panic, darting toward the hallway before he closed the door behind him.

She struggled with how to proceed. She didn't want to assault him with a tumult of emotional accusations. She needed to present her suspicions logically, to appeal to his sense of decorum and not give him a chance to dismiss her as an impulsive idiot.

"First of all, there was that phone call that you wouldn't tell me anything about. Then, that night at Backstreet, I saw the head of the Rainbow Theater give you a check for ten grand."

At this, Chris's eyebrows shot upward, but he remained silent.

"Then, I just happened to see you and Greg Newcombe having a rather intense conversation outside our building. And after that…"

"What? What after that?" Chris looked even angrier now, his face nearly purple.

"Nothing. Well, maybe something. Have you been making any anonymous phone calls lately?"

"You've lost me, Katie. Exactly what are you implying?" He threw his hands up at his sides.

"I think you know. I'm not sure how or why, but it sure looks to me like Greg Newcombe was trying to bribe you or pay you for something, and the only thing that makes sense to me would be for making Viva Latina go away. You said yourself it was unwelcome competition."

He was again silent for a long moment, mouth agape. "You think I burned down that building." It was statement, not a question.

"You said as much in that phone call! You said something about starting a fire. You even said you ended a life!"

"You eavesdropped on my personal phone call and now you're accusing me?"

"No! Not eavesdropped…I…" No. She couldn't let him put her on the defensive. She had to stand her ground and make him see she wasn't just a snoop. Her hands curled into fists, mounted on her hips.

"Okay what about that threatening call to Jorge?"

"Jorge? *Dr. Ramirez*?" He was shouting at her now. "Damn, Katie. Probably ten people a day make threatening phone calls to the clinic. Why on earth would you think it was me?"

The outrage on Chris' face was so raw, so real, that Katie almost missed the flicker of fear that registered in his eyes. There was something there, something important he was hiding, something that frightened him, but there was no way she would get it from him now. Their confrontation had hit a stalemate. Her mouth went dry as she searched his eyes again. *What exactly had he done? What kind of trouble was he in?* Despite her anger, she began to feel sorry for him.

"I think you should leave." His voice was once again controlled, his gaze again steady. He placed a firm hand on the doorknob.

"I'm sorry. Perhaps I've made a mistake," she said, throwing him a small bone of comfort as she backed through his office door.

But there was no mistake. Chris was mixed up in something that scared him.

CHAPTER 35

Now that she had alienated Chris, Katie was more miserable than ever at work. All day Thursday and into Friday, her sense of unrest about her career swirled together with a growing sense of concern for Chris, frustration at the seemingly unsolvable mystery of the fire and murder and the unshakeable sadness in the wake of Jim's departure from her apartment.

She had no friends or allies left. Even Louise seemed cold to her, possibly disappointed in Katie's obvious lack of concentration over the past week and a half. Chris hated her, and all she wanted to do now was get to the bottom of that fire and help him if she could. She needed to make things right. Chris clearly needed help, even if he wouldn't ask for it. Who would help her if *she* asked for it?

Her instincts told her that solving the mystery of the fire was the only way to help Chris, but she'd made absolutely no headway there. Jim had discounted her theories about Porter, and Chris had thrown up a brick wall. And there was simply no way, *no way*, Jorge would have burned down his own building. What did it all mean? Where did it point her?

And even if she did somehow manage to unravel it all, she'd still need to find another job. She doubted that anything she learned would make this job a better fit. Even if she were right about everything, they'd never trust her again.

Jorge had mentioned following her passion. That sounded like good advice, but then again, what *was* her passion? She'd been wrapped up in other people's money for so long, she had lost track of her own priorities. What would really make her happiest? How could she be true to herself?

She pondered those questions, struggling to focus on her work as the deadline for making her grant recommendations inched closer. Even if she was planning to leave, she didn't want to go out like a slacker. If nothing else, she'd need a strong reference from Louise. By Friday, both her fingertips and her split ends were frazzled.

Then the lightning bolt struck. Jim was the key. Of course! He could help her figure out how to help Chris. He was the one person who could most help her—even *offered* to help her—and she'd pushed him away. The *real* question was, could she let go of her past enough to try again? Could she support his sense of ethics and confidentiality without interpreting it as an intentional slight? She had berated herself for being a fool by falling for him, but maybe, just maybe, she had truly been foolish by letting pride and insecurity get in the way of their relationship.

The more she considered this, the more she wanted him. She wanted to stop being so uptight about their work roles and focus more on their personal ones. She wanted to take a risk. She wanted to test herself and not just give up because it got difficult. She wanted to get out from under the ghost of Michael once and for all. More than anything else, she wanted to prove to herself, and to him, that she really *could* trust him.

On Friday afternoon, she picked up the phone to call him. She decided to suggest they get together over the weekend. They could start fresh and see where it all led. But instead of Jim, she got his secretary. He'd left for the weekend. Would she like to leave a message? She declined.

She tried his cell phone, but got his voicemail there, too. She didn't want to leave a message. She wanted to hear his voice in person.

That evening, after hearing his voicemail for the seventh time, she remembered he had mentioned something about going to South Carolina to visit his mother. She smiled now at his choice of words, "my mama," he'd said. Like every native-born Southern man she'd met, "my mama" always referred to the entire family.

A new idea came into focus. What if she surprised him? Landrum, South Carolina, was a three-hour drive, but wouldn't it be worth it if she could meet his parents after all? It couldn't be hard to find the residence for Bailey Hunter, Jim's father, since he was such a respected attorney in such a small town.

Her heart beat faster as she contemplated this plan. It was unlike her to simply show up, but what the heck? She'd been thinking of an entirely new career, so why not change some other things as well? It was time to break out of the mold, so to speak. Do something a little crazy.

She looked up "Bailey Hunter" in the online white pages. There was only one listing in Landrum. She copied down the address, then used a mapping website to find the way there from the interstate.

She went to sleep that night imagining the drive and her arrival, the surprise and delight registering on Jim's face when she confessed her change of heart.

***

Next morning, she awoke early. After a quick shower, she chose a black knit skirt and a wrap-around tank top under a denim jacket—comfortable, but nothing that would appear wrinkled when she met Jim's parents. She slipped on a pair of leather flip-flops for the drive. In an overnight bag, she folded in a nicer outfit (in case they went out to dinner or the parents were church-going types) as well as a pair of shorts and a T-shirt for the drive home on Sunday. After a moment of contemplation, she decided to throw in the sexy lingerie from the Highlands trip, then hedged her bet by adding a conservative pair of pajamas.

She left some food and fresh water for Babka and drove off in a flurry of excitement, impatient for a reunion. As the drive unfolded, though, she grew more and more doubtful. When she stopped at the state line to grab gas and a granola bar from a highway quick stop, she almost turned around. What if Jim had changed his mind? What if he was embarrassed to have her show up at his parents' house? What if…

No. No "what ifs." I'm doing this. She gripped the wheel of her Honda and steered onward, pressing a little harder on the accelerator.

Just past lunchtime, she found the exit for Landrum and before long coasted into a quaint little town square, complete with a courthouse and clock tower. She drove around the square, enjoying its picturesque quality, and was delighted to discover Jim's father's law firm directly across the street from the courthouse's west side. *J. Bailey Hunter, Esq. and Associates*, the sign said.

She parked to take a closer look, scanning the front of the building as if she could catch a glimpse into Jim's early life. The bright white window molding popped from the light gray brick façade, making her want to peek in through the shining glass. The wrought iron supports that held up a second-story balcony shaded the sidewalk below. Ivy spilled from planters under the windows and from pots on the balcony, suggesting years of growth and care. The walnut-paneled front door had a brass knocker and mail slot. It was very different from the haughty feel of Atlanta's large firms, but this building had a sense of permanence; the sense of solidity and honesty announced that the man who led this office had clout and respect.

What was it like to grow up with all this? She imagined Jim as a small child, stopping by on errands with his mother to witness the bustle of a busy firm. His family must have been one of the wealthier ones in this small town, but for some reason—maybe because of Jim himself—she didn't imagine that played a role in their place in the town's esteem. She pictured Bailey Hunter as a "people person," able to talk with anyone—rich or poor, old or young—and really make a connection.

She wondered if Jim admired his father as he grew through his teen years, or if he felt stifled or intimidated by expectations. Had Bailey been the kind of father who offered his son nurturing support or a firm hand or both? She remembered Jim had mentioned that he and his father had grown distant in the recent past. Maybe this visit was about mending fences. Maybe one day, he would return to this town to practice. Would she be there, too?

She stroked the wooden door for a moment, then turned back toward her car. Out of the corner of her eye, she thought she glimpsed someone familiar entering a small café across the street. A man with close-cropped gray hair and a stocky build. Could it be—what was his name, Fred? The car salesman from Highlands?

It seemed ridiculous, impossible. No one even knew she was here, and yet an uncomfortable prickling climbed up the back of her neck. She scanned the square, but couldn't find a green sedan that matched the one he'd been driving. *Why on earth would he be here, anyway? There had to be millions of short-haired, stocky white men in their fifties in the South.*

As if to prove that point, the door of the café opened, and a man fitting that description emerged, carrying a newspaper under his arm and a Styrofoam cup in his hand. From across the square, she couldn't quite make out his features; he could have been any of a thousand men, for sure. He didn't even glance her way, but instead strode off down the street in the opposite direction.

Quit imagining things and stick to business. Finding Jim right now was what was most important. She hopped back into her car and drove off to locate the Hunters' house.

Her directions took her along a main street, heading west from the square. The downtown shops gave way to large homes, many in antebellum style with columns and large plantation shutters. Understated signs for bed-and-breakfast inns hung unobtrusively in front of a few. Exquisitely maintained acres of landscaped yards gave the neighborhood a sense of well-ordered calm. After another block, the street changed a little. While the houses still seemed large, they weren't mansions, and they weren't quite as old. The lawns, though equally immaculate, were of a size more easily managed without a landscape crew.

She found the Hunter's address and pulled to the curb. She turned off the engine, studying the house. It was a pretty red brick place, surrounded by a manicured lawn outlined by a flowering border of small roses, irises and peonies. Two stories high, it had large casement windows and a steep slate roof. Its front left corner featured an octagonal tower that reached just above the top of the second floor. A parapet at the top, capped by a steep conical roof, gave it the look of a small castle. All it needed was a flag. How fun it must have been to grow up here—assuming they lived here when Jim was a boy. He could have spent hours pretending to be a knight or a king.

She glanced at her watch, almost 2:00. With any luck, a good time to catch them at home. She checked her hair in the mirror and smoothed her skirt as she emerged from the car. The street was quiet—no kids playing, no dogs barking, not even any other traffic on the road. Only the chirping birds and warm sunshine welcomed her.

Her heart fluttered as she walked up the walkway. She curled her toes as she pushed the doorbell. Its ring echoed inside.

Through the window beside the front door, she saw a young woman, probably in her early twenties, crossing the foyer to answer the bell. She wore jeans and a Clemson T-shirt, but had bare feet. Jim said he had no siblings. Was this a cousin? A friend? A…a…girlfriend?

The girl peeked through the door and, apparently deciding that Katie presented no threat, opened it. "Hi, can I help you?"

"I hope so." Katie smiled, hoping to look as friendly as possible. "I'm looking for Jim Hunter."

The girl frowned. "*Jim* Hunter?"

"Yes, Mr. Hunter's—I mean, Bailey Hunter's son."

The woman continued to frown, as if concentrating on a puzzle.

"Oh, I'm sorry. I must have the wrong house!" Katie exclaimed, her cheeks coloring in a blush.

"No." The girl shook her head. "This is the Hunters' house, all right. But they have two daughters, both married. They have don't have a son."

"This is *Bailey* Hunter's house? The attorney?"

"Yes."

"And you're telling me they don't have a son named Jim?"

"Look, I've worked in Mr. Hunter's firm for two years, and it's a small town. If he had another kid, I'd know. I'm just house-sitting for them right now while they're…away, but I know the family well." The girl crossed her arms and examined Katie more closely.

"But…" Katie stopped, at a loss for words. "I…I'm sorry. I'm looking for a Jim Hunter. I know he lives in Landrum, but I thought it was here. I guess I made a mistake." She took an unsteady step backward, as the girl's words took hold of her.

The girl reached out to her. "Are you okay?"

"Yes, yes. I'm fine. Thank you." Katie gathered herself, trying to think of what to do next.

"Sorry I can't help you. Hunter's a fairly common name around here, though. I'm sure you'll find the one you're looking for." She hesitated a moment and looked over her shoulder. "You need to use a phone or something?"

"No, no. Sorry to bother you." Katie turned and hurried back to the car, desperate to flee that house as fast as she could. She drove a couple of blocks, and then turned onto a side street and killed the engine. She sat there, heart racing, too surprised to do anything for a moment. Jim was not Bailey Hunter's son. He had lied not only to her about that, but apparently to everyone in Atlanta.

But if he wasn't the lawyer's son, who was he? And why did he lie about it?

A knot of tears crept up from her chest, but she struggled to force them down, taking deep breaths as she searched her mind for a rational explanation. There had to be one.

She decided to do a little investigating before she allowed herself to react further. First things first. Was he even *from* this town? She pulled out her smartphone and searched for the last name "Hunter" in Landrum, South Carolina. The search yielded a dozen listings. Cursing the small screen on her phone, she scrambled to get her bearings as she began to plot directions to each one.

Two were nearby, according to the online map, and she drove to find them. The first was only a few blocks away from the Bailey Hunter residence, She saw a young mother playing with two toddlers in the front yard. Katie watched as the woman watered a flower garden, periodically turning to squirt the children, who squealed with delight.

She rolled down her window. "Excuse me, but I'm looking for someone by the name of Jim Hunter. Would this be his residence?"

The woman nodded no and eyed Katie, casting a warning glance back to her children. "Sorry, I don't know of anyone by that name."

Katie waved her thanks and drove on. The next house lay a little farther from town. It wasn't nearly so well kept and had a "for rent" sign in front. It appeared empty, and no cars were parked in the drive. *Not likely.*

She checked the map on her phone for the next address. It appeared that if she stayed on this same road and followed it into the countryside, the next house wouldn't be too far.

The neighborhood fell away and in its wake, she saw rolling hills dotted with farms and the occasional cluster of low ranch houses. She slowed as she neared the address. Then she spotted it, a one-story brick ranch, rather nondescript, flying a string of Buddhist prayer flags between two oak trees. A number of contorted metal sculptures rose from the grass in front. A weathered post-and-rail fence separated the house and yard from the farmland beyond. To the right, a gravel drive led just past the house to a long, low shed with four cars parked inside. As her eyes scanned the shed, an involuntary gasp escaped her lips. All of the cars appeared to be vintage convertibles, including two Corvairs.

She'd never noticed cars much before, but a weekend in Porter's attention-grabbing wheels had at least made her recognize a Corvair. Neither of the two in the shed appeared to be in good shape. One was even up on blocks. Yet from the road at least, the shed looked tidy but dusty, as if no one had disturbed it in a long time.

She looked for Jim's Toyota, but she saw only the rear of an SUV sticking out from behind the house. She checked the name on this address again—J.S. Hunter. *J., as in Jim.* She pulled into the drive and parked a short distance from the road.

As she made her way toward the front door, she studied the sculptures in the yard. They appeared to have been fashioned mostly from old car parts. She spied what she thought was a muffler on one. On another, a side-view mirror caught the sunlight. Her curiosity about the house's occupants suppressed the prickling of nerves creeping up her neck. She knocked on the front door.

At first, she heard nothing inside, but then there was a rustle of movement and a woman's voice shouted, "Just a minute."

The handle turned, and she stood face-to-face with a pretty woman who appeared to be in her late forties. Her long, curly blonde hair, touched with gray, was bound up in a blue bandana. She wore overalls covered by a very worn long-sleeve man's dress shirt, both covered with paint splatters and smudges. Behind her, the doorway opened into a comfortable, but sparsely furnished living room. Bright colors burst from the large canvasses hanging on the walls, which gave the room a vibrant energy that drew Katie's eye. Music floated to her from somewhere in the back of the house. The woman said nothing, but raised her eyebrows, as if surprised and pleased at the same time.

Katie fought the urge to flee. She got the feeling that this woman was taking her all in—not just her appearance, but the confused young woman inside as well. "Um, hi," she said after a short pause. "My name is Katie Nelson, and I'm looking for someone named Jim Hunter. This wouldn't be his parents' house, by chance, um, would it?"

The woman smiled, a gleam of understanding in her eyes. "Ah, you must be the young woman from Atlanta. Yes, you've found the right place. I'm his mother." She held out her hand. "Camille Hartwell Hunter."

CHAPTER 36

Katie fought to make sense of it. This woman was so young compared to her own parents; it hardly seemed possible. But then she remembered the stories about Camille, a wild teenager who had run away at an early age and gotten pregnant. She must have been, what, sixteen or seventeen when she had Jim?

"Nice to meet you," Katie said, remembering her manners and taking Camille's hand.

"Jim's not here right now. He went to run an errand for me, but he'll be back shortly. I know he'll be glad to see you," she said. There was that knowing smile again.

"Oh, um, I'm not sure I can stay. I'm, uh…" *How do you tell someone that her son is a liar and that you don't want to see him, when you've obviously driven all this way to do so?*

Camille caught her confusion. She also caught Katie by surprise when she said, "I understand. He didn't tell you about us, did he?"

Katie shook her head.

"Come sit down for a minute. I think you deserve some answers."

Katie followed her to the couch and sat as instructed. Her heart climbed into her throat, then reached up to bang on her temples. She was afraid of what she might hear, but still desperately wanted to know.

"Will you have some tea?" Camille raised her eyebrows in invitation. "It's my own herbal recipe, all grown out back in my garden. Nothing illegal, though, I promise." She chuckled as Katie accepted.

Katie inspected the room more closely while she listened to the sounds of running water and a clattering of teacups beyond the living room wall. The paintings were all bright and dynamic, a combination of thick brush strokes and splatters, sophisticated, yet childlike at the same time.

On one wall Katie examined a few framed photos. There was Jim all right, next to Camille and a man she didn't recognize.

"Jim grew up in this house." Katie jumped as Camille breezed back into the room with a tray of fragrant tea. "His father James and I loved him very much—still do, of course. James was an auto mechanic and a sculptor and an all-around beautiful soul. I met him in San Francisco, and we bonded for life instantly."

"But I thought…"

"That Jim's father was Bailey Hunter?" Camille asked. "No. We aren't related to that family in any way, as far as I know. But they are part of Jim's story. Give me a moment and I'll explain what I can."

Katie nodded, her eyes growing wide, and sank onto the couch. She couldn't have left now if she tried. She had to know who Jim really was. As she took the teacup Camille offered, she watched her with renewed interest. Although she wore paint-spattered clothing, her posture was straight without appearing stiff and her bearing reflected her poise. On another woman, it might look somewhat prissy or regal, hinting at a childhood of strict training, but on her, it felt unforced and natural. She carried herself with confidence, but humility. Her eyes glowed with kindness.

Camille tilted her head toward a framed photograph on the end table next to Katie. "That's James," she said, with a little smile, her voice melodious, cultured.

Katie turned to look at the photo of a young couple in an embrace, cheek to cheek, as they mugged for the camera. The woman was Camille, with her golden curls cascading down her back and shoulders, a radiant smile on her face. The man was a younger version of the one on the wall—thin, with shaggy brown hair and a beard. He had the most soulful eyes that Katie had ever seen. She could see a little of Jim in both faces.

"I think Jim had a happy childhood," Camille continued. "He and his dad were best friends. They spent hours working on old cars and fixing them up. But when Jim got to be a teenager, he became more interested in material things, in money. That's not something James and I ever thought important, but I believe that you have to let a child go his own way, learn his own life.

"When Jim found out about my family, about the money I'd walked away from, he became furious. He said some hurtful things then, but I knew he'd eventually figure out that money is just an illusion when it comes to living a happy life. I had plenty of money growing up, but I can't remember any kind of happiness…" She paused as a shadow passed over her face.

"But it must have been difficult to just walk away from all that," Katie said.

"Difficult? No, not difficult at all. Perhaps I should explain about *my* father." She took a breath, held it, then let it out. "He had an enormous respect for wealth, but not much for human warmth. I suppose he might have loved my mother, but she died when I was just a baby, so I never saw them together.

"His obsession consumed him, and so he meant it to consume us as well. He reminded my brother and me every day how hard he had worked to build his fortune and how lucky we were because we'd inherit it someday."

She glanced around the living room, as if to remind herself of the present. Then she continued. "The problem was he attached so many strings to that inheritance. We had to do things *his* way, according to *his* plans. My father chose to measure his personal worth through the money he accumulated. He respected honor and integrity, but for us, he made it clear that his ultimate goal for us was to further increase the family fortune."

She refilled the teacups, then pointed to the paintings hanging in the room. "When I was growing up, all I wanted to do was paint. I loved art, but that wasn't what he had in mind for me. I was to become the star of Atlanta's social scene and marry well. There was no place for self-expression. I was to follow the rules and marry a man from a wealthy family."

She swept her arms wide and said, "Needless to say, my brother and I both rebelled. He escaped into drugs and ended up killing himself in a car crash, but I wasn't allowed to even mention that with my father. He became more and more obsessed with my every move, and we grew more and more at odds. Eventually, I just left."

She paused, staring into the middle distance with her cup frozen in front of her, then turned and gave Katie a soft smile as she took a sip. "It took me years to get over the anger I felt toward my father, to understand where he must have been coming from. When I finally returned to mend the fences, it was too late. He was very ill, and he wouldn't see me. I had his attorney make sure he knew I was married and had a baby boy, but apparently he didn't say anything when he heard the news. He died shortly thereafter. It didn't make me bitter; I just felt sorry for him. Here I had this wonderful child, the luckiest woman in the world, and he couldn't see the beauty in that."

"But he didn't change his will to keep Jim off the foundation board, did he?" Katie leaned toward Camille, but stopped herself from reaching out. It was clear that, despite her words, talking about her father still caused Camille some pain.

"That's true, he didn't. It's funny about the foundation. I always thought he created it out of spite or revenge. He had an attorney contact me when he founded it, to inform me that I'd have no claim of any sort on the estate. But the attorney said nothing about the rules for male heirs. My brother was already dead, so he must have meant to include my son, but I don't know if he made that provision before he knew about Jim or after."

"Oh, it must have been after, don't you think?" Katie grasped at the positive. "Maybe it was a peace offering."

"Maybe. But you'd have to know my father the way I did to understand why that's so difficult to believe."

"Money definitely changes people…"

"Well, that's certainly been my experience. I don't exactly believe that money is the root of all evil, as the saying goes, but it certainly can supplant the roots of happiness. Some families seem to manage just fine, but ours didn't do so well. All the money in the world can't replace time lost or love not given."

She gave Katie a pointed look. "The irony in all of this is that my father and I ended up on the same page about what to do with all that money." She chuckled, straightening her shoulders and taking a deep breath. "Even if he hadn't disowned me, I would have given it all away as soon as it was mine to give. It's doing more good now than it would have if I'd got hold of it years ago."

"You wouldn't have wanted it for Jim?"

"Oh, no!" Camille dismissed the idea with a wave of her hand. "The things James and I wanted for Jim had nothing to do with money. We both learned that love is measured just as much by what you give *up* for your children as what you give *to* them. We both loved the freedom of the nomadic lifestyle we shared when we met. We saw so many beautiful places and met some fascinating people. But we realized it was no life for a child. So we settled in here to give Jim a home and some roots. James' family all live around here, and they love Jim, too. We wanted him to have a solid base to start from as he figured out who he was."

"But you didn't tell him he was a Hartwell?"

"No, not for a while. I wanted him to know how to value himself in ways beyond money. Besides, he was a Hartwell in name only. No one in this family has a claim to that fortune any more. I had no aunts, uncles or cousins, so *you*, my dear, have more connection with the Hartwell fortune than I do."

Katie thought for a moment that Camille was the least bit bitter, but the woman's laughing eyes and warm smile belied that assumption. She truly seemed to have no regrets about the path she had chosen and the wealth she had turned her back on. *But what about Jim?* "Jim didn't necessarily agree with your thinking." It was more an observation than a question.

"No, he was deeply upset—and I have to admit, I didn't see that coming. I still don't know where he got the idea that the money was that important. Maybe that's just what we teach our children as a society, despite our individual efforts as parents." She stared at the photo of her and her husband. "James didn't like the way Jim talked to me. He was adamant that he not go down that road. They started to fight, and Jim started spending a lot of time away from the house. He started hanging around with the wealthy kids at high school, talking about going to law school to become rich himself. He worshipped Bailey Hunter, a big attorney here in town. He even dated the eldest daughter—Meghan was her name—during his junior and senior years. That ended badly, though. I think she realized Jim was perhaps more interested in her money and in impressing her father than he was in her. Smart girl."

She paused and looked at Katie with a mix of resignation and dread. "He won't want me to tell you this, but it got ugly at one point. She claimed Jim tried to assault her. Attempted rape, they called it. He was innocent, of course, and the charges were never officially filed, but it devastated him."

Attempted rape? Alarm bells went off in Katie's head and she sloshed a splash of tea out of her cup. She looked down to dab at her skirt with a napkin as she struggled to maintain her composure and pay attention.

"After that, Jim just brooded in his room and fought with his father until he left for college. While Jim was at Clemson, things got a little better between them. I thought they might finally make peace. Then Jim announced he was going to go to law school in Atlanta. James refused to help him out with tuition, and they pretty much quit speaking. When Jim was in his last year of law school, James was killed. Drunk driver."

"Oh!" Katie's eyes flew open wide. "I'm so sorry. I had no idea."

"No, it's okay. I figured Jim hadn't told you. He was still angry with his father after the accident. When he decided to stay in Atlanta after law school, other lawyers at his firm made the assumption that his Hunter name and Landrum address meant he was related to Bailey Hunter—and Jim chose not to correct them. It makes me sad that he sometimes pretends the beautiful, deep relationship we both had with James never happened…It makes me sad that he doesn't honor that…but like I said, I'm not going to push him. He'll eventually find the right path."

"But what about you?" Katie couldn't help but ask. "Why did you play along with his story?"

Camille laughed: a bright tinkling noise that reminded Katie of a cool breeze on a hot summer day. "Oh, honey, it's not like I've ever had the opportunity to meet anyone from Jim's life in Atlanta. He's gone to great lengths to keep his world there and his world here completely separate. I don't even know where he lives."

Katie scowled.

"It's okay," Camille continued, taking Katie's hand. "Like I said, each of us has to figure out our own path. I always figured Jim would turn around, and I think maybe now he's starting to." Her vibrant blue eyes gave Katie a look of approval. "You're a positive force for him."

Maybe, but it's a one-way street. Who was the real Jim now? The man she had come to know and almost love? Or the man with the attempted rape background who had deceived everyone, including *her*? She struggled for something to say. "I'm sorry that Jim and his father never got the chance to reconcile."

"Oh, Jim's slowly coming around," said Camille. "He spends a lot of time out in that shed when he's here. He and his dad used to spend hours out there working together. Jim knows a good bit about cars himself. I think maybe his turning point came when the car he inherited was stolen in Atlanta."

"Oh?" She answered without thinking, something to say. Inside, her stomach tightened into knots as her mind whirled with the story she'd just heard. It blindsided her. She'd been completely fooled, just like everyone else. No, even more so.

"It was about three years ago, I think." Camille continued. "Not too long after he'd started with that law firm. I know it must have been a crushing blow for him, even though he said it was no big deal. He and his father worked on that car every day after school when he was younger. Every day. And it was a beautiful car, it really was." She looked wistful, her mind rolling back into the past. "I remember how much fun they had together out in that shed. They rebuilt it from nothing. When they finished, it was perfect. A 1965 Corvair convertible. One-hundred-forty-six horsepower flat six. Cherry red. A once-in-a-lifetime kind of car."

Katie gasped, placing a hand on her stomach to keep it from leaping out of her throat. That wasn't Porter's car that took them to Highlands. It was Jim's. What *else* hadn't he told her?

She had to get out of there, *now*: get away from this house, away from Camille Hartwell Hunter, away from everything having to do with Jim. "I…I'm sorry. You've been very nice to share all this, but I…I really need to go," she said, almost dropping her teacup back on the tray before standing abruptly and turning toward the door.

"Oh, please stay! Jim will be back soon! I know he wanted to tell you all of this. He told me he had invited you up here this weekend to explain it all!"

"I don't think there's anything left to explain." Katie spoke in even tones, forcing control over her voice while the emotional torrents raged beneath the surface. "At least, not to me."

Camille sighed. "Oh, Katie, if there's one thing I've learned in my life, it's the importance of forgiveness. I never got it from my father, and I never gave it either until it was too late. The same thing happened to Jim, but he's starting to understand it all. He's not a bad person…"

"I'm sorry," Katie said, stumbling toward the front door. "But I don't know *what* kind of person he is."

She ran out the door and jumped into her Honda. Gritting her teeth, she backed out of the driveway, tires spinning and gravel flying. Her temples pounded as she slammed into drive and screeched away. In the rearview mirror, Camille stood stock-still in the yard among her husband's sculptures, her hand raised in a wave—or perhaps a blessing of peace?

CHAPTER 37

Katie drove back toward Atlanta, hounded by thoughts that raged as fast as, maybe faster than, her car. Despite all the answers she'd received, some to questions she hadn't even asked, the pieces refused to make sense. For two hours, as she drove through South Carolina, she turned everything over and over again in her mind. The red convertible was Jim's, not Porter's. But everyone in Highlands who had described the driver had described Porter, not Jim.

Perhaps they shared it. She pictured them at a bar somewhere, privately laughing over their drinks about the women they'd seduced with that cherry-red ragtop. Maybe they shared more than just the car, too. Details from the past few months slammed into her head like a thunderbolt, creating a clear picture. How quickly Jim took on Jorge's case after the fire. How he continually pushed Katie away from making accusations about Porter. When she finally made it clear that she knew something was up, how he used his so-called "ethics" to close her out. How convenient.

Maybe Porter and Jim concocted this whole thing together. They had sabotaged Jorge and then tried to ensure his silence, should he ever suspect anything, with $10 million. Jorge suspected Jim, she realized now. He had tried in his way to warn her, but she had misunderstood and followed her heart deeper into Jim's deceit.

Then there was the assault on Angel. Jim had been accused of attempted rape before, as a boy. As a boy! Angel was attacked in a Midtown building. Could it have been? Is he that kind of devious monster? Her mind simply couldn't connect the gentle, patient lover she knew him to be with someone who could attempt rape. But then again, she really didn't know him at all, did she?

Another wave of nausea surged forward and she gripped the steering wheel with all her might. She may have slept with someone who was a violent criminal. "My God," she breathed. For the first time, she realized that she might herself be in danger. A cold sweat broke through her skin. She pushed the accelerator as much as she dared; she wanted to get home and lock herself in her carriage house.

The evening sun had dipped below the horizon, and a deep purple twilight descended as Katie crossed the border into Georgia. The other cars on the road changed from solid forms into pairs of headlights and taillights, either zooming past her or disappearing in her rearview mirror as she passed them.

She needed to hear a friendly voice to calm down and think straight. She could call Rita. Best to push the buttons when there weren't too many other cars around. She checked her rearview mirror as she reached for her phone. A car approached on the left to pass, so she slowed to let it clear before pulling up Rita's number.

All of a sudden, her Honda was spinning in circles across the highway. She sat glued behind the wheel, but she could do nothing except watch, frozen in shock, as dark shapes and light flashes spun across her windshield.

For a long, terrifying moment, the Honda skidded out of control. In slow motion, the car clattered over the shoulder and bumped sideways through tall grass and dirt.

A thought came to her, and she slammed her foot down on the brake pedal, half-expecting it to do no good. The car bucked once, tilting up on the two left wheels, before coming to a stop.

With a shaking hand, she reached forward and turned off the ignition. She concentrated on taking deep breaths, wiggling her toes and fingers and turning her head from left to right. She felt no pain, but had the strange sensation of watching herself from above.

She heard the sound of car tires on gravel from somewhere behind her and then a voice. It seemed so far away.

"Hey! Are you all right?" A young-looking man, maybe a teenager, appeared at her driver's side window. He knocked once. "Ma'am?"

She peeled her fingers from the steering wheel and reached to open her car door. The young man, seeing her movement, opened the door from the outside. She tried to climb out but discovered she couldn't move. Something was holding her back. Oh God! Did she have some kind of spinal injury?

"You gotta unbuckle your seatbelt, ma'am," he said, seeing her struggle. "Can I hep you?"

She nodded, too frightened to move.

He stretched across her and unhooked the shoulder belt at her hip. Then he offered her a hand and helped her climb out, supporting her weight as she tested her limbs. "Yes, ma'am. Yes, ma'am. Doin' good, ma'am. You sure you're okay?"

She stood there, shaking. "I…I…Yes, I think so," she managed to say.

"I saw that car sideswipe you, ma'am, but I didn't get no plates."

Sideswipe? For a moment, she couldn't remember what happened. She started from the beginning. "I was trying to get my phone…" she murmured.

"No ma'am. I saw the whole thing. It were the other driver's fault, ma'am. He sideswiped you. I can call the cops if you want." He cocked his head at her. "You sure you're okay, ma'am?" His eyes swept her up and down, looking for evidence of some injury. "I got some coffee in my truck. You look like you could use some. Would you like that, ma'am?" He gestured up the small slope to the shoulder of the highway, where she saw a large pickup truck, complete with yellow flashing lights on the top.

She nodded, still in a daze. Her car, she realized, had skidded into the wide center median, but she had no idea whether it faced north or south. In the space of several minutes, she had lost her place in the world. It had been flung off into the distance as her car had spun. She followed the man up to his truck, where he pulled out a thermos of coffee and poured her a cup. The warmth helped ground her feet and clear her head. "Thank you," she said.

"Yes, ma'am. Mah pleasure, ma'am. Glad you're okay," he smiled and pointed to the name embroidered on the front of his shirt. "Name's Rob. Work security at the outlet mall in Commerce." He tilted his head in the direction his truck was facing. "I was on my way to my shift when I saw what happened. I still cain't believe it ma'am; you don' look like you even got a scratch."

"I really appreciate your stopping," she said, feeling better and stronger with every passing second. "I feel much better now, but I'm not sure about my car."

"Yes ma'am. Want me to take a look, ma'am?"

"Please."

He reached into his truck and pulled out a huge flashlight. Then he left her standing on the shoulder as he waded into the grass.

As she watched him check for damage and pop the hood, Katie noticed a highway patrolman pull off into the median strip on the opposite side, lights flashing. The sight of the officer sent a wave of relief through her—so much so that tears began to form in the corners of her eyes. She wiped them away with the back of her hand.

"Anyone hurt?" she heard the officer ask. He and Rob spoke for a moment, and Rob pointed up to where she stood by his truck. Not wanting to cause any concern, she raised her arm and waved. The officer came over and took her report, his large frame so reassuring that she had to refrain from hugging him.

After some minutes passed, with traffic backing up on both sides of the highway, she heard Rob start the engine of her Honda, then ease it up the bank and onto the shoulder. She heard a distinctive clunking sound as the car made its way through the grass. Once on the shoulder, Rob turned on the car's hazard lights and came over to where she stood with the patrolman.

"First, I'll need to pull off a hubcap, ma'am. Then I think I can wire your bumper up enough to clear yer tires. You got one heckuva dent in your driver's side, but she still runs," he said, as much to the patrolman as to Katie. The officer nodded.

Rob returned to her car to remove the damaged hubcap. She groaned when she saw the damage to the side of her car. It started in her driver's side front quarter panel and worked its way down the full length of her car. She was surprised that the door still worked, although it protested loudly every time Rob forced it open.

"Yes ma'am. You're good to go now. You need to get her to a body shop tomorrow though, ma'am. Some uh the fixes I did won't hold up fer long."

"Thank you so much, Rob. You're a saint. I really don't know what I would have done without you."

"Oh please don' mention it, ma'am. Part uh my job." He hooked his left thumb in his belt and stuck the fingers of his right hand into his shirt pocket, producing a card that he handed her with obvious pride. In raised letters it said:

Rob Whitmire. Security Officer. America's Outlets. Commerce, GA

Seeing the phone number and address on the card, she decided she would call Rob's boss the next day and praise his assistance. Maybe she'd also send him a box of cookies. *And I swear I will never, ever make fun of a mall cop again!*

A few minutes later after another "thank you" and "good-bye" from Katie and a half-dozen more "yes ma'ams" from Rob, and she pulled back onto the highway with the patrol car and the pickup truck close behind. Both vehicles followed her as far as the exit for Commerce, fifteen miles down the road. Then, apparently satisfied that Katie and the car would make it home, they turned off the highway and left her to finish the trip alone.

More than anything in the world, Katie wanted to be home. She fought to focus only on driving, giving wide berth to other cars until the volume of traffic inside Atlanta's perimeter made that impossible. As she regained the safety of the city lights, a growing fear joined her anger, frustration and betrayal. Maybe that collision was no accident. But who would want to hurt her that badly? Jim?

Despite the anger and disappointment she felt toward him, she could not believe he would purposefully put her in danger. She couldn't have imagined his gentleness and sincerity from those moments in Highlands. He couldn't have been faking then, could he? And he was so upset when she nearly fell…or was that a lie, too? A tremor ran down her spine. She stared into highway ahead, willing the lights of the city to emerge on the horizon.

What about Porter? He was loud and brash, but even he wasn't so ruthless as to cause her bodily harm. Threats and intimidation were more his style.

But if not one of them, then who? Chris? It wasn't impossible, but exceedingly unlike him. Jorge? She couldn't even process that thought.

It was after midnight when she arrived back at the carriage house. She had to brace her feet and shove her shoulder against the sagging car door to force it open, which it did with a reluctant groan. Her legs wobbled as she got out of the car, but she somehow managed to get her bag up the steps. She collapsed in a heap on her couch, where Babka jumped into her lap. Petting his long, soft coat helped Katie calm down.

"I need to think, fat kitty," she said to Babka, settling him on a cushion before she got up to pace. Just as she hit her stride in front of the coffee table, her cell phone rang. She saw Jim's number and froze. Then the stories, the tension and the trauma of the past 24 hours all welled up in a huge wave of anger and hurt. She didn't need to talk to Jim ever again. She wouldn't. She turned the phone off.

For the rest of that night and throughout the following day, Sunday, her mind was a blur. She slept better than she would have expected—the stress of the day taking its toll. When she awoke, every muscle in her body was sore, but she could find no bumps or bruises from the crash.

She ate barely at all. Instead, she paced. What could she prove? Whom should she tell? What would happen if she did?

Jim was right about one thing. She only had accusations and scattered evidence. No hard proof. She could share her suspicions with Louise, but she'd insist on full evidence before taking the matter to the board. Besides, given the Viva Latina grant's unanimous (and private) approval, there could be other board members involved in this as well.

She could go to the police or to the arson investigators perhaps, but that might blast the whole thing out of the back room and into the papers. She couldn't do that until, again, she had proof. And if she were wrong…

On Monday morning, weak and exhausted, she called in sick to work.

By now, the enormity of her wounded career and lost love hovered over her like a thunderhead. She could no longer work at the Hartwell Foundation, for reporting her suspicions would more than likely get her pushed out, while pretending everything was fine and dandy simply wasn't something she could manage. Given what she'd learned and the events of Saturday night, it quite possibly was no longer safe for her.

And damn it, even though she hated Jim and the lies he had told her, she mourned the loss of what had felt like the real thing. How could she have been so stupid and gullible…*again*? Jim's betrayal felt just as bad—no, worse—than Michael's, and the empty hole of loneliness she had tried to ignore after Michael had now grown to a yawning chasm.

The pity party didn't last long. Her mind wandered back to the clinic fire, the dead woman and Porter's—or Jim's—potential role.

She needed to talk it through, and Jorge was the only other person who was involved enough to understand. Reaching out to him would seal her fate in terms of working at the Hartwell Foundation, but she couldn't give a damn about that now.

She turned on her phone and called him, but once again got only voicemail. She didn't leave a message. As she started to turn the phone off again, she noticed a voicemail waiting. She called and was relieved to hear Jorge's voice, but he sounded urgent.

"Katie, please listen carefully. I have just learned that the attack on Angel happened in the Kinsey & McMillan offices in Midtown. We still do not know who the perpetrator was, but I think you should be very, very careful. I…just wanted you to know. Please be careful."

She looked at the phone, mouth agape, as if waiting for it to explain. There were dozens of attorneys who worked in that office, but only one that she knew of who had been accused of attempted rape in the past.

She had no idea how long she sat there as the news soaked into her head. When Camille had first told her the story, she couldn't quite process the idea of Jim as a rapist—in fact, the idea made her ill—but the evidence kept mounting up against him in too many ways. When the phone startled her back to the present, she answered it without thinking.

"Katie!" Jim's voice sounded desperate.

Damn! She cursed herself for not turning the phone off again after listening to the voicemail.

"I have nothing to say to you." She prayed that the ice in her voice masked the quiver that shook her body. She stretched a finger toward the "end" button.

"Wait! I have to talk to you. It's important. I need to tell you about…"

Beep went the phone as she ended the call. She turned it off before he could call again.

"There's nothing you could tell me that I'd believe," she said aloud. She sank into the couch and turned on the television to distract herself. There was nothing on, mostly sitcom reruns and game shows. She settled in to watch a tear-jerker of a chick flick on a movie channel, but found that instead of constantly wiping her eyes, she was fighting to keep them open. She fell into an exhausted sleep.

When she awoke, it was dark outside and inside as well. The only light came from the television set, which she had left on. She switched it to the news channel, turned on a couple of lamps and padded to the kitchen to pour herself a bowl of cereal.

Her mind felt hazy, yet teetering at the edge of it was the problem of what to do next, how to work herself out of this state of limbo. There must be some missing piece of the puzzle. What was it?

Something else pricked its way through the noise in her mind, pulling on her sleeve and demanding attention. What was that on the television? She stepped back into the living room with her cereal. The newscast showed a scene from somewhere in the Middle East. Armored vehicles faced off with a crowd of protesters or rebels of some kind, a flaming building to one side.

"The explosion is said to have killed two civilians and injured several more," the reporter said.

It was something else. What was on before that? She picked up the remote and used the system's DVR feature to rewind the scene. As she watched, people in the crowd hurled flaming objects toward the building, and the reporter said, "A protest in the West Bank today turned deadly as demonstrators hurled stones and Molotov cocktails at a police headquarters…"

Molotov cocktails. She heard Chris's voice as clearly as if he were in the room with her: *It's not a drink…He was referring to something explosive…*

She rewound the news report again and again, looking closely at the flaming objects flying across the screen. They looked like glass bottles stuffed with fire. They *were* glass bottles.

Her eyes fell on the empty milk bottle on her coffee table, and her eyes grew wide. *They said that it looked like two separate "incendiary devices" came through a back window.* Jim had told her that. She even remembered him making little air quotes with his fingers. And two bottles were missing from the garage in Highlands.

She rushed to open her laptop, jumped onto the Internet and searched for "Molotov cocktail." There it was, a simple bomb made by pouring something as common as gasoline or kerosene into a glass bottle and inserting a piece of cloth as a wick.

Katie stared at the screen, hands shaking as they reached for her hair. Such a device would have been easy for Porter or Jim to make and easy enough to smash through the clinic's glass windows. The fact that she had seen Porter that night in Atlanta meant he could have thrown the bombs. It couldn't have been Jim, though, could it? After all, she had been with him that night.

Then another thought sent an icy cold knife down her spine. She had left Jim's apartment by 2:30 a.m. on the morning of the fire. He had called her at 7:30. Five hours. Plenty of time for him to make the short drive downtown and start the fire. He wouldn't have even had to get all the way home. He could have called her that morning from anywhere.

"Oh my God!" she wailed. "I'm his freaking alibi!"

But why had he been so insistent on keeping her away from Porter? And Jorge? Jim had repeatedly inserted himself between her and two potential suspects. Was he protecting her or himself? Or someone else?

Would people assume she had been in on it as well? After all, Jim had insisted that she take a bottle as a souvenir. Her prints were all over it. Still, it was odd that he'd allow her such free access to evidence.

But that was a minor detail. The main thing was that she was absolutely certain now that Porter and Jim were somehow responsible for the clinic fire. Her breath came rapidly, and she resumed her pacing to try to calm down and think. What should she do? Whom should she call?

Rita. Of course. Rita worked at a law firm, and even though Katie didn't know exactly what she'd do next, she was certain that sooner or later she'd need a lawyer.

So even though it was late, she turned her phone back on and began dialing her friend's number. She'd pressed only half the buttons when a pounding on her carriage house door made her jerk. Her phone slipped from her hand and crashed to the floor, where it skidded out of reach under the sofa.

CHAPTER 38

"Katie? Katie, please open the door," a man's voice yelled.

She froze. It was a deep voice, not Jim's but someone else's, familiar somehow, yet different.

"Katie, it's Guy Porter. Please, I need your help."

Her heart began to hammer. She should call the police. Quietly, she dropped down to her hands and knees to retrieve her phone, feeling around blindly under the sofa. As she searched, her shoulder bumped the coffee table just enough to send her spoon rattling out of her cereal bowl, where she had left it precariously balanced.

The pounding stopped. There was a brief silence, and then Porter's voice again, calmer this time: "Katie, look, I know you don't like me, and you have good reason not to, but I'm here about Jim. He's not who you think he is. He's not who *I* thought he was. I think he's lost it. He's gone over the edge. The people he paid to start that fire are coming after him, and he's desperate."

What? She now realized what made Porter's voice sound so different. Was he *crying*? She got up from the floor and approached the door. Her senses were on high alert, but she was desperate to know more. "What are you talking about?"

"The fire. Look, Katie, I know you thought it was me. I even know you saw me on the night of the fire. I *was* down there, only I was trying to stop it. I was trying to get to Jim's people before they started it." He paused, and then said with a muffled sob, "But I was too late."

"What do you mean?" After making sure the safety chain was secure, she unbolted the door and opened it a tiny bit. She needed to see his face.

It wasn't pretty. Sweat glistened on his forehead, and his hair looked disheveled, as if he'd been running his hand through it over and over. The tear streaks were easy to see on his cheeks.

"Please, let me explain," he said, eyes wide, pleading. "I'm not proud of the part I played in some of this, but I want to make it right, even if I lose everything. I know you don't trust me. I know I treated you badly, but I need your help now."

"Why don't you go to the police?" She pushed the door forward, minimizing the opening to a mere sliver.

"I plan on it, but I wanted to make sure you knew the whole story first. I know Jim hurt you with his lies. He fooled me too. I want to make sure you know everything before it all becomes public." Then he peered through the sliver in the doorway. "And I wanted to make sure you were okay. Enough people have been hurt."

"Who ran me off the road?" She studied his face for a response.

"Wha…? When?" He hesitated. It sounded as if he were genuinely surprised. "Oh, Katie. That must have been Jim's doing, too. He's not who he says he is, and he's got other people working with him, including…" He paused for a breath. "Dr. Ramirez."

"What?" *That couldn't be true.* "How are they working together? What do you mean? Why…"

"For the money, of course." Porter sounded matter of fact, as if it were the most obvious answer in the world. And as he told his story, she realized that it was indeed quite obvious.

"Jim wanted to get as much out of the Hartwell Foundation as he could. He never got over the fact that his grandfather disinherited him. His father's not even a lawyer, like he claims."

That was true. Jim must have been lying to Porter as well.

"Jim convinced Dr. Ramirez to work with him. They arranged for the fire so Dr. Ramirez could get the insurance money; then Jim pushed through the grant. He plans to take his cut through fake legal fees. I didn't figure out what they were up to until after the grant was approved."

"Why didn't you say something then?"

"There was no hard evidence." Through the sliver in the doorway, she saw him hesitate and look away. In a hushed tone, he added, "Plus, Jim has something on me I'd rather not discuss." He turned back at the crack in the door. "But now I don't have a choice. Look, could I at least come in so I don't have to share my dark secrets out here in front of the neighbors?"

There were no neighbors who could see him on her stoop, she knew, but she felt sorry for him, tears and sweat mingling on his clammy face. Letting him into her apartment went against all of her instincts, but they hadn't been so accurate lately, had they?

She was about to suggest that she meet him in a few minutes at a neighborhood coffee house when Porter, sensing her hesitation, threw his massive shoulder against the door. The safety chain snapped instantly, nearly catching her eye.

"Thanks," said Porter, pushing through the threshold and forcing her backwards toward the living room. "I knew you'd see it my way." In a flash, his expression transformed from tearful and penitent to smug and snarling.

Her throat went dry and her heart hammered at her rib cage.

"Lots of people know I played football. Very few know I was also a great actor. You've been creating some fas-cinating stories about me, young lady. In fact, you've been incredibly right about almost all your suspicions. Your mistake was sharing them with Jim. Oh, I know he's not been quite truthful about his past, but he left out one really important detail. I *own* him. He's basically my bitch on the foundation board and in the firm. All I have to do is snap my fingers, and he'll be absolutely nothing in this town—or anywhere else—ever again."

Still backing away, she cast about the apartment for something she could use to defend herself. A kitchen knife? A frying pan?

He continued his advance toward her. "Maybe you started to suspect something after your little visit to his mom. Nice lady. Jim told me all about your trip this afternoon. Really wasn't such a good idea to go up there."

With Porter blocking the door, she mentally swept through her apartment for another way out. Had she left the bedroom window open? It was close enough to the dogwood tree that she might be able to jump and climb down. If she hadn't left it open, though, she was trapped, unless she could think of a way to stall him long enough to raise the sash and get through. She began to inch that way.

"Uh-uh, you can't leave right now." He lunged at her. He was surprisingly fast for his size and girth. His powerful hand clamped tight around her arm, making her cry out in pain.

"Let me go!" She struggled to wrench herself away.

"Oh no." He grabbed her other arm. "You need to listen to what I have to say. You need to understand something about life, missy. The fact is, I'm the one with the money, and that means I'm the one with the power. I have the power to make people's little dreams come true or to tell them to go to hell. I have the power to take *what* I want, *who* I want, *when* I want. Your job was easy. Hell, I even told you flat out. All you had to do was be *loyal*. How fucking hard is that?" He shook his head, as if stunned by her disobedience. "But nooo. You couldn't do it, could you? You had to mess with things. Well, I'm not going to let some little bitch like you fuck it up for me."

His mouth contorted into an evil grin. "You see, it takes a special perspective to understand how to use money and power effectively. Like with your precious little clinic. I got what I wanted, and that spic doctor got a brand-new building. Everybody wins—until you start digging around and fucking it up."

"But it's not your money!" She spat out the words despite the fear that gripped her as tightly as his hands.

"The hell it's not!" he bellowed. "I decide how it's spent, how it's invested and who gets to play. Little shits like you just get in the way!"

He pushed her backwards, hard, knocking her into the coffee table. The cereal bowl, the spoon and the milk bottle rattled and fell over, then rolled onto the floor.

Porter's glance followed the sound, and she took that instant to make a run for the bedroom.

"Get back here, you fucking bitch!"

He caught up with her at the bedroom door. He grabbed a fistful of her hair from behind and twisted one arm cruelly up behind her back. Then he crushed her breastbone into the doorframe, looking past her at her unmade bed.

"Is that how you want to play it? Maybe we'll have time for that," he said with a low chuckle as he pressed his body against her back, "but first, you've got some explaining to do."

She shuddered, wondering if it had been Porter, rather than Jim, who attacked Angel.

Keeping his grip on her hair and sharpening the twist on her arm so that she cried out again, he wrestled her back into the living room to where the milk bottle lay on the floor.

"Now, you can start by telling me where that came from. That's not the kind of thing one just finds in the grocery store, now is it?"

Her mind raced. "I found it at an antique store," she said through ragged breaths. "I needed a new vase."

"Bullshit!" he screamed. He whirled her around and slapped her hard across the face. "You got that from *my* house! *My* house!"

Pain slammed into her cheek as she scrambled to keep her footing. "It's not your house for long!" She knew she was in deep trouble, but she couldn't help herself. "Your wife is taking it back."

He registered surprised, but then his fury intensified. "What the hell do you know about my wife? She's not taking *anything*! Do you hear me? Why do you fucking bitches always think you know everything?"

With a scream of rage, his face turning purple, Porter lunged forward, grabbing her hard around the neck and squeezing with both hands. She struggled against his grip, but was no match for his brute strength.

Her lungs began to burn and her head spun. As her vision went dim, she heard a scream followed by a loud crash. Then she felt a blinding pain on the side of her head just before everything went dark and silent.

CHAPTER 39

As through thick cotton gauze, noises began to penetrate the silence. She heard voices, although none she recognized, and the sound of a chair scraping the floor. She stirred and opened her eyes, blinking as a bright light—the sun?—shone from above.

"Wha…?" She wanted to ask, but a sharp pain in her throat cut off her words.

"There you are. You're all right now; you're safe. Here, drink a little water."

She turned her head, grimacing at the pain in her neck, to a woman with a friendly, pleasant face. The woman handed her some water in a paper cup.

She took a tentative sip. It hurt to swallow, but the water helped. "Where am I?" she whispered. Her head felt fuzzy and throbbed all along one side.

"You're in the hospital, honey, but you're going to be just fine," the woman said.

Katie noticed that the woman's nametag said *Nelson*. "That's my name, too," she said, her voice hoarse. "I'm Katie Nelson, and I…" Her muscles tightened as memories of the past few days came flooding in. Jim had betrayed her. Porter had tried to kill her. She struggled to sit upright.

Nurse Nelson placed a comforting—and firm—hand on her shoulder. "Shh, shhhh…it's okay," she said in a reassuring tone. "You're safe. Do you remember what happened?"

Katie nodded. She would never forget.

"The police caught the man who attacked you," the nurse said. "He beat you up pretty good, and you got a big bump on the head when he dropped you, but he won't bother you anymore." She removed her hand when Katie stopped struggling. "The police have been waiting to ask you some questions. I always think they should wait a little longer, but you know how they are. They've kept insisting. Do you feel up to talking to them?"

Katie nodded again, reaching her hand up to feel the painful marks on her throat. Oh yes, she'd definitely talk to the police.

The nurse patted her shoulder and stepped to the door. She spoke quietly to someone in the hallway, and then stood to one side as two officers entered the room. The first—a rather handsome, older African-American man—wore a suit with his badge on a lanyard around his neck. A dark grey fedora perched on his head.

The Hat Squad.

The other, younger officer was in uniform. Tall and slender, he walked with a stiff gait, as if uncertain how to behave in such a situation.

"Good morning, ma'am," said the plainclothesman. "I'm Detective Tate and this is Officer Perrin. I know you've been through a rough ordeal; please excuse our interruption." He looked her over carefully as if memorizing every detail. "You should know that we've apprehended the man responsible for this, and he's given us a confession. We just need to get a statement from you, if you feel up to it."

She nodded and told them her side of the story as best she could. The detective asked a few specific questions, and she had a few of her own. Porter had confessed to setting the fire, so she merely had to provide the supporting details. She confirmed that she had seen Porter in Atlanta less than an hour after the time the arson investigators determined the fire was set. She explained how she and Jim had discovered the old milk bottles in Highlands and how she had begun to put it all together when Porter came to her apartment.

The detective asked how Porter had gained entry to her apartment, what he had said to her and where he had injured her. It was more difficult reliving the incident than she thought it would be. She felt helpless and afraid all over again. She began to cry.

Then she thought of Angel. "Did Porter confess to attacking the woman who died?"

He looked surprised. "Attacked? No ma'am. We have no report of an attack. Do you know that he attacked the deceased woman?"

No, she realized, she didn't know, and she couldn't send the police in search of Angel's cousin either. There would never be a case. She would never know for sure who attacked Angel, Porter or Jim or someone else. Just as she would never know for sure whether or not Jim was involved—or whether or not she could ever really trust him. She sighed and shook her head "no" in answer to the detective's question.

"I know this is difficult, ma'am," he said, perhaps taking her expression of despair as one of fear. "But the good news is, because of the perpetrator's confession, you won't have to tell this story in court. He'll go away for arson and felony murder for a long, long time. Once we finish here, you can get on with your life."

What life? She almost smiled at the absurdity of it all. Would she still have a job at the foundation, or anywhere in the nonprofit world, after this became a public scandal?

"Thank you for your time, ma'am," the detective continued. "Your information corroborates what we got from the man who rescued you. He's been very helpful."

The man who rescued her? She threw a quizzical look at the detective. She had assumed the police had somehow rescued her.

The detective caught her look and added, "Mr. Hunter. He's spent the whole night giving us his statement and confirming Mr. Porter's activities leading up to the attack. He's been pacing out there in the hallway for hours, waiting for you to wake up." He pointed toward the door.

"Jim?" She had difficulty forming the word.

"Yes, ma'am. He's the one who called us about the attack. He was the first one on the scene—and it's a good thing he arrived when he did."

Her heart leapt. Jim had saved her! He made sure that the police knew about Porter! He wasn't in league with Porter after all...

"Would you like us to send him in, ma'am?"

She hesitated, then nodded yes.

The detective pulled out a couple of business cards and placed them with a snap on her nightstand. "Here's my card. The boys at the office may need to follow up on a few details, but you can always get a hold of me, anytime. The other card is for a good therapist, in case you want help with your recovery, psychologically, from the attack. Well, good luck to you, ma'am."

She stared at the cards while the policemen left the room. *I might have more to recover from, psychologically, than just Porter's attack.*

There was a tentative knock at the door, and she raised her eyes to see Jim in the doorway. His suit looked like he'd slept in it, if he'd slept at all. His eyes were ringed in red. "May I come in?" He appeared cautious. With his wrinkled clothes and mussed-up hair, he looked almost feral.

She nodded yes and covered her throat with her hand.

"Good God!" he said, seeing her lying there. He glanced to the ceiling and rubbed his shoulders before he gazed down on her again, more composed this time. "I can't tell you how happy I am to see you."

"Uh-huh." She knew she probably looked horrendous. "I want a mirror."

Jim dashed out and returned a moment later with a tiny compact mirror. She angled it in all different directions as she studied the bruises on her face and throat and a taped-up gash on her temple. For once, she was glad that she couldn't see her whole face. The bits and pieces made her feel queasy enough.

"I guess I don't look so hot, huh?"

"You look absolutely beautiful to me."

She pursed her lips and glared at him. "Really."

"Look, Katie, I know I have a lot to explain. I didn't tell you the whole truth about my background. I lied about who my father was…to everybody. But everything you've seen since we started dating is the real me. I was gonna tell you—that's why I asked you to go to meet my mom—but then when we had that fight, I thought maybe there was no point. When Mom said you showed up at the house, I realized whether we stayed together or not, I had to set things right and tell you the truth, and I had to do the right thing about Porter."

"What *did* you know about Porter?"

He let out a breath and stepped to her bedside.

She knew that if she reached out her hand, he would take it, but she kept it next to her, fingering the blanket at her side.

"I knew he was a manipulating asshole. I've always known that. He's had a thumb pressing down on me for the last three years. Learned about my past not long after I joined the firm. Came up with this plan of taking over the Hartwell Foundation board with his own people, including me. Wanted to turn it into his personal bank account and use me as a way to do that. He thought I'd carry more weight as the founder's grandson, that the other board members would do what I suggested. Don't think he counted on the resistance he met behind closed doors, though. There's some good people on that board, Katie."

She thought about the other board members, whom she'd often dismissed as kindly and well meaning enough, but not very assertive or courageous. Perhaps she'd not given them enough credit. "But what about the fire?"

"I didn't know any more about that than you did. In fact, you're the one who connected the dots. When you put it all together, I knew he must've done it. Spent the last week doin' some research to confirm it all. He *was* in bad shape financially, and he *did* really need for Jorge's clinic to go away. Your instincts were right on target. I should have listened to you sooner—then he wouldn't have had a chance to..." He stopped, his voice breaking. He stared at the floor for a long moment before looking back at her.

"How did you know he'd come after me?" She swallowed back the pain as she again replayed the night's events.

"When I returned from my mama's, I decided to confront him. I waited until late in the day on Monday and went to his office. I told him what I knew, and he said he would ruin me if I said anything. Somehow, he knew about you and me. Guess we weren't as discreet as we'd thought, or maybe his wife said something. Hell, he coulda had us followed. Wouldn't put it past him."

Fred Harmon, the car salesman.

"He said he'd make sure you didn't tell either, then kicked me out of his office. I ran to my office and got on the phone, called everyone I could think of that I should tell before I told the cops—other board members, Louise and the firm partners.

"The partners were the hardest, Katie. They called me into their private conference room and grilled me for two hours. I told them everything, including about how I lied to them about who I was. They asked me not to call the police until they had a chance to talk to Porter themselves. I told 'em I'd think about it. One of 'em went to get Porter. I was bracing for the big showdown, but he'd already left.

"That's when I realized he'd most likely come after you. I bolted and headed toward your place. Tried to call you, but you hung up on me. Called the cops, too. When I got there, I heard the yelling and the noise coming from upstairs. Saw the door open. Then I saw Porter with his hands on you, with your eyes closed and your face blue and…" He stopped again and pinched the bridge of his nose while he took a deep breath.

Katie said nothing, waiting for him to finish.

"Saw that bottle on the floor, the one we got in Highlands. Didn't really think. Just picked it up and broke it over his head. Didn't knock him out or anything, but it did make him drop you. Your head hit the edge of the coffee table, and you were just…so still. Then he started swingin' at me. I'm not sure what happened next. I must have fought back—I was pretty mad by then. When the cops arrived, he just, I dunno, kind of…deflated. Like he knew it was over. Started blubbering about how unfair everything was. It was strange, surreal and comical, all rolled into one. Once the cops had him cuffed, all I cared about was gettin' to you, but the cops wouldn't let me anywhere near you…until now." He dropped his head into his hands. He wasn't crying, just breathing, like he was just thankful to be close to her.

When he raised his head again, he inspected her face, as if to reassure himself that she were really there, really alive. When he appeared to be satisfied, he continued. "Arson investigator has been here, too. Turns out Porter used those bottles we found in Highlands to make the clinic bombs. It's the same kind of glass they found in the investigation. That old glass is so thick, there were still big pieces of the bottles with the etched areas on them. Those bottles, along with Porter's confession, will put him away for a long time."

"Did you know about the bottles then? Is that why you were so insistent that I take one?"

"When I noticed two were missing already, I had my suspicions. Thought it might be a good idea to take one, case it came in handy. Was hopin' you wouldn't make the connection and do anything rash until I figured out more." He shook his head. "Just think, Katie. If you hadn't happened to see Porter in Atlanta that night, they'd probably never have a way to solve this case."

"Other than the fact that he confessed." The cuts on her face hurt when she moved her mouth.

"Yeah, but he only did that 'cause he knew you had him. You're the hero here."

She didn't feel like a hero. She felt like a victim—but not as much of a victim as Angel. "What about the woman who died? Angel? Did Porter say anything about her?"

"Says he had no idea she was in there. When I confronted him, he called her 'collateral damage.' I don't think he meant to kill her, but also don't think he really cared that he did."

She swallowed hard, not wanting to ask the next question. "Did you know she was attacked in *your* offices a few weeks before? When someone tried to rape her?"

"Huh? No!" His surprise seemed genuine. "How'd you find that out?"

"It doesn't matter." She didn't want to call any more attention to Angel's cousin. "Do you think it could have been Porter?"

He shrugged. "Could be, but he'll never confess to that. Honestly, it could have been any number of people."

Yes, including you.

She stared at him for a moment. It felt like staring at a stranger. The weekend in Highlands, the visit to his mom, even the fire that started it all were like things she had imagined or read in some book.

"And what about the Corvair?"

Jim looked confused for a moment, then nodded. "That's really mine. Porter appropriated it for his own use when he discovered my secret. It kills me to think of what he did with that car. My dad—my *real* dad—and I worked on that car for years."

"I know. Your mom told me all about your father. I…I'm sorry."

"Yeah." He looked down at her arm lying near him on the bed. "I was a real shit to him. He didn't deserve that. He was a good man."

He paused, then looked at her once again. "He's not the only one I was horrible to. Katie, I'm so, so sorry. You didn't deserve any of this, and it's all my fault. I want to make it up to you, if you'll let me."

She looked at her hands, unable to meet his gaze. Might as well deal with this now. "Your mom also told me about your old girlfriend. I know the story. I can't help but make a connection between then and now. I can't help but wonder about Angel." There, she'd said it. Whatever happened now, at least she had spoken what was on her mind.

He looked stunned, stunned and hurt—as wounded, she realized, as he may have been by Meghan's original accusation.

But he brought his gaze down to meet hers and held it. Then he said, "I deserve that question, and you deserve an answer. I can't conceive of committing that kind of crime. I hope you'd know that. Meghan was furious at me, and rightly so, for using her to get close to her father. I never laid eyes on Angel. I swear it on my life." He held up a hand as if swearing on a Bible.

She realized she had no idea what to think. Then, another realization settled on her shoulders: she had no intention of deciding anything about Jim until she was ready.

He looked down at his shoes. "I know it's a lot to ask. But can you believe me? Forgive me?"

"I don't know. I'll need some time to think."

He nodded once. "Fair enough. Just happy that you're talking to me right now."

An awkward silence settled between them.

She had to change the subject. The prospect of continuing their relationship just wasn't something she wanted to consider at the moment. "So what will you do now?"

"Honestly I have no idea. I'm done at Kinsey & McMillan, for sure. They won't fire me, but there's no way they'll trust me to protect the firm's interests now. I'd just rot in place if I stayed there. Guess I'll have to look around, find another firm that'll have me for a while 'til I'm ready to do my own thing."

Nurse Nelson knocked on the doorframe and smiled at them. Katie couldn't help but smile back.

"Hope I'm not interrupting, but there's someone else here to see you, a Mrs. Porter. Are you up for another visitor?"

"Um, sure," Katie said, exchanging a puzzled look with Jim.

Nurse Nelson left and Mrs. Porter appeared in the doorway, sniffing with mild disapproval at the room before entering. Jim politely stepped aside, but she ignored him after one sidelong glance.

"Please excuse us," she said to Jim without looking at him further. After he slipped out, the doyenne of Atlanta society turned her steely gaze to Katie. "Heavens!" she said, her wandering gaze absorbing Katie's injuries. "You look positively frightful. I can't believe my beast of a husband would stoop so low. You have my sincerest apologies."

Katie dipped her chin, unsure of what, if anything, she was expected to say in response.

Mrs. Porter didn't wait for an answer. "My dear, I came here to thank you for making my separation from that worthless excuse of a man much easier than I had anticipated.

Thanks to you, he'll have no leg to stand on when I file for divorce, and I've avoided a potentially costly and most definitely very public domestic battle. That and his jail time are more than I could have hoped for."

"You're…welcome?"

"Don't make statements sound like questions, my dear. They make you seem weak, and you're anything but."

Was that the slightest hint of warmth in her tone?

"That's the other reason for my visit. I want to discuss a business proposition with you. You've proven by your actions that you are a woman of strong convictions and courage, and that your instincts are very much on target about people.

"Now that I've wrested my assets from the clutches of that barbarian, I'd like to create my own charitable foundation. I have no children, but I would like to leave a legacy in this city. Atlanta has always been good to my family, and we have always felt a strong conviction to support it, to give back. My father especially would have approved. I'd like to honor his memory by helping others in perpetuity."

She paused, pursing her lips while she tried to frame her next words. "The fact is," she continued, her tone softening ever so slightly, "I don't have a clue how to do that effectively. I've always supported the society causes, but I merely did what was expected. I don't think I've done a good enough job of making a *real* difference. I want to be more strategic, and I want you to help me."

Katie stifled a happy gasp. "I'd be delighted to," she forced herself to say without too much zeal. She sensed that Mrs. Porter would frown on an enthusiastic display of emotion. "Who…with whom would I be working? Have you chosen someone to lead your foundation?"

Mrs. Porter frowned. "I've chosen you, of course. I'm asking you to help me start it from scratch. Please don't make me think I've chosen incorrectly."

"Oh no! I'd love to! I mean, I'd be honored."

"Good. That's settled," said Mrs. Porter, nodding with approval. "We can discuss the details later, when you've recovered sufficiently." She fluttered the air with one of her hands. "I should warn you that I'm not the most agreeable person with whom to work, or so I've been told. But I will expect you to push me, to challenge me and to be ready to defend your recommendations at every step. I may have much to learn, but I've also acquired a bit of knowledge in my lifetime."

"Thank you," Katie said, smiling. "I won't let you down."

"Here's my card," she took a step forward and handed Katie an embossed rectangle of high-end stationery. "I'm told you'll be out of this place by tomorrow. Take the time you need to recover"—she gestured at Katie's face with a look of distaste—"and then call my secretary. We'll make all the arrangements for you to get started." She took one last long look at Katie in the hospital bed, then turned to leave.

"Mrs. Porter?" Katie called, just as the older woman reached the door.

"Yes?" Mrs. Porter seemed impatient to leave the unpleasantness of the hospital.

"Who will provide the legal representation for your foundation?"

"I haven't decided. Certainly not my ex-husband's firm. God, it feels good to call him that. If you've someone in mind, you can present your proposal when you start." At that, she slid out of the room with an elegant toss of her head.

Jim sneaked back in as soon as Mrs. Porter had disappeared down the hallway. He shot her a big grin. "You'd better keep your eye on that lady."

"Oh, I think I can take care of myself." She smiled back and watched as his eyes lit up with hope.

He returned to her bedside. They were both quiet for some time. He appeared exhausted and lost in thought, but she was thankful for the silence. She simply didn't have the energy to sort it all out. Trying to solve the mystery had pulled her in so many different directions…

"Oh no!" She dropped her head into her hand.

"What?" Jim leaped to her side, a worried look on his face.

"Chris! I completely made an ass of myself! I accused him of having a hand in all this! I'm such an idiot!"

"Oh, no." Jim relaxed. "It's okay. Chris was here. I called him when I could. I thought you'd need a friend…you know…if you didn't want to see me. I told him what happened while we waited in the hall, and then he told me something, too."

"About Greg Newcomb?"

He nodded. "He asked me to share this with you. Apparently they dated for a few years. Even bought a house together last year, and Chris had an old cat that he had to put to sleep because Greg was allergic to it. He said that part would probably make sense of a conversation you overheard?"

He looked confused, but Katie just nodded. He continued.

"Then Greg got the executive job at the Rainbow Theatre and started pressuring Chris for grant money. Long story short, that put a strain on their relationship, Chris moved out and now they're arguing over how much he should get from Greg for his half of what they'd put into the house. He said you'd understand that, too."

Katie nodded again. "He's not in trouble, is he?"

Jim snorted. "Chris? Of course not. I see that all as personal business that he handled without involving the foundation in any way. I agreed that no one else on the board needs to know. It's a private matter."

Katie lay back and exhaled. Hopefully, she and Chris could remain friends.

They returned to an awkward silence again. Jim looked exhausted, and eventually, she convinced him to go home and get some rest.

"Jim?" she said, as he stopped at the door. "Thank you for saving me—again."

"My pleasure," he said. He smiled and was gone.

She fell into a deep sleep, but woke later to the sound of voices. Jorge was there, chatting with Nurse Nelson. She smiled to see Katie awake, then left the room with a little wave.

Jorge came to her bedside. He was wearing a white lab coat with "Dr. Jorge Ramirez" embroidered on it. *Quite handsome*, Katie thought.

"Katie, how are you feeling?" His voice was full of tender concern.

"Um, I'm okay, I think. Are you my doctor?"

He chuckled, a warm, enveloping sound. "No, no. But I do have privileges here. I have been watching your case ever since Jim called me."

Jim again, looking out for her. She shifted in bed, trying sit upright without moving her neck too much. It still was sore.

"I wanted to thank you, Katie," he continued. "You are a very brave young woman, and I owe you a great debt. You risked a great deal to push for the truth. You also have closed the circle on Angel's death, and that means a great deal to several people."

At least three, she thought. *Me, Jorge, Angel's cousin and how many other friends or relatives? Maybe Angel wasn't so faceless after all…*Then a thought hit like a bolt of lightning and made her sit up straighter. Maybe Angel's cousin couldn't tell the police who attacked her, but would he tell Katie? She couldn't believe her luck when Jorge continued.

"In fact, Angel's cousin Ramon is here. He asked me if he could thank you himself."

She agreed, and Jorge stuck his head out in the hallway and murmured something in Spanish. A short, surprisingly young Mexican man tiptoed in and smiled shyly at Katie. Jorge translated as he thanked her for helping find his cousin's killer. Katie responded with her condolences and was just about to ask about the attack, when the young man's attention turned toward the muted television playing in the corner of the room. His face reddened as he pointed to news footage of Porter being transferred from the back of a police car into the courthouse downtown.

"¡Es él! ¡Es él! Ese es el hombre que atacó a mi primo!"

She looked to Jorge, who wore a deep frown. Pointing to the TV set, he said, "He claims that's the man who attacked his cousin."

She fell back onto her pillow, causing pain to shoot through her face, but also releasing a huge wave of relief. Porter may never have to admit to that particular crime, but he would definitely pay for it. And it proved that Jim wasn't responsible. He might be a complete dumbass, but he wasn't a criminal. Tears slid from her eyes.

Jorge hurried Ramon out of the room and came back to her side. "I hope you will let me suggest people to help you through this trauma," he said.

She blushed despite herself. "I'm okay. Actually, all things considered, I'm better than okay. I think I just realized that I can trust my instincts."

Jorge smiled, and she continued. "Remember the discussion we had the other day? The one about my being frustrated with the Hartwell Foundation?"

He nodded.

"Well, as it turns out, I was just offered the executive directorship of a brand-new foundation. I get to build it up from scratch and do the kinds of things I've always wanted to do."

Instead of congratulating her, he raised an eyebrow. "And whose money will you be using?"

"Actually, Mrs. Porter's. She's the wife of the guy who…" she stopped. *That wasn't really the question, was it?* "But it will still be someone else's money."

"Ah, I see. That sounds like it could be a great opportunity. But perhaps it is not your only option," said Jorge. "I could use a strong development director at Viva Latina, and you could perhaps use some time to explore what you are most passionate about."

"Are you offering me a job?"

"I am just saying that perhaps you should take this time to consider *all* of the possibilities that are out there for you." He smiled. "At least there is one good thing about you leaving the Hartwell Foundation."

"What's that?"

"If you are no longer my program officer, I can get to know you better as my friend." He patted her hand, sending a wave of warmth up her arm. "Now, you rest and get well again." He glanced at her chart once more and then left the room.

Katie's mind swirled in the endless possibilities that were opening up for her. In her half-awake state, she saw a vision of the dark-haired woman again. This time, she looked right at Katie with a smile of contentment on her face. She raised her hand as if in greeting, then spun around and walked away.

The daydream pulled her back into consciousness and she smiled to herself. Maybe it was the painkillers, but with the mystery solved and justice done, she could finally let go.

After the ordeal she had just survived, she should have curled up in a tiny ball. Instead, a strange sense of power coursed through her. She kept turning Jorge's words over in her head:

"Perhaps this is the time to consider all of the possibilities that are out there for you."

He was right. She still had a lot to explore, a lot to learn. There were many, many ways to contribute to the world, ways that were driven by her passion, whether it involved other people's money or not.

She would take her time deciding.

CHAPTER 40

It's done now. Porter, the idiot, has confessed to everything. Hunter, by some miracle, managed to not get himself killed. The kid means well, but what a dumbass!

The funny part is, Porter actually thinks he's the one who pulled all the strings. As usual, he thought this whole thing was all about him, when in reality, it was all about a higher power.

Mr. Sutter pulls all the strings in this town, plain and simple. The beauty of it is no one even realizes it. Mr. Sutter understands that true power is dead quiet. You fill a room with silence until it becomes unbearable. Someone has to break the silence, and it's always the weaker man who speaks or acts first.

Mr. Sutter also understands people. Knows how they think. Understands what most of them don't about money. See, most people think that money gives you power and gets people to do what you want. But truly powerful people like Mr. Sutter know how to get people do to what they want with or without money. He has a gift for controlling people without them even realizing it. Like, for instance, if he wants to build a building, and someone doesn't want to sell, he can think of a million ways to change their minds. Maybe they get hurt accidently, or maybe they decide it's better to sell a property and take advantage of a better investment.

That doesn't mean money's not nice to have, and Mr. Sutter has more money than anyone in this town even dreams of. No one knows exactly how much, and Mr. Sutter likes it that way. He understands that money sometimes garners too much attention.

The other thing Mr. Sutter understands is the power of distance. He keeps almost everyone at arm's length. That way, he can watch them more objectively, see what they're up to. That way, he can adjust accordingly.

That's how it was with Porter. Porter thought he was part of a close partnership with Mr. Sutter, even though he never met face to face. He worked through me, and I reported back to Mr. Sutter. When Porter's financing fell behind, I dropped the hint that if the building went up in flames, it would solve a lot of problems. But let's be clear; I never told him to commit arson. In his mind, he came up with that idea all by himself, just like Mr. Sutter said he would.

The problem was, he used those antique bottles. Still, they should never have been able to trace them back to the garage in the mountains. Only one other person besides Porter could make that connection. Turns out, she had the evidence she needed but neither she nor I realized it at the time. I thought she'd bought that bottle at the antique shop. She didn't recognize how it could have been used to make a Molotov cocktail, at least not until the night Porter lost it.

When he realized a bottle was missing, he went crazy. I tried my best to calm him down, but he was sure she knew. He wanted me to go after her. I agreed to tail her just to shut him up. I even followed her to South Carolina. She must be learning about the boyfriend, I realized. Disappointing for her, but not my business. And then, on the way back, it hit me. She had all the evidence she needed—she just required a little push, so to speak, to take it to the cops. That would get Porter off my back and out of Mr. Sutter's hair.

She'll never know how close she actually came to dying. I'm not talking about the car thing; there, I was just tying to shake her up, get her to focus, point her in the right direction, get her to call the cops. I needed her to concentrate on Porter, to point the finger at him before he went off the deep end and started naming names. He was getting frantic, and he could have caused a lot of serious problems.

But she still didn't do it. I sat outside her apartment for two days, willing her to put all the pieces together. I figured it was tough for her; to make a call like that would shake up her comfy life. But if she didn't call, I'd have to consider her a loose end. Mr. Sutter doesn't like loose ends.

Turns out, she was lucky. Porter came to her apartment to end it himself. Stupid fuck. No planning, no thought. He would never have gotten away with it, and her life would have been wasted. But the boyfriend showed up, with the cops—finally! It was a regular cavalry charge.

Now everyone thinks Porter was the mastermind, including Porter himself. Classic. Beautiful. I made *sure he saw me in the shadows when the cops drove him by. Just so he'll know that Mr. Sutter is still watching and will always be pulling the strings.*

I hope the girl will never question the way things ended. The cops will tell her that Porter confessed, and that will be enough. No one has a reason to question Mr. Sutter's role, and that's just the way he likes it. He asked me if I needed to get rid of the girl, and I said no. I said I'd keep an eye on her for a while longer, just to make sure.

But there's another reason I want to keep watching. I want to know that she's okay. She went through a lot. She's brave. She deserves to be happy and safe. Like I said before, I'd like to take care of her.

About the Author

Elizabeth Russell has been telling the stories of foundation and nonprofit clients for twenty years. During most of that time, she served as a marketing and communications consultant to the Southeastern Council of Foundations, a membership association of 350 foundations in 11 Southern states. She has also worked for high-profile national foundations. Through this work, she has developed an in-depth knowledge of the "real life" issues that face foundations and the individuals who work in them. Her fiction is drawn from her insider's knowledge of the good and the bad of the foundation world, and woven with a creativity that makes the field intriguing and engaging to all. She lives with her husband and two children in Asheville, North Carolina.

Murder, romance and unexpected twists and turns continue for Katie Nelson in Elizabeth Russell's *Donor Intent* from Moonshine Cove, coming soon.

Learn more at elizabethrussellfiction.com.